Seeing Things

Blessings!
Pattie Hill
II Cor 5:7

Seeing Things

a novel

patti hill

B&H
PUBLISHING GROUP
Nashville, Tennessee

Printed in the United States of America

978-0-8054-4751-4

Published by B&H Publishing Group
Nashville, Tennessee

Author is represented by Books & Such Literary Agency,
Janet Kobobel Grant, 52 Mission Circle, Suite 122, PMB 170,
Santa Rosa, CA 95409-5370, www.booksandsuch.biz.

Dewey Decimal Classification: F
Subject Heading: APPARITIONS—FICTION
\ MACULAR DEGENERATION—FICTION \
FAITH—FICTION

1 2 3 4 5 6 7 8 9 10 • 13 12 11 10 09

Dedication

Geoff and Matt—
You're still opening my eyes to wonders
beyond my seeing.

Acknowledgments

Dennis, my beloved husband, best friend, cheerleader, and patron. Your love keeps me grounded and free to fly. You're my hero, babe.

Janet Kobobel Grant, agent and friend, thanks for saying what I need to hear. We'll always have Sonoma!

The creative folks at B&H Publishing Fiction Group made *Seeing Things* a beautiful reality. My heartfelt thanks to all, especially Karen Ball, who supported me with wit and wisdom.

David Webb, my intrepid editor, fearless with the red pen, and yet, he never draws blood. Thanks for finding the story, wise one.

I observed twenty-first-century teenagers in Brigham Leane's classroom. The students amazed me, and this master teacher entranced me with a lesson on exponents. To add or multiply, that is the question.

The brave folks at mdsupport.org generously shared their stories, including the triumph and challenge of living with AMD. Daniel L. Roberts is their fearless leader and author of *The First Year: Age-Related Macular Degeneration: An Essential Guide for the Newly Diagnosed,* a compassionate and practical handbook for those facing such a disruptive diagnosis. He read *Seeing Things,* along with Barbara Smith and Fiona Hall, to make sure I portrayed life with AMD. Any mistakes are solely mine.

I gleaned all I know about broken ankles and growing up in Denver from Mimi Frank and Rebecca Frank, mother and daughter extraordinaire. Another cup of tea?

I find the prospect of writing a novel without my critique group absolutely terrifying. I love you Sharon Bridgewater, Muriel Morley, and Darlia Sawyer! Death to the extraneous word!

Helen and the ladies of the low-vision group entertained me royally at The Center for Independence in Grand Junction, Colorado. They demonstrate a brand of courage beyond my dreaming. Thanks for the honesty and the laughs, girls.

When I needed to know about collisions involving air bags, Allison Bottke, Dave Lambert, and Tom Morrisey shared their harrowing stories. Hope those bruises have healed.

Wade McDowell helped me understand elder care on a personal and compassionate level because that's the kind of man he is.

Jennifer Murrell and Eusebia Garza filled in the blanks of my Spanish skills. *¡Muchas gracias, mi amigas!*

Coralie Bloom of the National Park Service at Great Smoky Mountains National Park enthralled me with the early history of the park. I'm going back there someday.

O my Strength, I sing praise to you; you, O God,
are my fortress, my loving God. (Ps. 59:17 NIV)

"Some things you can't find out; but you will never know you can't by guessing and supposing; no, you have to be patient and go on experimenting until you find out that you can't find out. And it is delightful to have it that way; it makes the world so interesting."

Mark Twain, *Eve's Diary*

Prologue

You're talking to the queen of skepticism right here.

I roll my eyes over newspaper stories where teary-eyed folks report they've seen Jesus in a potato chip. That sort of hogwash sends me straight to the comics for a dose of reality. You don't have to worry about me. I know Alley Oop doesn't slide through time, but the inhabitants of Moo remind me of my friends in Ouray with their common sense and heave-ho attitudes, something sorely missing among the potato chip crowd. Honestly, someone isn't rowing with both oars in the water.

Let's proceed with this understanding: God shaped the Grand Tetons with the power of his Word. No overcooked potato chip evokes that kind of awe. Sadly, some people fritter the good sense God gave them on happenstance and wishful thinking. Despite my adventures into the whimsical, I'm not one of them. Not that anyone can prove anyway.

Because I've lived among the wild things all of my life, it's not my habit to shrink back from anything. I've thrown snakes out of the house by their rattles and snatched a toddling son from the path of a charging moose, and there's nothing meaner in nature than a moose cow if she doesn't like the way you look. And I won't shrink back from telling my story as soon as I hit my stride. You see, I like to think I'm a reasonable person. Chatting up my problems with a literary character scoots me several degrees east of rational as far as I'm concerned, so I'd kept mum about my visits with Huckleberry Finn. Until now.

Who can keep a secret like that?

Once word leaked that I chatted with Huck, the offers came pouring in to write my story. I suppose with so many Boomers out there sitting in orthopedic waiting rooms and making transoceanic flights, there's a call for old-lady stories to make those folks feel better about themselves. Well, my story will certainly do that.

One name-dropping literary agent wanted to represent me something fierce. She declared old-lady stories all the rage among reviewers and New York City publishing houses. It's about time, is all I can say. Before I knew it, she'd sent me an old woman's memoir about her life in Iowa during the Depression. Someone who thinks pretty highly of himself declared the book one of the best written last year. I don't mean to cast aspersions on the author, but for a woman in her eighties she sure remembers a lot of details from the year she turned five years old. I can't remember what I had for lunch yesterday, although I ate a piece of peach pie with a dollop of whipped topping afterward. I love that about getting older. I'm on my way to looking like Buddha, and I don't care one lick.

That's enough stalling. The telling of this story won't get any easier if I chase every stray thought, so I'd better get to it. Promise to give me a fair hearing and proceed.

Chapter 1

I stood at the top of the stairs kneading the newel post. The oven timer groaned from the kitchen below. Four pies—two apple, a cherry, and an elderberry—filled the house with a nutty sweetness, meaning the crust was golden and the sauce had thickened around the fruit. I'd finished my shower and started toward the kitchen long before the timer sounded, but now I stood frozen like a raccoon in the beam of a flashlight. Such bold marauders.

Below me, the stairs were a mountainside of wildflowers—a swath of starry edelweiss and buttercups, lupine and red gilia—all growing among granite boulders and spiked grasses from the second-floor landing to the first floor. A breeze that neither lifted my apron nor jostled my curls, whipped the grass and set the flowers dancing.

The timer grew more insistent. Nutty sweetness turned bitter, a sign the pies' crusts had edged beyond golden to toasted. I closed my eyes, but the mountainside remained. I knew better. A few weeks earlier I'd sat on the top step, enjoying the deep purple of the lupine and watching a deliciously red ladybug crawl across a boulder, but I hadn't had pies in the oven that day, only a load of towels in the dryer.

The timer groaned on, sounding a bit tired from its unanswered call. I slid my foot down the step's riser, willing my brain to ignore the flowery slope and to think of stairs, predictable and ordered. One step. Two steps. A boulder?

"You're not there," I said to the boulder. "I can walk right through you, yes I can. And I will."

Fooling myself proved harder than I thought.

I overstepped and missed the next stair. My ankle twisted and cracked like kindling. I fell forward, reached for the railing that had belatedly reappeared, but my knee hit the wooden stair hard, and my head bounced on the last two risers before I came to a stop. A hot poker of pain seared my ankle. I fumbled with my sneakers and screamed with the movement. With reluctant fingers, I felt a lump rising over my ankle bone. My foot lay at an unnatural angle. I writhed like a landed trout on the floor. I needed help, but moving only intensified the pain.

Bee's dog door slammed shut, and her claws tapped eagerly across the floor. She stopped, tilted her head as if to ask: *What kind of game is this?* She held a tennis ball in her mouth.

You've got to be kidding. "Not now, Bee. Go away!"

She slunk toward me, dropped the ball in my lap, and nosed my hand.

My ankle screamed and so did I. "Bee!"

She lapped at my face and made to sit across my lap. I pushed hard on her chest, but she lowered herself slowly to straddle my legs, all seventy pounds of her. With my ankle crying for attention, I debated who to call. I hated to make a fuss, but I knew the EMTs in town; Tom and Veryl liked nothing better than sounding the sirens.

Then twinkling lights danced before my eyes, and the decision left my hands.

Chapter 2

It had taken no small amount of cajoling on my son's part to convince me to recuperate at his home in Denver. Denver is a good three hundred miles from Ouray and light years from mountain living. Andy eventually agreed to bring Bee along, and I promised to bake him a strawberry-rhubarb pie once I felt up to it. In the end the fact that there's a toilet on the ground floor of his home persuaded me, but Andy didn't know that.

My daughter-in-law Suzanne—Andy's second wife of eight very long years—had already purchased an adjustable bed for my use. More than once over the years, while waiting for the Mylanta to do its trick around midnight, I'd reached for the telephone during a Craftmatic commercial. Anyway, that's how I found myself ensconced in eiderdown pillows in my son's fancy-schmancy guest bedroom with an attached bathroom.

I lay flat on my back with Suzanne standing over me, hands deep in the pockets of the lab coat she wore over algae-green scrubs. She no longer wore her nearly black hair cut to her chin. Instead, she sported a Cleopatra do with thick, blunt bangs and hair that slid over her shoulders like silk. Andy stood with his back to me, looking out a glass door into the night. Tall, broad shouldered. So like his pa. Yet so not.

"I've arranged everything," Suzanne said. "You have a series of post-op appointments arranged with Dr. Milner. He's known internationally for his work with world-class athletes. Fortunately his wife's breast augmentation went splendidly, and he owes me. You'll see him Tuesday."

What day is this? "Thank you for going to so much trouble, Suzanne."

She demonstrated the functions of the bed. With a hum, I rose to a sitting position. Much better. Bee nuzzled my hand. I fingered her ears like a worry stone. Another hum and my feet rose. A human taco, but the ache in my ankle receded.

"Everything you need is on this nightstand," she said, her voice a mix of Florence Nightingale and Old Mother Hubbard. My chest warmed. "Ring this bell for Lupe, our housekeeper. You may have to ring twice, but she'll come eventually, or you're to let me know. Here are your pain pills—it's important to take them as scheduled. You don't want the pain to get away from you, so even if you're feeling good, take a pill at the scheduled time."

I'd already heard this speech innumerable times by my surgeon and a bevy of nurses.

She continued. "And drink lots of water. Lupe will keep you supplied with plenty of chilled Evian." She shook something rod-like at me that rattled. "I've divided out your blood pressure and cholesterol meds into a pill organizer."

I'm not helpless. "You're very kind."

"No problem," she continued. "And I've taken the liberty of prescribing a stool softener. Surgery can wreak havoc with digestion and elimination, especially since you won't be very active for the next eight weeks."

"*Six* weeks," I said a tad too eagerly. "I mean, my surgeon said six weeks."

Andy walked to the foot of the bed. "He said six to eight weeks, Ma."

"I'm a quick healer. Remember? I have the bones of a thirty-year-old. That's from all the hiking and dancing."

Andy spoke slowly. "Ma, the break was bad. Both the fibula and tibia. We're going to take this one day at a time."

Where's the phone?

"And Mom," Suzanne said, presenting a walker at the bedside. "My nurses tricked out a walker for you—a water bottle holder, a zippered pouch you can use as a purse, and this little pouch works like a pocket. I hope you like it. Andy suggested the royal blue. He says you love color. Any questions about how to use the brakes?"

Physical therapists had pressed me to take one more lap around the ward with a walker during my hospital stay. The Continental Divide now separated me from their bullying. I smiled. "I don't think so. I've used one before."

My ankle throbbed. I wanted to be alone, but Suzanne, obviously proud of the preparations she'd made for me, yammered on. "Now, in the bathroom, you'll find a wheeled stool to help you move around. Also, the plumber installed a handheld shower and a grab bar."

A plumber? "I had no idea my stay would create such a problem . . . and expense. I don't know what to say."

Andy patted my good foot. "Ma, we're happy to do it. Just relax and enjoy."

Could I do that?

"How long since your last pain pill?" Suzanne asked.

I covered my eyes to concentrate. I took a pill at the pharmacy, didn't I? And another when Andy stopped for gas in Edwards, I think. "I'm not sure."

Suzanne expelled a long sigh. "Are you hurting?"

What a question. "Yes."

"On a scale from one to ten?"

"Seven-point-three."

Water sloshed into a glass and the top popped off a pill bottle. "As I said, you've got to stay on top of the pain," Suzanne said with some irritation in her voice. "What are you thinking?"

What was *I* thinking? I wanted to be in my own bed where pain in or out of control was nobody's business but my own.

"Andy, help your mother take a pill. I'm beat. Rounds come early." She bent to touch my cheek with hers. "We'll take good care of you." And she left.

In the dark, after Andy left, I found the telephone and held the handset to my chest, wondering who I should call. Josie, my best friend in the world, slept like a brick. Besides, she hated talking on the telephone—she feared developing brain cancer from the receiver. I wouldn't talk to her until I returned to Ouray.

My daughter, Diane? I didn't dare. That girl would hop a plane without packing a bag and fly all the way from Dublin to drive me home. Just knowing she was out there somewhere settled my racing heart.

Emory? Too complicated. Very appealing. Maybe later.

It didn't matter. The telephone handset turned out to be the television remote. Fine. I pushed a row of buttons before the television snapped on and the room filled with blue light. Without my telescoping glasses, the images were mostly lost to me. That left listening to the news or infomercials. The announcer passionlessly read about an insurgence here, a coup there, the falling dollar. Another missing child. *Click.* "Age spots and deep wrinkles melt—" *Click.* "Kobe Bryant—" *Click.* "Not one Magic Bullet but two, and for our late-night viewers only—" *Click.* The familiar voice of Jimmy Stewart filled the room as he addressed the U.S. Senate.

Mr. Smith Goes to Washington. Perfect.

I listened until the pain pill soggied my thoughts and I fell asleep.

Chapter 3

Under the influence of painkillers, time suspended and surrendered its grip. A stout woman with a thick accent escorted me to and from the bathroom and coaxed me into drinking chilled water. Another woman, quite voluminous, breathed sherry and peppermint in my face as she bathed me perfunctorily each morning. At least, I think it was morning. Even in my stupor, I regretted accepting Andy's invitation. My weakness embarrassed me terribly. Not being able to tell one day from the next completely unnerved me, so I flushed the pain pills down the toilet. From then on, Tylenol was my drug of choice.

Back in bed, I listened as someone poured coffee just a few steps from my room. I raised the bed and clicked on the bedside lamp, hoping to signal Andy, an early riser from birth, that I was eager for a visit and most definitely in need of a cup of coffee. Maybe he would refill the ice pack too.

"Fletcher," Andy roared. "Meeting in ten minutes."

"I'm walking," Fletcher countered, more a question than a proclamation.

My stomach tightened.

Andy parried, impatient and biting. "We've had this discussion before."

I threw the only thing within reach at the door—my Bible. Footfalls pounded toward the bedroom. Andy leaned into the room. "Ma? What's up? Are you okay?"

"Me? Yes, I'm fine. It's just that I haven't seen Fletcher yet."

Andy stepped inside the threshold and lowered his voice. "I have a big meeting this morning, and I didn't want to worry you, but Fletcher has cut school a couple times. If I drive him, at least I know he gets there."

Bee moaned from under the bed.

"Have a good meeting, Son."

I BRUSHED MY TEETH twice and waited for Fletcher to arrive home from school. He entered the house with the energy and stealth of a disgruntled Clydesdale. The refrigerator opened and closed.

"It don't matter that you are hungry. *Su abuela* wants to see you. Get in there and say hello." I imagined Lupe pushing Fletcher toward the door and winced.

"Is she in her pajamas?" He sounded like Andy. My hand went to my heart.

"The nurse lady comes every morning to give her a bath and dress her," Lupe said. "*Su abuela*, she smells a whole lot better than you."

"What do I say?"

"Ask her about her ankle. Old people love to talk about their aches and pains."

"Fletcher," I called. "I have an early birthday present for you."

Something heavy thudded to the floor. "Hey, Grandma." A flash of arm, pale and thin. Fletcher was a wispy one, like his father at that age. He moved too fast for me to make much of his face. Bee rushed him, tail pounding the bed, the nightstand, his legs.

His voice slid higher. "Will it bite?"

"Bee? Of course not. Open your palms to her. Let her sniff you." This was sad business, a boy unfamiliar with dog etiquette. Unwilling for Bee to ruin the moment, I added, "Be good, Bee," like she would ever take that kind of direction. She'd earned her name, Ms. Bee Haven, honestly. "I mean it, Bee."

Fletcher stepped back. Bee followed. He muttered, "Dazzy Vance, Hall of Famer, class of 1955. Pitcher. New York Yankees. Pittsburgh Pirates. Brooklyn Dodgers. St. Louis Cardinals. Cincinnati Reds. First pitcher in National League to lead in strikeouts for seven straight years. Most Valuable Player 1924."

No one resisted Bee for long. Fletcher sank to his knees to scratch the sweet spot between her shoulders. She was such a conniver. To tell the truth, I envied her lavish exhibition of affection and the response she got from Fletcher. All I needed was a twenty-pound tail and a lightning-quick tongue. Until that happened, I used Fletcher's preoccupation with Bee to see what I could of him. Glasses. Thick chestnut hair like his grandfather. Too long. Lots of neck. Huge Adam's apple. And since I couldn't read his expression, I imagined he sparkled with delight to see his grandmother. What male teenager wouldn't?

Fletcher sputtered, and I knew Bee had managed to lick his tonsils. "Is Bee your Seeing Eye dog?" he said, wiping his face with his sleeve.

"Thank the good Lord, no. I'd be dead in a week."

Bee nosed my hand.

"She knows you're talking about her," he said with a hint of wonder in his voice.

"She's showing off for you. She's as dumb as a stump."

"Suzanne was expecting a lap dog."

"Bear bait? One of those yappy puffballs? Bee's a galoot, but she's right there with me all through a hike. We've never been bothered by bears, so I guess she's good for something."

Fletcher flopped in the recliner at the foot of the bed. "You hike?"

I savored the surprise in his voice before I brought Fletcher up to speed on my age-related macular degeneration—AMD for short. More than anything, I didn't want him to think of me as an invalid, never mind the broken ankle.

"Fletcher, I have low vision, but I'm not completely blind. A gray fog blocks my central vision. Point is, the rest of my vision is relatively sharp, at least for now. What I see is like flipping through a magazine I'm not sure I want to buy. I catch transient images and ephemeral impressions, unless the object is something familiar. Then it seems my brain fills in the blanks. If, while flipping the pages, I come across something I want to see more fully, I have to study the image.

"Now, Fletcher, you must forgive me for switching metaphors."

"Metaphor?"

"Never mind. To truly see the object of my desire, I must look through a knothole of sorts, like you might look through a fence. Let's say, just for illustration, that an African elephant stands behind my fence and the knothole is quite small. To see the great, twitching ears, I must shift to look through the hole at an angle. Likewise, to look at the elephant's tail, I shift again. Looking right at you, like I am now, your face is completely hidden behind the fog, but I can tell you've grown quite a bit and you're wearing a T-shirt with a hockey mask on the front."

"It's a skull."

"You're a tough guy?"

"Nah, Grandma, just camo."

"Who are you hiding from?"

"No one in particular. New school. I'm flying low. It never pays to stand out in high school."

I knew about high school from the national news. Shootings. Drugs and alcohol. Girls in skimpy outfits. Overcommitted kids. Flying low sounded like a good plan. "Only two more years," I offered as encouragement.

"Two years, three months, and six days."

"A detail man." I pulled an envelope from a pile of books on the nightstand. "A friend of mine has introduced me to eBay. He thinks I got Gil Hodges for a pretty good price."

"Gil Hodges?" Fletcher gathered sprawling legs and arms to come to me. "What year? Had he driven in a hundred runs yet?"

"You'll have to see for yourself."

Fletcher opened the padded envelope with a deliberateness that warmed my heart. "Oh man, this is great, Grandma. I don't have this one." He flipped the card over. "No date, but he's a Brooklyn Dodger, so this card must date before 1958. He played for eighteen years. Over 100 RBIs for six consecutive seasons. Career batting average .273."

"Impressive. Have you told your father about your aspirations yet?"

Fletcher kept his attention on the baseball card. "Maybe when they paint my name on the door to my office."

"You'll make a great commissioner of baseball. No one knows more about the game than you."

Lupe entered. "I'm leaving early today. My high-and-mighty sister, Pilar, is bringing her girls to the house while her and her husband go to a dinner for electrical people. Did they offer to pick me up? No, I'm taking the bus home and watching their bratty girls for nothing." She shuffled out but kept talking. "See you in the morning, but don't expect me to be no Señora Sunshine tomorrow."

"Oh man, it's late," Fletcher said. "I have to go, Grandma. I have tons of homework."

Shame on me. Starved for his company, I asked the first question that came to mind, hoping to snag him for a few more minutes. "What classes are you taking?"

"Pre-calc . . . chemistry . . . French."

"You're a smart one."

"Depends on who you ask."

A vocal stop sign halted that line of conversation. No problem. "Are you taking a literature course?"

"You mean death by analysis? Yeah, I'm taking Literature B, like every other poor-sucker sophomore."

"What are you dissecting these days?"

"*Huckleberry Finn.*"

Secret caves. A runaway slave and a couple of rapscallion con men. Nocturnal floats down the wide Mississippi. "I love that book."

He hefted his book bag to his shoulder. "Have you read it lately? I mean, the book's pretty controversial. Some kids are refusing to read it. They say it denigrates their race and lowers their self-concept."

"What do you think?"

"Seems to me people don't appreciate satire anymore or understand the culture and times Huck lived in."

"Well said."

"Listen, I still have a calc test tomorrow and a paper to write." And he was gone.

I called after him, "See you later!"

Bee's claws clicked on the wood floors behind him.

"Bee! Come!" I demanded. Of course she didn't return.

Obedience had never been Bee's strong suit. Oh well, if I couldn't follow him, Bee was the next best thing.

Lupe came to the door, wearing a sweater and carrying a purse as big as Texas. "You should have seen the smile on that boy's face with that dog following him. I haven't seen him smile like that since . . . I don't think he ever smiles like that."

I'd already learned that Lupe exaggerated like an old fisherman. I changed the subject. "I think I can make it to the dinner table tonight. What time do they eat around here?"

"Dinner table? There's no dinner table in this house. I mean, yes, I polish that hunk of wood in the dining room, even though I can barely move the chairs. The family, they don't eat together. The mister and the miz bring something home from a restaurant, whatever time that might be, I think around eight or nine. Mostly they eat on their bed, watching TV."

"And Fletcher?"

She shrugged. "He eats in his room, but I'll remind him to order something for your dinner tonight since I won't be here. I hope you like pizza."

Chapter 4

Bee jumped from the bed to bark at the door, her tail thumping the nightstand like a drum. A quick rap of knuckles and the door opened. The cuff of a sweatshirt. A book bag. Fletcher! A book landed in my lap, and I reached for a magnifying glass.

"It's *Huck Finn*," Fletcher said, breathy.

"Won't you need—?"

"No lit today. Assembly." The door clicked shut. Fletcher's tennis shoes squeaked across the wooden floor toward the front door. The house shuddered when he slammed the door.

Lord, help him to fly low today.

Bee stood at the glass door that led to the patio, and beyond, the lawn, her dumping ground so to speak. "Just a minute," I said, surprised by the irritation in my voice. But why shouldn't I be grumpy? It took over an hour to get out of bed, showered, and dressed. Stupid ankle. Getting ready for my wedding didn't take that long.

Bee pawed at the door.

I reviewed the steps of getting out of bed: Roll onto side. Push slowly with arms into a sitting position. Wait for blood to redistribute through my body, especially the brain. Despite my best efforts to focus on the task at hand, the usual inventory played like a litany: Back aches. Neck aches. Calves ache. Shoulder complains. Broken ankle feels perfectly fine. I felt a hundred years old, and I didn't know what day it was, except that I'd been getting out of bed per the physical therapist's instructions for about a week. I counted back to the day I fell.

"This must be Friday. What say you to that, Bee? We should be hiking with Josie today. Lots of fat bunnies live along the Ruby Canyon trail. The creek will be flowing. How does a stop at the Red Rock Grille sound? You know I'd share my hamburger with you."

Bee wasn't listening. She whined at the door. The beat of her tail against the recliner intensified.

"I hear you, you troublesome bag of bones." I slipped the hospital-issued, skid-proof slipper onto my good foot. I'd come to terms with the walker. Without the contraption, I was limited to walking where I could support myself with furniture or counters. Much to my chagrin, the walker provided the little freedom I enjoyed, so I arranged the walker in front of me and hefted myself to standing. I hop scooted to the door. "You're not covering that door with snot art, are you? Lupe doesn't appreciate your artistic talent." I opened the door and prepared for the *thwack* of her tail against my leg as she exited, but her tail hit the walker instead. "Hey, I could get used to this."

I pressed the button on top of the alarm clock. The metallic voice said, "Seven-oh-three a.m."

"I'm getting lazy."

At home I welcomed the coming of morning. I left Bee in bed and felt my way downstairs to coax a flame out of the stove before adding a log. While the coffee brewed, I stepped onto the porch for a jolt of the bristling cold. Before the birds started their chattering from their roosts in the piñons, the cold, like a snap of a wet towel, shocked all the aches and pains right out of me and hailed me back to a time when I'd walked into the burgeoning morning with Chuck, his lunch and thermos in hand. In the early years at Yellowstone, he leaned down from his horse, Samson, to kiss me good-bye. In the Everglades, I shone a flashlight under his truck to make sure an alligator or snake hadn't spent the night under the muffler. Most mornings on the Olympic Peninsula we kissed with mist-dampened faces. Although I can't conjure his face, I can still taste our good-bye kiss—bitter with coffee but oh so warm.

TO SAY DENVER'S SPRING weather is fickle is like saying Napoleon possessed minor ambitions. Spring came to the Front Range like a lamb, then a lion, then a lamb again, and then like a Tyrannosaurus rex. Today the sun was a friend's caress, comforting and familiar. The bright sunshine provided the best possible situation for me to read, so I coaxed Lupe into dragging a chaise lounge to the middle of the lawn. I lifted my face to the sun to encourage liver spots and wrinkles to multiply as they may.

I focused my magnifying glass on the pages of *The Adventures of Huckleberry Finn* and read. Shifting the glass around the page slowed my progress, but Huck hooked me with his keen eye for hypocrisy and his careless naiveté. I laughed out loud, which was more of a snort I'm afraid, when he told Miss Watson he wished he were in the bad place because it appealed to his sense of adventure, whereas sitting on a cloud playing a harp did not. As for me, I believed God created us for purposes that crossed time into eternity. When I anticipated the Father finding worth in my lackluster talents to serve the purposes of eternity, goose bumps rose on my arms. Maybe I would bake pies for the wedding feast. For sure, I would need a bigger oven.

I stopped daydreaming to return to the story. Flecks of ash floated across the page. Odd. I scanned the sky for a telltale column of smoke. Surely a fire burned nearby. The sky was a baby-boy blanket, soft and pale. I shrugged, the mystery of ashes less interesting than Huck's adventures, and returned to the book. The magnifying glass revealed a charred hole in the pages.

I'd gone and burned a hole in Fletcher's book.

I snuffed out the smoke with the hem of my sleeve. "Oh, for heaven's sake!" Bee barked, thinking I'd started a tug-of-war game with my sweatshirt. "Shush up, now. I have a situation here." My pinkie slid through the blackened edges of twenty pages or more.

IIIIIIIIIIIIIIIIIIIIIIIIIIIIII

I SAT AT THE kitchen counter with Fletcher, finishing an eclectic selection of *dim sum* from the Snappy Dragon restaurant, Fletcher's choice, and the food was indeed snappy. Wads of spent napkins cluttered the countertop.

I dabbed my forehead. "If they charge you for the *Huck* book, I'm paying. Should I write a note to your teacher?"

"It's no big deal, Grandma," he said and popped a dumpling of sorts into his mouth. "I'll download the story onto my iPod. It'll be easier for you to listen anyway."

An iPod sounded beyond my technological abilities, but for now I beckoned Fletcher to push the dipping sauce my direction and talked around the pot sticker in my cheek. "Back home we have to drive two hours to get Chinese food worth eating. This is wonderful!"

"There's one more shrimp and scallop *shu mai* left. You really should try it. The mango sauce rocks."

I'd given up seafood after eating spoiled sea bass on a Mexican Riviera cruise. "Nah, it's your favorite. Take it."

"Dad says you didn't let him leave the table without tasting everything."

"I was a coldhearted mother, and I've regretted being so every day of my life."

"*Dim sum* means 'to touch your heart' in Chinese. This mango sauce will definitely warm your cold, cold heart." He tipped the gaping take-out carton toward me. "Just one, Grandma."

My own grandson taunted me with the same ruthlessness I'd used to cow Josie into trying a spicy jellyfish salad in Thailand. But Fletcher said my name with such affection, I stabbed at the shu mai with a fork and swirled it in the mango sauce, knowing I'd live to regret my extravagance.

My tongue burned. My nose ran. A tear escaped each eye.

"I like it," I said.

Chapter 5

I woke with a branding iron searing through my back to my ribs. Heartburn. A little belch and the shu mai received full credit for ruining my sleep. The motor that raised the head of the bed moaned, and so did I. Bee, caught in the valley between the raised head and foot, whimpered and jumped off.

"I've got a medical situation here. Have a little heart," I told the retreating dog. Her toenails clicked against the bathroom tile, and with a groan, she fell to the floor where she whimpered again.

"Good riddance."

I'd asked Andy to pick up some Mylanta from the drugstore, but that had been days earlier. I understood. The man left for work before seven and dragged in while I prepared for bed; Suzanne wasn't much better. Besides, I hated being a whiner.

I reached over to turn on the light and there he was: Huckleberry Finn.

Precious Jesus! My heart thumped like a kettledrum.

Huck sat on the back of the recliner, elbows to his knees. His legs crossed at the ankles, all relaxed and lackadaisical like, not a thought in his head about his muddy feet on the chair. He chewed on the end of a corncob pipe and looked straight at me. Like the mountainous staircase and the purple flowers I had seen sprouting from sidewalks and the like, he wasn't real. I can't say how I knew that. I just did, but he looked as real as anyone I'd ever known. A smudge of ash on his chin. A scab on his elbow. Eyes the color of the sky on the first rainless day of spring, the brightest color I'd seen in a long, long time. I stared into those eyes for a good long while, drinking in the brightness, praying he wouldn't evaporate. I studied him like a Monet or Cassatt painting, hoping to hold his image forever in my memory.

His shirt wouldn't do for a dusting cloth, it was so thin and frayed. It had been red once, that was plain enough; but one sleeve missed a cuff and the other was rolled to his elbow. I winced at his fingernails, jagged and packed with black dirt as they were. He'd been away from the Widow Douglas for some time.

A mixture of kindness and devilishness danced in his expression that made me want to reach out and ruffle his hair, but I dared not upset the mystical juxtaposition that brought him to me. From all those days on the river, when school got too binding for him and he played hooky to go fishing, his skin was ginger with a constellation of freckles on his face and arms. Fortunately he'd left his catch of catfish on a string somewhere else. I must have smiled because he winked at me.

"What was that for?" I asked.

He cocked his head, and I thought he might say something. When he didn't, I kept talking.

"Do I remind you of the Widow Douglas?" If he heard me, he didn't answer, so I kept talking on as if the sound of my voice anchored him in place. I didn't have any trouble finding a topic. With a father like Pap, Huck needed advice. "You shouldn't let Pap discourage you from learning how to read. Unscrambling all those words seems like an awful chore to you now, but you won't regret being able to read on a cold winter's night. That's when I do my reading. Otherwise, I bake pies or strap on snowshoes to go walking with my dog." I caught myself. He didn't need to hear old-lady stories. His pap menaced him something awful. "Pap's just jealous. He sees you turning into a fine young man, gifted with common sense and a bright future, and he knows his chances to do the same are lost forever."

Huck wiped his nose with the back of his hand, and I stifled the urge to scold him. Maybe he'd get talkative if I found a subject he liked. True, I'd never been part of a robber gang like him and Tom, but I grew up in the wilds of New Mexico and Tennessee and California.

"When I was a bit younger than you, I sneaked away with my sister to sleep under the stars, just like the Indians. By that time, my pa worked as a ranger at Yosemite, a place with granite cliffs, lush valleys, and heart-pounding waterfalls. Bears and mountain lions lived there too and worried Pa. If he'd known we left our beds like we did, he would have walloped us good, but we couldn't resist the pull of the night sky, not even Miss Prissy Pants, Evelyn. She was the one to stay awake until Pa's snoring rattled the windows because she was older and tossed and turned most of the night anyway. Then she'd wake me, and we snatched our winter quilts from under our beds to tiptoe out of the house.

"I agree with you, Huck, the sky is biggest when you're lying on your back, trying to make patterns of the stars. Even though she begged me not to, I told Evelyn scary stories I'd thought up while drying the dishes. I scared her bad enough that she returned to the cabin more than once. And then a twig might snap, or the wind moaned through the tops of the sequoias. That got me thinking about bears and mountain lions, and I loathe admitting so, but I soon followed her inside. On the nights we stayed under the stars, I woke up Evelyn while the moon still hung in the sky to go inside before our parents woke—Pa to mount his horse,

General, to patrol the back country, and Ma to try to keep her girls civilized, just like Widow Douglas did for you."

Huck crossed his arms and leaned back. I waited. His stories surely outpaced mine for adventure and danger. He played with the mouthpiece of his pipe but didn't utter a sound. I kept talking.

"I have a grandson a little older than you. He's built like a scarecrow with hair about as wild and the color of, well, General, a handsome dark chestnut. I'm sure you've seen some fine horseflesh during your day."

Huck scratched his chin but seemed content to listen.

I rambled on about the time I'd sewn the legs of Evelyn's underwear closed up tight before I left for Sunday school camp. I thought it was a pretty good story, especially since I'd remembered to leave the underwear on top unstitched. The prank dimmed my homecoming some as I wasn't allowed to play outside for a week, and I had to do all of Evelyn's chores until I could apologize without smirking. That took a good long while.

Hearing my voice, Bee returned to bed, and as I talked, I stroked her long back. The motion clarified my memories. When I looked up, Huck had disappeared.

I'd gone and bored an imaginary boy to death.

Chapter 6

There's a huge difference between an English Labrador retriever and an American Lab. It's what you would expect. The English version is a phlegmatic fellow with a square head and body and the disposition of an old soldier—strong, loyal, and a comfort to have around, not that he ever forgets how to be a puppy. Not so the American. Bred for field work, the American Lab owns the single-mindedness of—well, a bird dog—all with paws the size of oven mitts. Bee is an American Lab. She woke me up pawing at my shoulder.

"Ouch!"

Undaunted, she pinned me to the mattress to wash my face. I tightened my lips as I pushed against her chest. I glimpsed a slice of sunlight outlining the window.

"Get off, Bee."

I tapped my alarm clock. "Nine-oh-nine."

"For goodness sake, Bee, I'm sorry. Your bladder must be busting."

Bee jumped off the bed to bark at the door.

"Okay, okay. I'm coming. Don't get your tail in a knot."

Lupe knocked and walked past me to let Bee out. "I thought maybe you had turned into Sleeping Beauty or something."

I ran fingers through my hair. "I smell coffee."

"Miz Doctor Lady insisted I make a fresh pot. She's upstairs talking to herself."

At the mention of Suzanne, I remembered Huck's muddy feet and headed for the recliner, as if a woman hopping with a walker could outpace Lupe's sharp eye. She leaned against the doorjamb, oblivious to my dive into the chair.

"She messes up my routine when she works at home. She watches me like I might steal the silverware or something. Does she think I'm dumb enough to steal something while she's watching? Don't answer that. I know the answer."

I ran my hand over the recliner's arms. No mud. Had Huckleberry Finn come to call or not?

Lupe shuffled away. I called after her, "At home, I'm up before five every morning to bake pies."

"Whatever."

Fresh from the shower, I settled into the recliner to study my Amsler chart. I held the graph of small squares at arm's length, looking for bent or distorted lines that weren't there the day before. No matter how many times I looked at the chart, I still held my breath. The fog remained within the boundaries I'd marked.

Thank you, Jesus.

Bee trotted into the room with a lump of something—a tree limb? a car fender?—and dove under the bed. Suzanne screamed from the other end of the house. Lord help me, I thought of howler monkeys. She stormed in, waving a length of fabric, heavy and dark, maybe brown. I couldn't tell. She stopped to push an end with an irregular edge at my nose. The odor of dog food and slobber wafted from the fabric.

Suzanne spoke from a fiery place, raw and deep. "Where is that stupid, stupid dog?" She walked into the bathroom. "Where is it? I want it out of here today. Do you hear me? Out of here. Gone."

This would have been upsetting if Bee hadn't been banished almost daily since our arrival.

"What happened?" I said, trying not to sound bored.

Huck walked out of the bathroom to stand behind Suzanne. I sat up straighter, blotted the sweat from my forehead with my sleeve. What was he doing here?

"It chewed the skirt off of a ten-thousand-dollar sofa, that's what it did," Suzanne said, stomping her foot. "I'm calling a kennel."

Huck put the back of his hand to his forehead in a mock swoon, and I must have smiled, because Suzanne asked, "Is this funny to you?"

"No, absolutely not. Your furniture is very important to me." Despite Bee's eccentric brand of loyalty, putting her in a kennel was out of the question. But even more than that, I didn't want Suzanne to turn around. Huck mimicked her stance, hand on hip, shaking the other as if waving the ruined sofa skirt.

"Putting Bee in a kennel won't be necessary. Bee and I will be out of here by six," I said evenly, although I had no idea how to make good on my promise.

Suzanne's arms hung limp at her sides. "Birdie—*Mom*, I'm trying really hard to be reasonable. The sofa isn't the only problem. The dog is scratching the floors terribly, but that isn't the biggest point. Andy won't be happy if you leave. Can't you control that dog?"

Huck wiped away a fake tear with the back of his hand.

I sucked in a breath to stifle a laugh. "Not always, but I'm willing to try. I'll keep the bedroom door closed." I wasn't sure I promised this to keep Bee in or to give Huck and me some privacy. "I'm very, very sorry about your sofa. If there's anything—"

Suzanne stepped closer and I totally lost her behind the fog. I checked her location with a slight dip of my chin and fixed my gaze in her direction. My ankle throbbed like crazy.

"To be completely truthful, I've never been around dogs much," she said as if gliding on ice.

"Bee's a pussy cat, in a manner of speaking."

"I'm allergic to cats."

"You've never had a pet?"

"They're messy."

Huck stuck out a pouty lip and laced his fingers under his chin.

I willed myself to look at Suzanne. "You don't have a thing to worry about. From now on, Bee won't venture from this room, unless, of course, she's outside. Cross my heart."

I waited for Suzanne to leave, but she didn't. Instead, she ran her fingers lightly over my ankle. "How is your ankle feeling?" she said with a kindness that tipped me back on my heels.

"It aches a little."

"Are you still taking the pain pills?"

"Just Tylenol."

"How often are you getting out of bed?"

"Every hour. I'm walking to the end of the front walk and back."

"Good. Throwing a clot is the last thing you want." She slipped the icy disk of her stethoscope between my blouse and skin. "Take a deep breath and let it out slowly." She moved the stethoscope to my back. "Again. Again. Again."

Huck puffed up his cheeks, holding his breath until his face reddened.

"Are you sleeping okay?" Suzanne asked.

"Perfectly. Couldn't be better." Now please go.

She took my pulse at each ankle and wrist and checked my blood pressure. Then she palpated my stomach, digging deeply enough to check the firmness of the mattress. When she asked if my bowels were passing every day, Huck covered his ears. I grunted.

"Everything sounds great." She turned to go but stopped. "It would kill Andrew to know we'd argued."

"Please, Suzanne, it was all my fault. I should have kept a better eye on Bee. I really am sorry about your sofa. All that was said today is between you and me. You have my word."

"Thank you," she said as she closed the door with the faintest thud.

I turned to look for Huck, but he'd already gone.

"I DIDN'T WAKE YOU, did I?"

Emory's voice triggered a butterfly stampede in my gut. I ran my hands through my hair and licked my lips. "It's almost noon, for goodness' sake."

"You sound hoarse, is all."

"I had a bout of heartburn in the middle of the night." And I'd talked an imaginary boy into oblivion.

"I could overnight some Mylanta tablets."

"That's terribly sweet of you, but I ate something I shouldn't have. Fletcher ordered dim sum from a Chinese place. You wouldn't like it. A bit spicy, I'm afraid."

"Is your family treating you well?"

"Bee ripped the skirt off of Suzanne's sofa, so we're sequestered in the guest bedroom."

"You can't leave the bedroom?"

"Technically, I can, but Bee can't. The problem is, if I close the door on her, she'll claw straight through the wood. So unless she's outside, I am stuck in this room."

"That won't do. It's not healthy. Let me come get you. We'll figure something out. I'm sure Josie would stay with you . . . or you could stay with me."

"Emory!"

"You'd have the whole downstairs to yourself. You wouldn't even know I was here, unless of course you needed me. And Bee would have the run of the mountain."

My face warmed. Honestly, I had no business acting like a school girl with Emory McCune. Thirteen years my junior, he was; I could have changed his diapers back in my babysitting days. I patted my chest, hoping to settle the beating of my heart. Still, I wore flats in deference to his height and found comfort in the restrained strength of his lead on the dance floor.

"You have too many coyotes up there," I said.

"Then we'll set you up at home. I'll stop by before and after work, bring something from Elsie's for lunch."

"I can't do stairs."

Emory sighed.

My heart flip-flopped. "You're worrying like an old hen. Bee and I are doing just fine. Suzanne, while she has her quirks, is keeping a good eye on me."

The peppermint Emory always held in his cheek, clacked against his teeth. "It's been six months, not that I've been counting. I'd planned on proposing—"

"*Emory—*"

"Please, Birdie, hear me out."

His voice was a warm blanket, a skill he'd developed from reassuring mothers everything would be fine once a little fella took his antibiotic. Little old ladies like me stopped stewing once he told us a stool softener takes a few days to work. Even burly truckers sighed when he explained how Lipitor lowered cholesterol.

He said, "I'd planned on proposing after the tango competition. I figured you couldn't say no to me then, not with a medal for us to share. Yes, I'm younger, but even my mother said I was born an old man. Ask any of my brothers or sisters. I wore wing tips to junior high. I'm the one who's robbing the cradle here. You won't catch me hiking up a fourteener. You're all the adventure I need." He paused and I held my breath. "I've been waiting for you my whole life."

Had I not just purchased nonrefundable passage on a Columbia River cruise, I would have said yes immediately with just as much thought as accepting a cookie warm from the oven. Irresistible. Wondering if Gladys Conner would buy my ticket gave me pause to question myself: Do I want to be married again? I wasn't sure. No doubt about it, Emory enticed me with many fine qualities typical of the better males of our species. After all, I wasn't dead yet. As fuzzy and cushiony as Emory was, I would no longer need to dress like a Sherpa to go to bed in the winter. My heart thumped wildly.

Hold the phone!

Men liked meals at certain times of the day. And, hey howdy, they loved their meat. Emory ate steaks as big as roasts, with hash browns and dinner rolls on the side; I slapped peanut butter and apricot jam on slices of Elsie's bread and called dinner done. And then there was the laundry, and telling him everywhere I went, and that sad-puppy face saying *wherever you want to go* when he really wanted us to sit like bags of salt in matching recliners to watch *Bass Fishing World*. True, we danced twice a week now, but the Hoopers had dropped their Moose membership within weeks of their wedding. I like to travel when I'm good and ready to go, and I'm inclined to go with whomever I please. Emory claimed he liked to travel, but in all the years I'd known him, he hadn't ventured farther than a yearly pharmacological convention. Sure, he ended up in some swanky resorts, but that wasn't traveling. Travel should be unsettling enough to test my mettle and beguiling enough to raise my heart rate. And most discouraging of all—feel free to check this with any woman married more than one year—men have egos as fragile as robins' eggs.

I'm done walking on eggshells!

"You've taught me how to live," he was saying, "and quite selfishly, I don't want the lessons to stop." Emory spoke from a deep well. "I want to be more than your dance partner, Birdie. I want to be your husband. I live for the times you walk into the pharmacy. I'm so muddled I can barely count to ten when you're in the room." I heard him swallow. "Marry me, Birdie. Give this old bachelor a reason to wake up in the morning."

Oh my. "Can I have some time to think about this?"

"I waited six months like you asked."

"You did. You certainly did. It's just that . . ."

"I never intended to ask you over the telephone. I'm sorry, Birdie. You deserve better. I promise, not another word until you get home."

"Don't apologize, but we do have a lot to talk about. I'll be home in no time. We can sit on the porch and talk all we want."

"I would climb a fourteener for you. I just want you to know that."

"I know, but you don't have to."

"I guess I better go," Emory said, his voice dragging the floor for dust bunnies.

I'd wanted to delay this conversation to gain clarity, perspective, not pull the plug on Emory's manhood. See what I mean about those eggshells?

He said, "Have your daughter-in-law prescribe something for heartburn. Nexium won't interact with any of your other meds." Is this a dream guy for an old lady or what?

"I'll ask."

"I miss you, Birdie."

"I miss you too." And I did.

Chapter 7

The surgeon and assistant entered the exam room, a flurry of white coats and rustling papers. I'd prepared myself to dislike the man, sure that he expected me to worship the ground he walked on. After all, he'd left me alone in an exam room for more than an hour, which he kept chilled to just above freezing. Surprisingly, he didn't fill my expectation as a hard-bodied athlete, angular and terse. Instead, a shiny pate and an ample stomach sidled up to the exam table where I sat like a turkey in a meat case, only colder. I rubbed at the goose bumps on my arms.

"Good heavens, it's like a meat locker in here." He spoke to the assistant whom I hadn't determined as male or female yet. "Get this poor darling a warm blanket, and tell Hannah to call maintenance. The air conditioner has turned renegade on us again."

The doctor scooped my hand from my lap and held it between his warm hands. "I'm Dr. Milner. Please forgive my tardiness. I've been out of step with the world since I pushed the covers back this morning. Despite a frostbitten nose, how are you feeling?"

"Well, my ankle's fine. Aches a little now and then, especially when I've been moving around more than I should."

He hummed "Moon River" as he clipped my x-rays to a light box, and I ached to waltz across the dance floor with Emory.

"Fabulous," he said. "The bones are perfectly aligned. A gifted surgeon put you back together. The plate and screws are well placed, although not quite the way I would have done it. Surgeons, and I'm no exception, have healthy egos, Mrs. Wainwright. Please forgive my lack of humility."

The assistant returned with the warmed blanket. Short-cropped hair. A hint of lavender. I made a tentative diagnosis: female.

Huck filed in behind her, shivered, and hopped to sit on the counter. His shirt pocket bulged and wiggled. He pulled out a glorious frog, nearly as big as his palm, khaki colored and covered with chocolate spots and sergeant's stripes on its legs. Golden eyes with pupils of onyx looked about for the nearest pond.

"Mrs. Wainwright? Are you with us?" Dr. Milner asked.

I directed my attention to my wounded ankle. The doctor bent low and turned on a bright light. I squinted against the glare.

"I don't like the look of these stitches," he said. "Are you on a blood thinner?"

Red lines marked my ankle. "Yes, Plavix, should I be worried?"

"Have you been staying off your ankle?"

"I use a walker and hop around; do most things sitting down."

"These stitches aren't ready to come out, but no, you shouldn't worry. No two people heal the same." He fingered the skin around the incisions. "No swelling. No unsightly pus oozing from the incisions. The skin just isn't knitting together as I'd like."

I imagined myself lying in Andy's guest room until Christmas and shivered. "What does that mean?" I said with panic squeezing my voice.

"It means you'll be back to see me in a week or so, and I'm going to put you in a supportive boot. You won't like the looks of it, if you're the least bit fashion conscious, but you'll love the way you feel wearing it."

He spoke to his assistant. "Gary, go get an air boot. Size large." He leaned against the exam table and crossed his arms over the shelf of his belly. "The boot will help reduce your swelling. It's right out of *Star Wars.* Your grandkids will love it. Most folks complain about the added weight, but they all end up thanking me."

The frog leapt from Huck's hands onto the floor. He rolled his eyes and jumped down from the counter after it. The frog hunkered behind the trash can. Huck plucked it up and deposited the frog back into his pocket. He sat on a chair, head in hands, looking as smug as a bug.

"Mrs. Wainwright?"

I snapped my head around.

The doctor shuffled through papers. "Now, what sort of discharge instructions did your doc give you?"

"First of all, no dancing."

"Obviously not a person familiar with the melodious tunes of the swing era. My deepest regrets."

"Do you dance?"

He patted his stomach. "Not nearly as often as my doctor or my wife would like." He turned to study my x-rays again.

Huck pumped the blood pressure cuff. An inquisitive fellow.

"What about weight-bearing restrictions?" Dr. Milner asked.

I confessed to the gruesome sentence my surgeon in Grand Junction had passed. "No weight on the ankle for six to eight weeks."

"You know, Mrs. Wainwright, you could be a pinup girl for bone density. If you're amenable, let's adjust those orders to 'weight as tolerated.' Now, that won't get you onto the dance floor tonight, but getting around should be easier. Once Gary gets you fitted, I want you to ease your weight onto the injured ankle.

If the pain is between a two or three, proceed with caution." He tucked the clipboard under his arm. "I hear from Suzanne that you're a hiker."

"I've climbed nineteen fourteeners, and I didn't start until after my husband and I retired."

"That's truly humbling, but I must make you promise to save number twenty until you've completely rehabilitated that ankle. I don't want to see you airlifted off a mountain on the ten o'clock news. You're out for this season, young lady."

"Next year?"

"If you're a good girl and do what I tell you."

"I suppose I could try being a good girl if it gets me back on the mountain."

He stopped at the door. "You probably already know this, but Suzanne beats me out as surgeon of the year on a regular basis—but only by a few votes." He said this with a wink in his voice. "Your daughter-in-law knows how to relate to hurting people. She's truly gifted."

"Thank you, doctor."

Gary returned with the boot. The sound of Velcro ripping made me shudder. He held the boot for my inspection. I saw the shape of a black, knee-high boot, period. Rather than ask to feel it, I listened. Old ladies have healthy egos too. "When your ankle gets to aching," he said, "press this bulb to pump more air into the boot. You'll figure out quickly what makes you feel better."

Huck watched over Gary's shoulder as he adjusted the many Velcro straps. Once I'd proven my boot-pumping skills, I looked around for a congratulatory wink from Huck, but he was gone, probably chasing after a corn snake somewhere along the river. And, oh, how I longed to be with him.

I'M NOT MUCH OF one for lying around in bed, even if it's a fancy bed that adjusts this way and that. Since sequestering myself in the bedroom as Suzanne ordered, I'd got to thinking of the bedroom as a cell. After a few days of living under house arrest, Bee and I ventured out to the living area while Lupe busied herself cleaning the upstairs bathrooms. Unless I wanted a matching cast on my right foot, I needed to locate area rugs, power cords, footstools, anything that would send me hurling. Besides, this was my first chance to snoop around a bit, see the house as more than a glance of wood here and a glimmer of stainless steel there.

Just outside my bedroom door, the great room lay to the left, the kitchen straight ahead. I shuffled my way toward the great room sofas until I caught my toe on an area rug. The exuberance of red poppies woven against a white and green background well nigh toppled me. Leave it to Suzanne to find the thickest rug on the market, one that couldn't be ignored even by the legally blind. The rug rose a good two inches from the floor. Bee nosed my hand.

"You stay off this rug. Do you hear me? Don't shed whatever you do. A muddy paw on that white, and you'll find yourself in a maximum-security kennel."

Bee whimpered. I scratched behind her ears. "You know better than that. No dog of mine will be sent off to live in a cage." I bent to be thanked with a wet kiss.

Finding the light switches proved easier than usual, pounded out of copper as they were. And besides a set of leather chairs with ottomans, the room proved easy to negotiate. However, glass vases and mica lamps topped every table, perfectly within range of Bee's tail.

"We better keep moving. Now, show me the dining room, girl."

Against the oak paneling, the light switches proved more difficult to find. I felt the wall on either side of the entrance until I found a row of switches and a dimmer. On the rug under the dining room table, royal blue and rust fronds of the tropical kind danced around the border, but more importantly, the edge folded back with a push of my toe.

"Here's a rug to watch," I told Bee.

I stepped onto the rug to get a feel for the thickness and steadied myself with one of the chairs. I prayed I'd never have to move that chair. It weighed as much as my Volkswagen, maybe more. I rubbed at the tabletop with the cuff of my robe, knowing I'd left plenty of smudges on the glasslike top.

"We better move on before Lupe catches me undoing her work."

I followed the tapping of Bee's claws toward the front door. Another rug, a runner this time, nearly filled the hallway and silenced Bee's progress. "Stay with me, you sorry excuse for a hound dog. My ankle's starting to ache, and I still want to see the kitchen." I paused at the bottom of the stairs that led to the family's bedrooms. At home I'd marked my stairs with orange tape to differentiate one step from the next. The Wainwright staircase was nothing but an oaken slide to my sorry eyes. I wouldn't be going up there any time soon. I turned back to the kitchen.

I found the refrigerator quite by accident, thinking it was the pantry. My mouth watered with anticipation of treasures within. No such luck. Soy milk. Brown rice. Tofu. The pantry, when I finally found it, was bigger than my garage, but not one thing sitting on the shelves appealed to my sweet tooth. The raisins were hard nuggets.

I must confess that I coveted the double ovens under a sea of burners. Just think of the pies I could bake in all that space! Elsie begged me to increase my output on a regular basis, and the extra income would buy paints and watercolor paper.

"Lord, if it would make you smile, I'd love a double oven. Of course, you're going to have to add on to my kitchen too." My tummy did a tumble when I thought, quite involuntarily, about Emory's double wall ovens. Even I wouldn't marry a man just for his ovens. Would I?

Before settling back in the bedroom, I scanned the space for any sign of Huck. Nothing. I sighed, surprising myself.

"Come on, Bee. Paula Dean is on in a few minutes."

ANDY APPARENTLY SLIPPED INTO the house as I scribbled notes on cinnamon rolls from Paula's show. Bee snored at my feet.

"Fletcher, come down here now!" he called.

"Andy?" I called out.

The clock announced the time: "Four-thirty-nine." Early for Andy to be home. Very early. He entered the room, slapping a piece of paper with the back of his hand.

"What's up?" I said.

"Your grandson is getting a *B* in English Comp. He missed an assignment."

All this drama over a *B*? I chose my words carefully, "Can you sit with me for a minute?"

"Are you in pain?"

"No, I wanted to show you my new boot."

He whistled. "Impressive."

"And I can put weight on the foot."

"I suppose you want to go home?"

"Do you want me to?"

"No, not at all." He shuffled around a bit. "Suzanne told me about the sofa."

"Bee can be a beast. One minute she's an angel; the next minute she's gnawing a leg off a table. I should have been watching her more closely. I'm so sorry." Men are the toughest of the species to read through the fog. So often, and I learned this before I lost my central vision, they believe they've answered a question when they haven't uttered a word. More than once, Chuck swore up and down he'd replied to my inquiry when, in truth, not a word passed his lips. Sitting there with Andy, no doubt, he believed he'd just said: *Think nothing of it, Ma. I hated that sofa. You did me a favor.*

I continued as if he had. "What's up with Fletcher?"

"I don't know. According to all the tests, he's brilliant. But unless I keep a fire under him, he loses interest."

"Like the time you built a volcano the night before it was due?"

"It's different now. Competition is fierce for the best colleges."

"He's fifteen. A boy. Boys get distracted . . . as I remember."

Andy stood. "I won first place in the science fair with that volcano."

Fletcher stepped into the room. "Yeah?"

Andy expelled a long breath. "I received this letter from your school today. Life isn't a game, young man."

Fletcher spoke like a plodding plow mule. "I turned the assignment in. We had a sub. She was new. Everyone got a letter."

The two of them stepped out of the bedroom and closed the door. Faster than I thought possible, I was up with my ear to the door. Andy dressed down Fletcher, more like the boy had invited pirates to pillage the family treasures than missing an English assignment. I turned and reached for my walker. Stopped.

Huck stood outside, leaning against the white bark of a birch. He raised a finger to shush me. I waved him closer, but he slid down the tree to lean against its trunk and tapped his pipe on the ground.

Hmph.

I moved toward the window. Bee, ever vigilant about visitors, twitched in her sleep. "You're missing a chance to play with a boy," I said. That's how utterly real Huck seemed to me. After all, I was leaving my battling son and grandson in hopes of some conversation. That didn't seem right, even to me. "See you later, Huck."

I peeked out the bedroom door to see Andy and Fletcher now toe to toe. Andy barked orders at Fletcher. "This assignment. On my desk. In one hour!"

An edge sharpened Fletcher's voice. "You won't be home in an hour."

Andy stabbed at Fletcher's chest with a finger. "One hour!"

"Dad," pleaded Fletcher open handed, "it's only a vocab assignment, worth five stupid points. I did it in class. I have a chem lab due tomorrow and a test in calc the next day. I can't redo the assignment and get it all done."

"That'll teach you to screw around when you have work to do. If you're going to make anything of yourself—and as my son, you will—nothing can slip by. Trust me, there will always be someone to step into your place. Remember that." And he slammed the office door.

Fletcher took the stairs three at a time, mumbling something about Johnny Bench winning ten Gold Gloves for the Cincinnati Reds.

Father, let your love reign here.

Chapter 8

I'd surrendered my dream to run the Olympic marathon a few years earlier. A seventy-something woman outpacing long-legged runners was such a cliché anymore, but I experienced the same sense of triumph ambling down to the corner for the first time, albeit with a walker. The cold biting my cheeks only magnified my sense of accomplishment.

A steady rumble of tires and engines sounded from the main north-south road only a few blocks away. On the trip to the surgeon, I'd seen buses loping along with the rise and fall of each intersection. Surely one of them ended up at the Greyhound station and on to Ouray. Forget that I couldn't walk more than—I looked over my shoulder—twenty yards, maybe, or that carrying luggage was out of the question, or that Bee hadn't learned her bus manners. I deflated as surely as if someone had poked me with a pin. I returned to the backyard to throw a ball for Bee.

"Hello there!" came a call through the fence. "Is that an actual dog barking?"

I called over my shoulder to the inquisitive voice. "I'm sorry. She's riled up. I'll try to keep her quiet."

"Don't you dare! There's not a happier sound than a barking dog."

I didn't know what to say to that. Besides the birds chirping and the drone of traffic, the neighborhood had remained ominously quiet. The voice called again. "Say, do you have time for a cup of tea? I've just put on the kettle. I'll meet you at the front door." The bushes rustled and a door slammed.

Anyone who loved barking dogs would be interesting at best, paddling her rowboat with only one oar at worst. Or she could be an axe murderer. Still, under the ice pack, my ankle felt perfectly fine. No problem. I called for Lupe.

IIIIIIIIIIIIIIIIIIIIIIIIIIIIIIII

"YOU POOR DEAR," THE woman cooed as I shuffled up her front walk. "If I'd known you were wounded, I would have brought the tea to you."

Lupe grunted as I leaned on her to take the last step inside the front door.

The woman, no bigger than a mite and bent at the shoulders, pushed aside the coffee table to give me room to pass with the walker. "Take this seat and I'll bring you an ottoman."

Before I could object, the woman disappeared into the fog and, I assumed, into another room.

"I've never seen so much green," Lupe said. "It's like living in a Coke bottle."

"I thought you had toilets to clean."

She turned toward the door and waved halfheartedly over her shoulder. "I'm getting queasy anyway."

The woman introduced herself as Ruth as she lifted my leg, boot and all, onto the ottoman. "I'm so pleased you accepted my invitation. Neighbors don't seem to want to be neighbors anymore. I know what I'm talking about. We bought this house just after Don graduated from DU. He'd been in the Pacific, like so many other boys. We cashed in a life insurance policy to make the down payment and walked away from the bank with a mortgage and fifty cents left for groceries. We were the two happiest people on earth."

Ruth sat on the edge of the sofa. She sported a salon hairdo as white as clouds on a summer sky. I'd yet to meet anyone who fussed over their hair who actually managed their side of a conversation. If Ruth thought I'd come to compare shampoos, she had one big disappointment coming.

"Now, Birdie, I have a cupboard full of tutti-frutti tea bags. My girls make sure I'm well supplied with the latest flavors. Name your fruit, flower, or mood. I have a tea for it."

"Do you have black tea?"

"That's my girl. I like nothing better than a strong cup of Lipton's with a pinch of sugar and milk. I'll be right back."

Drawers opened and closed in the kitchen. The kettle whistled and stopped abruptly. Somewhere a grandfather clock ticked like a metronome, steady and reassuring. Flouncy curtains framed the window by the front door. And Lupe was right: Ruth liked green. Carpet the color of moss, walls of spring sage, and upholstery as pale as cabbage gave me a sense of lolling about in Farmer Pearcy's hay field when the stalks were no higher than my knee. I felt sleepy.

Ruth moved from the kitchen to the living room with lithe movements I instantly envied. The china clinked as she set the tray on the coffee table. She handed me a cup and saucer. I dipped my finger in the hot liquid to judge how full she'd filled the cup.

"Did I fill the cup too full?"

Observant. I liked that. "It's perfect." I blew on the tea.

This was the moment I dreaded when meeting people for the first time. Do I tell them I have macular degeneration, accept their pity, or spill tea all over their prized furniture? "Ruth, I should warn you that I have low vision. In fact, a patch of gray fog blocks my central vision. I can't even see your face."

Nary a heartbeat passed before she said, "No problem, sweetie. I look just like Marilyn Monroe."

I played along. "And I run the hundred-meter dash in under ten seconds."

Ruth snorted then belly laughed for a good while, and I joined her. When she spoke, her voice was clogged with tears. "You remind me of Helen. Nobody made me laugh like Helen. She lived right next door where your family now lives. Such a silly girl, but I can't count the times she came to my rescue. Everyone should have a friend like Helen." We sat quietly for a long moment. "Birdie, I have AMD too, in my right eye, the dry kind. I was diagnosed when I was fifty, but it's not nearly as bad as yours."

"I'm so sorry."

"Don't be. It's not much more than an annoyance at my age. My heart's fine. A dose of ibuprofen soothes the arthritis in my fingers. My children are scared to death I'll live forever." She patted my knee. "Do you believe in divine appointments, Birdie?"

"Yes, but I never—"

"Will you be here for a while? A small group of ladies with AMD meets here every Thursday. We call ourselves the Three Bs, short for the blind bats in the belfry. I know, it's awful. Some folks at church objected, thought the name disrespectful. When it's just us, we call ourselves the Bats. If you can't have fun with a disease, what's the point?"

I explained how difficult getting around with a broken ankle had proven.

"That won't do for an independent lady like you. You're my new hero, Birdie, coming for tea at an unfamiliar house with a broken ankle and limited vision. I won't let you go nuts in that house. Like it or not, you're one of the girls now."

I swallowed down a lump. I liked the idea of belonging to a group of ladies more than I dreamed.

"The girls and I will get you here, no problem. You'll love them all. I've known them for—oh my goodness!—one for over sixty years, the others for at least thirty. Each one lives within a block or two, although Betty is living with her son in Lakewood. He takes off work to drive her to our meetings."

"Can I bring a pie? That's what I'm known for in Ouray."

"Do you use lard in your crust?"

"That's my preference—with a chunk of butter added for good measure."

"Birdie, I proclaim you an honorary member, expired only by death, in the Bats, contingent upon your willingness to share your piecrust recipe. Are you in?"

"I'll start nagging my grandson to type up the recipe immediately."

Ruth set her teacup on the tray. "I used to see that boy walking to school but not so much anymore. That's one full head of hair," she said. "It's all I can do to keep my hands off the hedge clippers when he walks by."

"And he's trying to stay incognito at school."

"It's wonderful to have a young boy in the neighborhood. I know there are children around. I see them pushed around the neighborhood in their perambulators, mostly by nannies. But the streets are oddly quiet. There was a time when you could use the children's heads as stepping-stones around here. Someone was always shouting, and many a day I cleaned a knee of one of the neighbor children." She sighed. "I miss those days. Nothing topped the whoops and hollers when the ice-cream man came jingling down the street at two-forty-five sharp."

BACK AT THE WAINWRIGHT house, I stood nose to knocker with the front door, anticipating the suffocating closeness of the walls within. This was Monday. Back in Ouray, the Super Seniors Bible study had just adjourned. Super seniors, my foot! Florence was a diabetic. Joan took enough pills to choke an alligator, and I'd seen a mid-sized alligator swallow down a small deer. Audrey had no business living at 9,500 feet elevation with emphysema, but she wouldn't budge from her beloved Ouray. That left Josie, my hiking partner and best friend, the healthiest among us, although she'd been complaining about her knees lately. I brought up the rear of the Super Seniors, and I mean that literally. When the AMD went wet in the second eye within two years of the first, the fog appeared. Super or not, these ladies were the candles of my life, especially Josie whose footfalls I imitated to keep from landing on my keister on hiking trails.

From the church, we would amble toward Elsie's Diner for meat loaf night and a piece of pie. When Conroy made the cowbell jingle, fresh back from his weekly run to Durango, every diner looked up from their mashed potatoes and tomato gravy to greet him. Such congenial folks, content with the predictable rhythms of life—the coming and going of a friend, sharing a simple meal, laughing and loving.

"Home," I whispered as a prayer. But then I remembered Fletcher's pitiful litany of baseball statistics and pushed the door open.

LUPE LEANED AGAINST THE doorjamb as I sat on the bed unbuttoning my coat. "You know, this room, this is where the nanny will sleep. I should be so lucky to have a room like this."

"What nanny? Fletcher has a nanny?"

Lupe positioned the walker in front of me. It was uncanny how she knew when I needed the thing. I leaned forward and pushed myself to standing.

"Miz Doctor Lady, she's trying real hard to get pregnant. She buys those pregnancy tests by the dozen. You know, like my sister buys toothbrushes at Costco, only Miz Doctor Lady doesn't know that I see the little wand things in the trash, so I wouldn't go saying nothing. Anyway, she's not so happy about your dog sleeping in here."

Lupe jabbered on as I started my expedition to the bathroom. "She's all upset, says she'll have to totally redo the room."

I ignored Lupe, as much as you can ignore, say, a magpie outside your bedroom window. If I didn't, I knew I'd hear about her aunts and uncles, her cousins in Albuquerque who opened a restaurant, and the son who'd forgotten her birthday for the second time.

"Miz Doctor Lady says she can smell the dog from the front door. She wants maybe I should get him groomed."

"*Her.* Bee is a girl dog." I immediately regretted correcting Lupe's mistake. I'd been hooked as surely as if I'd swallowed an earthworm whole. What could I do? I stopped to reward Lupe with my full attention. As she talked, even I could see her heavy eyebrows rise and fall. Her hair blossomed around the gray fog as a coarse tangle of black and gray.

Lupe yackety-yakked. "I always wanted one of those apricot poodles, you know? My sister has one. He sits in her lap while she watches television all day. The dog messes in the bathroom—on the floor. Sometimes Dolores doesn't clean it up for days. And she wonders why nobody wants to visit her. I told her, 'María Dolores, it smells worse than grandpa's farm in here. I'll be back when you get your fat—'"

I shuffled toward the recliner.

Lupe dropped her sentence like a hot potato. She wrung her hands. “Mr. Wainwright, he says you’re very religious.”

Her statement was a question I wasn’t sure how to answer.

“It’s okay. I don’t like to talk about religion either,” she said. She moved in front of the window and threw up her arms. “Nothing but troubles. My sister the nun, Sister Corazon Barbara, never shuts up that we should be going to Mass every day. Of course, she doesn’t have to take a bus to the church like I do. She lives next door, and she doesn’t pay no rent. I’d go every day too if I didn’t have to ride no bus for two hours. It’s easy to judge when life is easy.”

I doubted Sister Corazon Barbara lived an easy life as a nun in a metropolitan city. “Lupe, if you have something to do . . .”

“I’m supposed to fix you dinner, although they didn’t hire me to cook. I hardly ever cook for the boy, but when I do, he loves my tamales. The mister and the miz, they bring food home from fancy restaurants—no grease on the stove, they remind me a hundred times a day. I’m good enough to polish the granite in the kitchen and all the bathrooms. They better not ask me to wash the windows in this place, all those little panes. I jam my fingers, and then my arthritis flairs up. Good thing they hire a company to come every week, especially with your dog. His nose is wet. Is he sick?”

Let it go, let it go.

“Miz Doctor Lady is some kind of crazy person about the wood floors. ‘Oh,’ she says, ‘is that a scratch? Lupe, call the floor guy and get him in here today, not tomorrow. Do you hear me?’”

She impersonated Suzanne very well.

Since Lupe wasn’t going anywhere, I steered the conversation away from dog slobber and Suzanne’s obsessions. “Where’s Fletcher?”

“He better be at school, that’s where he better be.”

“Andy told me he plays hooky.”

"I think he wants to skip high school and go straight to college—a college far away from Miz Doctor Lady."

"Does he have any friends, Lupe?"

"There were some boys in the old neighborhood. They came over when the mister and miz traveled, never when they were home, not that they were bad boys. They played cards all day, never opened the blinds. I didn't see nothing wrong with it. They didn't do drugs or nothing, I made sure of that. But the miz came home a day early without the mister, and she wasn't very happy. She kicked the boys out, didn't even call their mothers to come pick them up, and it was like three o'clock in the morning. She went and fired me but changed her mind before I buttoned my sweater. She tried firing me before, but no one will answer her ads. Word has gotten out."

The gossip about Suzanne tickled my ears. "I'm having dinner with Fletcher tonight. Why don't you go home, Lupe? I won't be needing you."

Lupe straightened. "And *Dr. Phil* is a rerun."

MY STOMACH GURGLED. I tapped the clock. "Eight-oh-nine p.m."

Fletcher had twenty more minutes to produce dinner, or I'd make myself another one of those hazelnut-butter-and-marmalade sandwiches on a pita, what stood in for bread in this household. In the meantime, I double-checked the door was closed to stare in the direction of the recliner, hoping Huck might reappear.

"I could use a little visit tonight, Huck," I whispered into the darkness. "I promise, no more stories about my family, but I've had some run-ins with wildlife that might interest you."

Come on, come on.

"I'll tell you how I got my name. It's quite a story. It involves raw meat and mousetraps, just the kind of story boys like to hear.

Of course, if you've got a story, I'd love to hear it. I've never lived as wild and independently as you. It's been a coon's age since I read about you and Tom finding the treasure in the cave. I was nothing but a girl. Won't you tell the story again?"

My cell phone rang. I jumped and knocked the water onto the floor. Pill bottles followed as I rummaged the nightstand for the trilling phone. By the time I answered, my breaths came fast.

"Are you all right, Birdie?"

"Emory." I said his name like I was ordering French silk pie, and my pits got sticky. "Just fine. I managed to walk to the corner this afternoon, and I've met the most interesting woman. She lives right next door."

"Can you talk? Are things going well with your son and daughter-in-law?"

Emory's deliberateness of speech annoyed me, probably a characteristic that made him an excellent pharmacist. Sometimes I wished he'd just slap me on the back and say howdy. He never would. But what could I tell Emory about a son who struggled, as we all had, to be a good parent and a grandson who recited baseball statistics like prayers?

"Birdie?"

"There's no easy answer to that question."

"Are they taking good care of you?"

"Quite lavishly, actually." Any other answer would have brought Emory storming over the mountains to rescue me.

"You aren't pulling my leg, are you?"

"I'm living in the lap of luxury. I'm considering adding thirty silk pillows to my bed at home."

"Birdie . . . ?"

I never could keep a secret. "Okay, it's a bit like walking on eggshells at times. Andy is tough on Fletcher, who's been a complete delight. We're listening to *Huckleberry Finn* together. Suzanne, well, is trying very hard to be accommodating. She has a lovely bedside manner, but I can't help thinking she carries an ice pick in her pocket. I'm probably being too sensitive." And Huck had added a sense of adventure to my life I never thought possible.

"Just say the word, and I'll be there."

The temptation of his offer pulled at me.

The doorbell rang and Fletcher pounded down the stairs—*dumpety, thump, bump, bump, thud.* "I've got it!" he yelled.

"Dinner's here," I said to Emory.

"It's nearly nine o'clock."

"I had a very late lunch. I'm a woman of luxury, you know."

"I love you, Birdie."

Fletcher appeared at the door with take-out bags smelling of soy and grease. "Are you hungry, Grandma?"

"I am, Fletcher." And to Emory I said, "Fletcher just arrived with dinner. I should go."

"I'm praying for you."

"Don't ever stop."

Fletcher made himself comfortable beside me on the bed as the narrator introduced chapter six—"Pap Struggles with the Death Angel." He handed over a take-out carton full of shu mai. I considered begging off. Suzanne hadn't delivered on the antacid yet, but heartburn seemed a small price to pay for a moment of peace and enjoyment with my grandson. That night Fletcher also introduced me to wasabi, a slurry of something green that made horseradish out to be a sissy.

Chapter 9

Huck wiped his upper lip on his dirty sleeve, darkening the tip of his nose. Regardless, his face was lovely to see. Freckles. The dimple in his chin. The ease of his gaze as he watched me studying him.

"Of all the nights for you to come. I'm nearly dying. No more shu mai for me."

Huck, clearly unconcerned that wasabi had seared a hole in my colon, chewed on his pipe.

I slung my feet over the side of the bed, eager to reach the Mylanta that Fletcher had loaned me from his bathroom. I pulled myself up, using the walker parked by the bed. "This won't take a minute," I said. "This isn't my usual speed, you know. I pass younger people on mountain trails all the time."

Huck pushed his hair out of his eyes, and it stuck straight up like an antennae. Come to think of it, his last bath had been a century earlier. I actually considered running a hot bath, but only a bar of Ma's homemade soap would clean that scalp. What was I thinking? Offering a bath to Huckleberry Finn was like suggesting Queen Elizabeth muck a stall.

"Have you ever seen a mountain, Huck?" I sat back down, suddenly concerned that stepping out of the room might dissipate the magic that brought Huck into my presence. "I don't know how this works, Huck. I'd hate to come back and find you gone." I rubbed the sore spot under my ribs. "Looks like you catch me when I'm least fit for guests." Since when did a little heartburn stop me from socializing with fictional characters? I suppose I should have been used to the oddities of my AMD-inspired visions, but Huck was special. He was responsive to my voice and close enough to touch.

"I hope you're in a more talkative mood tonight. I've been reading—well, listening—to your story with my grandson. And I must say, I admire your resourcefulness, Mr. Finn. How you lit out from Pap when he locked you in that shanty was pure genius—much better than any plan Tom could percolate, and I'm not sweet-talking you either. You took your destiny into your hands and turned an impossible situation to your advantage. I admire that."

Huck tapped his pipe on the back of his hand. A pile of spent tobacco hit the floor. If he'd shinned away from Widow Douglas for trying to "sivilize" him, surely he'd flee if I scolded him for messing Suzanne's rug. I kept silent on the subject, hoping his tobacco would disappear like the mud. This was all so new. I did the one thing that came most naturally to me: I kept talking.

"I failed miserably at running away myself. But then Pa wasn't coming after me with a hick'ry. My ma seriously wished he would. I was a sassy thing, always wanted the last word. I tasted more soap than I care to recount."

Huck's eyes caught the light and his dimples deepened. That was all the encouragement I needed to continue.

"I hadn't thought about that night in years, not since before Evelyn died. You remember me telling you about my sister? She loved reminding me, and anyone who cared to listen, about what a foolish child I'd been. I was only ten years old and sick in love with a horse named Pete. The farmer had posted a 'for sale' sign on the pasture fence just outside the park. Did I tell you my pa was a park warden? You might compare him to the caretaker of a huge estate where people of any station could come and visit. He patrolled the Great Smoky Mountains for moonshiners and poachers. Ma sat up darning long into the night when he spent the night on the mountain. Well, that doesn't matter one bit about why I ran away, only that Pa didn't make a whole lot of money and feeding a saddle horse was completely out of the question."

Huck leaned back, picked at the frayed edges of his pants at the knees. Bored?

"I concocted a plan Tom would be proud of."

Huck rested his hand on his knee.

"Ma and Evelyn went visiting the new ranger's wife in the Greenbrier District with a basket of pie, jam, and pickles. Ma made the best pickles. As soon as they stepped off the porch, I packed a bag of Ma's bread and some cheese. Then I snitched a half dozen apples from the cellar for Pete and hid the bag under my bed. When the moon came up that night, I shimmied out the window and took off on foot down a game trail. Floating down a river, now that's the way to travel, but the West Prong of the Little Pigeon sluiced down the mountain, tumbling boulders and roaring like a train. Any raft I made would be toothpicks in minutes.

"I carried a flashlight and a whistle in case I came across any bears. We hadn't been at the park but a year, but I knew all the trails and roads like the back of my hand, at least the trails in the Sugarlands District. We lived in a dandy old farmhouse, where Evelyn and I could have had our own rooms but Ma made herself a quilting room. We would have shared a room anyway. I needed her snoring to lull me to sleep."

Huck shifted his weight. I figured I'd better stick to the facts of the story.

"I found Pete standing out in his pasture, head hung low, switching flies in his sleep. He looked magnificent in the moonlight. Did I tell you he was a palomino? He was no Trigger, but I can't deny most of my affection for him paralleled my adoration of Roy Rogers. Evelyn and I fought over who'd marry Roy first, never mind he was already married to Dale Evans, that hussy.

"Pete whinnied as I approached and leaned into my hand under his mane. He looked a good deal bigger at night, I can tell you that. I left my bag with him while I went looking for a halter in the barn. Now mind you, I never considered myself a horse thief, and I think they still hanged horse thieves in Tennessee back in the 1940s. In my mind's eye, Pete needed rescuing from his days as a plow horse.

"Well, you've probably guessed the end of this story. As you say, I was a perfect saphead for thinking I could steal a horse. Pete went and ate all my bread and cheese and the apples while I hunted the halter I never found. There's one thing I always take care of, Huck, and that's my stomach. Not much has changed in that department. Pete ate clear through my schoolbag. My hopes of becoming the Queen of the West faded that night, along with any hope of hearing the end of my foolishness in my sister's lifetime.

"I threw the worthless bag in a creek. Just as I rounded the last curve toward home, Pa stepped out of the shadows and nearly scared me to death. He took my hand. We walked a good distance in silence before he asked me, 'Birdie, had you forgotten the commandment, *Thou shalt not steal*?'

"The moon lit Pa's face like a lantern. The shadows deepened the furrows of his forehead. I don't know how he knew where I'd been, but my heart nearly burst for the disappointment on his face. I said, 'I reckon that old horse will be ready for the glue factory in a day or two.'"

"'That's what I was thinking too, Birdie,' he said.

"He bought me a new schoolbag in Gatlinburg before Ma or Evelyn noticed it missing. I loved him extra hard for that. Well, that's it. Not much of an adventure, not compared to yours."

Huck leaned back to suck his pipe and scratch himself like boys do.

"One thing I wondered, Huck. Did you understand you could never go back home, not to the widow or the judge, once you got them believing you were dead?"

I bit my lip to keep quiet, hoping Huck would get talkative. In the chapters Fletcher and I'd listened to that night, Huck floated down the river in a canoe he'd hived from the shore. He lay on his back to watch the night sky slide by. How I wanted that kind of freedom for Fletcher. A boy hungered for the chance to thumb his nose at probability now and again, even if he didn't know it.

Then a memory sat me bolt upright. Huck raised his eyebrows but otherwise seemed unperplexed by my sudden alertness.

"My son, Andy, the man who owns this house, he once ran away for three days. I liked to died of fright. Him and his father knocked heads over . . . I don't know what they argued about. Neither one talked about their fight, ever. I'd never seen Chuck so agitated, watching and waiting for Andy to return. The whole state of California, or what seemed like it, looked for Andy. Ends up he'd hiked to Tuolumne Meadows and set up camp. When the search-and-rescue folks hiked him out, the media flashed their cameras and poked microphones in Andy's face."

I worried the mention of media and microphones might mystify Huck, but he blinked and scratched his chin. Still, I yammered on. The story shouldered its way into the present.

"I hardly knew my own son. Dark whiskers bristled his chin and sideburns. A few nights in the wilderness had transformed him." My eyes burned with tears. "Things changed after that. Chuck only spoke to Andy to bark orders. Andy turned sullen, started running with a tough crowd, or what we thought was a tough crowd. They were Boy Scouts compared to the kids Fletcher comes across every day." I blew my nose. "Andy slept in our house, but he lived a million miles away. We bailed him out of jail once, but Chuck wouldn't do it a second time. Andy stayed in that cell for ten days and nights. I didn't sleep a wink, laid awake praying but mostly scheming ways to raise bail. Top on my list was selling Chuck's snowmobile. In the end, I didn't do anything, and I've lived to regret my paralysis to this day." I pounded the bed with my fist. "With Fletcher, things will be different."

Huck sat up straighter.

"Don't go getting provoked on account of a grandmother's passion. As I remember, you had plenty of people on your side. The judge and the widow fought hard for you . . . and they prayed for you, didn't they? While folks were out looking for your remainders, you figured prayer out for yourself. I know you did. The bread floated straight to you on Jackson Island. The widow and parson had prayed, and God listened. The bread found you, and you made a good breakfast of it. There's something to prayer, all right."

Although my watch read three o'clock in the morning by this time, the Sunday school teacher in me came alert. "Huck, Jesus prefers hearing from sinners. You ought to give prayer another try."

He leaned forward. "There ain't no doubt but there is something to the notion of prayer—"

At the sound of his voice—well it was if someone had pulled the drain and I was a bathtub full of warm water, now suddenly empty and cool. He didn't take notice.

"That is, there's something in it when a body like the widow or the parson prays, but it don't work for me, and I reckon prayin' don't work for only just the right kind of person."

Huck exited my world as weightlessly as he had trafficked into it. But his words remained, illusionary, sliding in and out of what was real and what was hoped for. Perhaps I only remembered his words from the story. But the longer I lay in the dark, the harder it became to dismiss the timbre of Huck's voice, the playfulness mixed with sadness. I stared toward what I'd come to think of as his recliner for a long time, willing him to return to confirm or deny his words. When he didn't, I wrestled with the kinds of accusations you might expect from someone approaching a certain age where vulnerabilities of the cognitive kind become more probable: You're crazy. You must stop watching television. You haven't been taking your vitamins. Your Aunt Terzie called the sheriff regularly to report zebras grazing among the cows. Chuck gave you a crossword puzzle book, and you never even tried.

Bee stretched and rolled onto my side of the bed without missing a snore. "And you consider yourself a faithful companion? You can forget about any surprises in your food bowl in the morning," I said, playing with a silky ear.

To silence the incriminations, I moved out to the great room, a room with a television as big as a bus and lots of leather and wood over a deeply piled rug. Maybe TCM was playing a Jimmy Stewart movie, or almost as good, a Cary Grant flick. I settled into a recliner that cradled my back with kindness and turned on a lamp to study the television remote. The thing weighed three pounds but was equipped with the teeny-tiniest buttons imaginable. Thwarted, I clicked off the lamp to blink into the darkness. My mind swam with conflicting thoughts. I composed tirades to hurl at my son over his unfair treatment of Fletcher, and then I nearly crawled up the stairs for a chance to hold Andy to my breast.

I needed clarity.

Chapter 10

"I'm going to church."

More a cry for independence than a statement of fact, I stood before the Wainwright family, each with a section of the Sunday paper spread before them. Fletcher looked up from what I supposed to be the box scores sprawled across the coffee table. Andy let his section collapse in his lap. Suzanne returned a powdery pastry to a plate. The scene was downright Rockwellian. Honestly, the temptation to trade my Bible for the funny papers nearly toppled my resolve. This was the first time in all the days I'd been in the Wainwrights' home that they all sat in the same room—no small miracle.

Andy stood up. "I'm sorry, Ma. I should have remembered. Give me a minute and I'll drive you."

"Sit down. There's a church a couple blocks away. I'm getting my technique down. Next week, I may enter a marathon." I didn't dare tell him I would need an hour to get there with all the rest stops I'd take.

Fletcher folded the sports page. "Are you talking about the Jackson Park Church? I'll go with you, Grandma."

If Dick Clark announced Andy Williams's "Moon River" had topped the charts, I couldn't have been more surprised or delighted. I'd prayed for Fletcher since he'd swam in his mother's womb. I won't apologize. I claimed his precious soul for Jesus, and now he'd offered to escort me to church. My heart thrummed the strains of the "Hallelujah Chorus."

I said to Andy, "There now, you don't have to worry about me. I'll walk with Fletcher."

Suzanne cleared her throat. Andy stood stock-still. Shifting the fog a bit, I saw Fletcher's offer had caught Andy off guard. I hadn't seen his jaw dropped that low since I'd asked him if he knew the facts of life. "You've never shown any interest in church," he said to his son.

"Grandma shouldn't go alone."

"I'm not so sure about this," said Suzanne, creasing the newspaper sharply in half. "I'd hate to see Fletcher caught up in something that would compromise him intellectually. What's the point?"

Andy took a breath, but I beat him at the conversational draw. Let the record show, I spoke matter-of-factly, although my heart raced feverishly. "I go to church because I'm as dumb as an ox, charging through life angry and scared. Church is the place where my heart gets back on track. I'm reminded what's important about life and eternity. I arrive feeling like the world is crumbling under my feet and leave knowing I stand on a Rock." You can bet I was glad I'd read Psalm 73 that morning.

Suzanne reached for another pastry and grew very quiet.

I know, I know, I should have kept my mouth shut, allow the Spirit to whisper sweet words of love to her, but the quiet taunted me. I struck out. "Besides, the serious brainwashing takes place during the midweek service when the snake handlers perform. Sundays are for collecting cash." I smiled to show I could laugh at myself and my brethren.

Suzanne twisted her hair into a knot and secured it with a

pencil. Did this action mark the end of our discussion, or was she strategizing?

"I'm still taking you." Andy tossed a section of newspaper to the pile on the coffee table. "I'll be right back, Ma. Have something to eat." Fletcher followed him at a trot toward the stairs.

I called after them. "The service doesn't start for nearly an hour. We have plenty of time." I sat in Andy's chair with a sigh I hadn't meant to be audible.

"What are you up to?" Suzanne asked.

All I'd intended was to meet with people compelled by God Almighty to love me, a soothing balm to my battered soul. "Excuse me?"

"Don't play coy with me. I know people just like you. Worse than that, I work with them. They think they walk on water and I'm the Wicked Witch of the West."

Careful. Shift tongue into neutral. Breathe. "I know people like that too. They infuriate me. It's all I can do not to strangle their scrawny little necks."

"They talk about me like I'm not there."

"They make my blood boil."

"And they leave Bible tracts on my desk."

"A neighbor once told me I was hell-bound for taking the kids hiking on a Sunday." Indeed, another ranger's wife had marched across the street in her Sunday suit to shake her finger at me. The look of disgust on her face kept me and the kids out of church for years. What a shame.

"I fired the Holy Roller with the tracts. I don't need distractions like that. I demand collaborative teamwork of my staff."

I said a silent prayer for the zealous woman, asking that her evangelistic fervor be tempered by love. "I put bitters in my neighbor's sun tea," I admitted.

Awe filled Suzanne's voice when she asked, "Did she know it was you?"

"Not until I asked her forgiveness many years later."

Suzanne captured a loose strand of hair to tuck behind her ear. "Why would you do such a thing?"

"Jesus called the self-righteous of his day 'white-washed tombs,' basically nothing but containers for death. So whether you like it or not, you and Jesus agree on the distastefulness of religiosity."

"But why ask her to forgive you? She's the one who wagged her finger."

"Oh, Suzanne, it took a very long time for me to make that phone call . . . years and years. By that time, I realized I'd been forgiven so much that being spiteful seemed ungrateful. I called her out of the blue, on a Sunday, probably after a particularly pointed sermon. She didn't remember me, not until I told her about the bitter sun tea. I learned that day how powerfully the sense of taste paves a link to the past. Once she calmed down, I asked her to forgive me."

"Did she?"

"She hung up on me. Her name is Philistia Concordia Pawlowski. I've had her name written in the front of my Bible for about thirty-five years."

"Strategizing a counterattack?"

"Jesus expects us to pray for our enemies. Her name is there to remind me."

Suzanne said provocatively, "Do you pray for me?"

"I do."

I'd long considered Suzanne an enemy. Since she married Andy, my relationship with him had never been the same. And despite her recent, surprisingly adept, attempts to supervise my recovery, clearly she disdained my lifestyle. She patronized me. She hated my dog. But I did pray for her. I'm embarrassed to say what for, now that time has tempered my reactions a bit. I've never claimed to be anything but a work in progress, so here's how

I prayed: *Dear Lord, please help Suzanne to value my contribution to the family, and may she work long hours, at least while I'm staying with them.*

"We see the world differently, that's for sure," I said. "I ask God to bless you with his love." This may seem like a lie, but how else would she come to appreciate me?

Suzanne leaned back into the soft leather of the sofa to finish her pastry. Finally, she said, "Thank you, I think."

Andy and Fletcher bounded down the stairs. "Let's go," said Andy, tossing and catching his keys.

AT LEAST ONCE A month during the high season, the kids talked Chuck and me into joining the camp-side church services rather than drive into Gardiner, nearly a hundred-mile round-trip from our station in Yellowstone. I didn't mind one bit. Whatever saved me time in the car with two small children, meant less time refereeing Andy's smug comeuppances and Diane's screaming over injustices. Above all, in the age before disposable diapers, the camp-side services meant fewer wet or otherwise soiled diapers to change on the road.

Lay or retired pastors regaled the camp-side crowd with messages predictably safe within the middle ground of doctrine, invariably centered on the majesty of God's handiwork. With the Grand Tetons in the background, the point was easily made. The fellowship among vacationing saints was frequently sweetened with invitations to campsites for lunch. I always toted a pie. Even in the wilderness, a sensible woman didn't show up empty-handed. Over the years, we nibbled hot dogs and potato salad with Presbyterians, Episcopalians, Methodists, Pentecostals, Catholics, Lutherans, and Congregationalists from all over the United States and several foreign countries. Under the canopy of God's cathedral, our differences didn't matter one lick. The experience expanded my view of the church, and love for my Savior deepened.

Later, when I traveled with the Round Robins, a group of women who loved good food, good art, and more good food, I never missed a chance to visit a church wherever we happened to land on a Sunday. I've attended services where the rain dripped through a thatched roof in Zambia and pummeled a tile roof of a Lutheran *kyrka* in Sweden. But no church suited me better than the little band of faithful at the Ouray Baptist Church, where they did a drop-dead imitation of the love of Christ. We gathered in the basement of Mount Abrams Variety and Gifts where we sat on cold metal chairs, summer and winter, to hear the Word of God preached, although no one begrudged the calling of a potluck now and again, especially if Josie brought her funeral potato casserole.

The Jackson Park Community Church I attended with Fletcher that day spanned the past and the present with ridges of glass and steel. Quite substantial yet agreeable, the stone walls muffled the traffic noise from the busy street while backs of heads glowed green, yellow, blue, and red from the light shining through sweeps of colored panes. I wondered what color bounced off my platinum curls. Green overlaid Fletcher's heap of chestnut curls, not an altogether pleasing combination. I hoped for a splash of red. I'd always wanted to be a redhead. The redder the better.

As the church filled, Fletcher waved a pamphlet and said, "Is this the program?"

"Yes, you'll have to help me follow along. Hand me a hymnal."

He grabbed a Bible.

"The red book, I think, sweetie."

"Sorry, Grandma."

"You can't mess up here," I assured him. "This is church, not some hoity-toity club. Everyone here is a sinner saved by grace." I patted his leg. "You're sitting in the safest place on earth.

God's people understand mistakes." I handed the hymnal back to Fletcher with a bundle of sticky notes. "I need your help. Mark the hymns listed in the program." Never mind I'd forgotten my magnifying glass and wouldn't be able to see a word.

"There's three listed," he said like I'd asked him to clean out the toothpaste drawer.

"Hymns are the best part."

"No, I mean right at the beginning." He groaned. "There's two more later in the program."

I held the hymnal to my face, trying to decipher the first title, but the page was nothing but gray smears. My heart leapt when I recognized the introduction to "Be Thou My Vision." Fletcher stood as silent as a statue while the congregation sang, even during the next two songs that turned out to be praise choruses with plenty of guitars strumming and drums thumping. But truthfully, beholding the structure and rhythm of a church service, through his or anyone's uninitiated eyes, probably made church seem a strange place indeed. Where else did grown people stand and sing together—besides the ballpark during the National Anthem and the seventh-inning stretch?

When the pastor stepped behind the pulpit, my heart sank. Not because of anything he said or did. He could have been the Cookie Monster, for all I knew. No, Huck was there, holding his hat out to congregants in the front row, pleading on one knee for a bald-headed man to drop some cash into his hat. I must have gasped because Fletcher asked me if I was okay.

"Fine. Never better," I whispered.

Huck skipped across the aisle to beg with outstretched hands and a pouty face. Although I knew he performed for my eyes only, I listened for any tittering among the congregants. Besides the preacher and scattered coughs, the sanctuary remained silent. Fletcher's legs bobbed restlessly. I put my hand on his knee and whispered, "Thank you for coming."

He stretched out his long legs by shifting to one hip and slid down in his seat. "Sure."

Lord, open his heart to the message of your gospel.

Huck pulled his hat down on his head so that his ears stuck out like speakers. He scowled at the congregation before he sat on the steps in front of the pulpit. The pastor spoke into the microphone. "Turn with me to the thirteenth chapter of John and read along with me through verse five."

Verse five? The story doesn't pick up speed until Simon Peter sasses the Lord about washing his feet. By habit, I checked the bulletin, only to see gray smears. Huck scratched at a scab on his arm. When it bled, he sucked on the wound. I fought not to react by focusing on the pastor's words.

He read about Jesus knowing his time on earth was short. The pastor's voice had the quality of a mountain stream, exhilarating and fresh. I listened intently as he read about Judas's treacherous plans and how Jesus, although definitely perturbed about his fate, bowed to wash his disciples' feet, all because he trusted the Father to get him home.

"Dear ones," said the pastor, "I want you to focus on the end of verse one: 'Having loved his own who were in the world, he now showed them the full extent of his love.' Consider the men he's sitting with, riddled with the weaknesses and blessed with the strengths we attribute to ourselves and those around us. They, however, earned the privilege of having every foible and act of faith recorded for our instruction and edification. I'm thankful the good Lord omitted my faith journey from the Scriptures. Surely I would have ended up somewhere between Balaam's donkey and Job's friends."

The congregation laughed, and so did I, as I squirmed. Huck fell to his back, laughing silently, and kicking the air.

Don't look at him.

"Jesus knew these men, and he knew them well. Eleven of the

disciples stayed in the boat when Simon Peter walked on the water. Those who chose the safety of the boat missed the exhilaration of walking with the Lord in defiance of nature's laws and experiencing the deep love of God's rescuing hand. And those crazy sons of thunder, James and John—they wanted to call fire down on an unwelcoming Samaritan village. I've been tempted to do the same during rush-hour traffic. Another time, unnamed disciples complained to Jesus that their provisions had dwindled to one loaf of bread. Only days earlier, Jesus had fed thousands of people with a few loaves and fishes, not once but twice. And yet they'd forgotten. Again, Simon Peter stands out on this important night. Jesus knew that within hours of his last Passover meal, Simon Peter, the great burly fisherman, would deny he ever knew Jesus—not to the chief priest but to a young servant girl. And dare we forget Judas? He sat watching the preparations for the meal, making plans for his thirty pieces of silver."

Huck leaned against the pulpit, crossed his arms, and closed his eyes. Soon his breathing deepened and his head lolled to one side.

"To these men—flawed, greedy, contentious, faithless, ambitious—Jesus demonstrated the full extent of his love. He did *not* lecture them on faithfulness, or pound his fist on the table or lean over to Simon Peter to say, 'Don't make promises you can't keep.'"

Men behind me cleared their throats. The noise broke my concentration enough that I looked for Huck. He was gone. I looked to Fletcher, a reflex really, to see if he'd noticed. I needn't have worried. Fletcher had spent his time filling every blank space of the bulletin with doodles. My heart sagged.

The pastor continued. "This is what the Son of the Most High God did to demonstrate the full extent of his love: He became a servant. He removed his robe, wrapped himself in a towel, and washed his students' feet. Go ahead and add stinking feet to the disciples' offenses. One of them should have risen to wash the feet of the guests. But they were full of themselves, anticipating their grand futures as protectorates of the Jewish nation. Jesus did what they would not do for one another. And the bickering stopped."

The pastor stood silently for a long time.

"Whose feet is Jesus asking you to wash? Now, relax, I'm not asking you to strip down to your Skivvies and wash anyone's feet."

A nervous jitter filled the sanctuary.

"Maybe the Lord will, but I won't. No, I'm asking: To whom will you show the full extent of his love?"

"CAN WE STAY A little longer?" Fletcher said, stretching his neck to scan the congregation shuffling toward the narthex and the espresso bar.

"What time is it?" I said.

Fletcher bounced. "Dad will be here in ten minutes."

"Are you looking for someone?"

"I have a friend who goes here."

"From school?"

"Chemistry. There. I'll be right back."

Fletcher returned to the sanctuary, I presumed, since he disappeared into the fog. I swallowed down panic. Unfamiliar situations unsettled macular degenerates like me. The fog made finding a helpful sign or a place to sit a challenge, especially since I liked to look normal in such situations. As casually as I could muster, I shifted my focus to catch a length of wall to lean against, or better yet, a seat near the coffee counter. People milled all around me. The smell of dark roasted coffee and bananas wafted over the crowd. I prayed the prayer God had never left unanswered for me: *Lord, send someone to guide me.*

A woman trailing Estée Lauder and wearing a reassuring amount of denim sidled up to me and slid her arm around my waist. "Birdie! It's me, Ruth. We must get you a seat, dear. We're only a few steps away. I'm sitting with a group of friends you'll love, a couple of the Bats. I'm anxious for you to meet them."

"My ride will be here soon, Ruth."

She squeezed tighter. "I'm so sorry I didn't invite you to join me this morning. The church sends a van." We sat at a bistro table by the espresso bar. Ruth announced my presence to the table. "Hey girls, we have a new Bat joining us. This is Birdie. She's living right next door to me."

"In that *new* house?" a woman said with a hint of that anger.

Ruth ignored her. "She can't stay long, but I wanted to introduce you. She's coming to our meeting on Thursday."

"We're both happy and sad to meet you, Birdie. It's always nice to meet another sister in the Lord, but I'm sorry you got stuck being a degenerate."

"That's Betty," Ruth said.

"We mustn't forget to pray for Ruby. She goes for an injection tomorrow. Keep the prayers coming, girls!"

I knew exactly what Betty meant by an injection—an anticoagulant shot right into the eyeball with a needle. "I'm at end stage."

"Oh, crumb. Who's your doctor?" asked another woman at the table with dyed inky black hair, a pageboy with bangs curled as tight as cannoli.

I'd had this conversation plenty of times on cruise ships, hiking trails, and in dance halls. Yes, I'd passed up laser photocoagulation—think of an iron rod cauterizing an opened wound—and tried photodynamic therapy, which turned out to be nothing better than a Band-Aid. Technology hadn't kept pace with the progress of my disease, so I'd determined to outpace the disease.

"I live in Ouray," I said. "I drive to Grand Junction to see a retinal specialist."

Fletcher reappeared. "Grandma, Dad's out front. We better go . . . *now.*"

I rose. "I'm sorry . . ."

"Don't be silly. See you Thursday," Ruth said. "You'll meet Ruby too."

Riding the few blocks home, I felt buoyant for the first time in weeks. "Fletcher, did you enjoy the message?"

"The message?"

"About Jesus washing the disciples' feet?"

"Why'd he do that?"

Chapter 11

I'd fallen asleep with the words of the preacher stitching my thoughts: *To whom will you show the full extent of his love?* Limited as I was in movement, the answer proved singular, simple: my family. But how? These people don't do a thing for themselves. They sent their laundry out and employed Lupe to clean house, a friendly gardener named Roger, and a team of window washers who arrived every Tuesday. True to form, I woke at four, considered flipping on the television, reading my Bible, or listening to more *Huck*, but the kitchen called.

Clear glass containers filled the pantry, and if the containers were labeled, you couldn't tell it by me. I tasted powdered sugar, baking soda, and something that left a metallic taste in my mouth before finding the workhorse of the pantry, bleached flour. I found butter in the freezer but no lard or shortening. Suzanne stocked only raw sugar. Not finding tapioca—my thickening of choice—nearly bushwhacked my intentions, but this was no time to let pride get in the way. I had love to extend. I settled on flour and more butter, not a wholly disagreeable notion. Once I'd assembled everything I needed, including the apples, I studied the oven controls with a magnifying glass. I turned the knob to 425 degrees, and a red light shone. Congratulating myself, I cut the butter into the flour and salt with two knives.

Huck sat at the counter, his chin in his hands. Was his hair longer? "I should have guessed you'd show up with a pie on the way." Huck's appearance energized the zing of knife against knife through the dough. "That was some show you put on at church. Goodness, but you made it difficult for this old woman to concentrate."

A lopsided grin let me know Huck enjoyed putting on a performance.

I poured ice water into the flour mixture until the dough barely held together. "You know, Huck, something's been gnawing at me. The last time you visited me, I could have sworn I heard you speak." I rested my hands on the side of the bowl. "I wouldn't mind one bit if you wanted to speak your mind, anytime at all, day or night. What with your adventures with Tom and all, I'm sure you have stories worth hearing. I'm nothing but a grandma, Huck. You can't get in trouble with me."

Knowing that nothing clammed a boy up faster than a female gaze, young or old, I set to kneading the dough. When I finally looked up, Huck stretched toward the ceiling and yawned. His indifference miffed me.

"Don't go thinking you can bamboozle me, Huck. I've been around the block more times than I care to admit. I heard you talk. I know I did, so there's no sense in playing these games. Spit it out. What's going on in that shaggy head of yours?"

Huck left his seat, and I feared I'd overstepped the unspoken boundaries of our friendship. He slipped from the counter to lean against the cabinets and set to chewing the end of his pipe.

"Okay then, keep me company while I bake this pie. You're a joy to look at, I can tell you that. Those blue eyes of yours are going to be woman-slayers one of these days. Talk when you want to. I'm not going anywhere."

The stove pinged and I nearly jumped out of my skin. I read the LCD numbers with the magnifying glass. The oven had reached temperature, and I hadn't even rolled out the crust. I needed a rolling pin.

I felt my way through every cupboard, high and low, which proved no small task with my enormous boot. I'd used jelly glasses in the early years to roll out a crust, but all of Suzanne's glasses were cut crystal. My ankle ached. I pumped the boot up tighter. "You could help me," I finally said to Huck. "I'm trying to do something nice for my family with a broken ankle. If you know where the rolling pin is, let me know, won't you?"

He backed away from the base cabinet he'd been leaning against, and with a flourish, gestured at the cabinet door. My heart thumped. His gaze held me. The boy. The apparition. My own imaginary friend spoke to me . . . if you're of a mind to count gestures in reply to a question as I am. My hand trembled as I opened the cabinet door. I found the mixing bowls and a French coffee press and assorted baking pans, just as I had the first time I rummaged through that cabinet's contents. I stretched my reach and there it was—a tapered rod of wood. French. Of course. Once I held the rolling pin in my hands, the sting of fresh wood thrilled my nose.

"I'm awfully grateful, Huck," I said, but in his typical manner, he'd already moved on. Did he go back to the story? Was he floating under the moon on the Mississippi River? Was Jim at the tiller, humming a lullaby as he dreamed about reuniting with his family?

ANDY STRODE INTO THE kitchen about half past five, wearing a sweater over a golf shirt, probably a prototype for next year's line. "Good grief, Ma, what are you doing up at his hour? You shouldn't be on your feet," he scolded. Then, "Is that a pie baking?"

"Apple," I said, opening the oven. "Couldn't sleep. Too much on my mind."

"Suzanne can prescribe something." He poured coffee into a travel mug.

"Getting my hands into dough cleared my thoughts. I needed something to do." Andy sat at the counter while I cut the pie. "You're looking a bit casual this morning."

"I'm meeting a client for a round of golf in the Springs."

"Colorado Springs? Have you looked out the window? You might have a hard time finding your ball in the snow."

Andy cupped his hands to look out the kitchen window and swore. "This storm wasn't due until after lunch." He swore again.

"Think of this as a grand opportunity to spend some quality time with your mother." I pushed the pie toward him.

"Ma, I—"

"I heard about the storm on the news. It's swinging up from the south. Morrison Hill will be treacherous. Surely your client has already gone back to bed." I popped the top off the ice cream carton. "One scoop or two?"

"Pie for breakfast? I can't remember the last time."

I drew a curl of ice cream with the scooper and served him. "You should never eat pie alone."

He sighed and picked up the fork. I bit my lips to keep from smiling. I hate gloaters.

Andy studied the pie. I'd loaded it with fruit, using every apple in the crisper, latticed the top crust, and brushed the pastry with egg yolk and milk before sprinkling the top with cinnamon and sugar. No one walks away from a pie like that.

He gouged a bite and pressed the tines of his fork into the ice cream. Melted cream dribbled down his chin. "Hot," he said and moaned.

I sat beside him and stifled the urge to moan myself. My ankle throbbed, but pillows and ice packs would come later, after Andy left. For now, he sat where I wanted him, several compass points closer to the boy I remembered. I knew better than to spew sentimentality, but the warm pie and ice cream melding in my mouth seemed to open a door long closed. "I miss eating pie with you."

"Sorry I haven't been around much. My marketing VP was courted away by our biggest competitor. That meant starting a new campaign from scratch. I hope you've been comfortable, Ma."

To this point, the conversation had followed surprisingly close to my rehearsed plan. But now I met a conversational fork in the path: Should I ask Andy about the argument he'd had with his father all those years ago, try to gain some closure, which might actually reopen a gaping wound? Or should I stick to the here and now, deal with the subject at hand: Fletcher?

"I'm a little concerned about Fletcher," I said.

Andy laid his fully loaded fork back on the plate. As surely as if a mason had blown through the room, a stone wall filled the space between us. He pushed the plate away. There went the breezy lecture I'd prepared about boys needing fun and freedom. I took a conversational back step. Any wall erected could be torn down again. "He's been absolutely wonderful to me. He walks Bee and does a great job. Bee can be a hellion on a leash. She's more responsive to him that she is to me; it must be his confidence."

"Fletch?"

"Bee smells weakness."

Andy picked up his fork. "It's just that . . . we've had our problems with Fletch lately."

"Boys can be inconsistent."

"He's lazy, doesn't give a thought to his future."

As a toddler, when Andy woke in the darkest hours of the night in an inconsolable fit of terror, caught between sleep and wakefulness, I'd learned to speak like a river of honey to soothe him. I hadn't forgotten that trick. "If boys care too much about tomorrow, the ladies snub them. They've lost their mystique."

Andy pressed against the counter with his palms. "Look, Ma, things are different now. In middle school, getting good grades and staying out of trouble was enough. Back then, Fletch walked in sand along the beach. Whatever he did, good or bad, got washed away once he entered high school. Now he's walking in wet cement. The impressions he makes will stick forever. Every grade. Every activity. Every sport. College recruiters from the best schools will be looking at his footprints. Good grades aren't enough; he needs a résumé. But Fletcher doesn't give a—"

"Perhaps I can add the perspective of longevity. What mattered to me when I was younger, the things that kept me up past midnight and woke me at the crack of dawn, don't matter a lick to me now. Perhaps the two of you could find something to do together."

"Are you talking about your county-fair quilts? For goodness' sake, Ma, you're comparing apples to oranges. As the general manager of Rocky Mountain Golf, I employ more than two hundred people. I export products to thirty foreign markets. I'm not making a pretty blanket in hopes of winning a blue ribbon. Those two hundred people represent two hundred families, all looking to me for their security."

Evidently, we were talking about Andy.

"Quilts and golf togs have one thing in common: they both burn. When they do, all that's left are satisfying relationships—or regrets. It's up to you."

Andy stared into his coffee. I'd gotten him thinking. I should have kept my mouth shut, let him figure out his relationship with Fletcher, but I didn't do that. "Don't forget Fletcher is still a boy—a dear, dear boy who seems to be trying as hard as he can and still has time for his grandmother. That's an amazing young man in my book."

"Ma, don't."

"It's as plain as the nose on your face."

"Ma . . ." Andy pushed himself from the counter. "I'll finish the pie later."

When hiking, Josie and I sometimes left the established trail to bushwhack cross-country. Many times we were rewarded with a panoramic view of mountaintops or by a rare wildflower find. On rare occasions, we found ourselves dead in our tracks at the base of a stone abutment or knee deep in soppy marsh grass. At times like that, we turned back toward the trail, a bit chagrined, mildly disappointed. Something had bushwhacked this conversation. Time to backtrack to the trail. "Fletcher needs his driver's license."

"Ah-ha! Fletcher put you up to this."

"Nope. This is my idea. I could use his help getting around, and he could follow his interests, build his résumé. You know, walk in cement."

Andy sat down and pulled the apple pie closer. He scraped it clean with the side of his fork. "This isn't a good time. Work is crazy. Maybe in the fall. Colorado requires parents to drive with their kids for fifty hours before they issue a license. It's all self-monitoring. The two of us will drive around a little, and then I'll sign off."

"Maybe you would have avoided rolling the truck if we'd driven with you for fifty hours. Besides, that's fifty hours spent with Fletcher. Time with your son will be harder and harder to come by the older he gets."

Andy's words darkened the room. "We'd kill each other." He rose to look out the window. "This storm is nothing. If I don't make the effort . . . thanks for the pie, Ma."

I spoke toward the door after it closed. "This may be a busy time for you, but I have nothing but time."

Chapter 12

I held the apple pie out to Ruth. "Will this feed the Bats?"

"We'll cut the slices in two. Most of the girls don't eat that much. If Betty wants seconds, I have brownies in the freezer."

"Is there anything else I can do? I came early to be of some use." This was my first visit to Ruth's kitchen, a cave of a room with painted orange cabinets and varnished scalloped trim. Beyond these bold details, the dimness of the room concealed its character. I was about to suggest Ruth turn the lights on when I saw that, indeed, a glowing globe of light hung from the ceiling. This kitchen would never do for me. I'd chop my fingers clean off.

"You're kind to offer. The dust may be thick enough to write in, but honestly, I don't know or care. I prefer relaxing with a cup of coffee. We have a good half hour before the Bats start showing up."

Ruth ushered me to the living room to sit in a chair by the window. I played with the rise and fall of its damask fabric. She returned from the kitchen with the coffee to lean back in her chair with her cup poised at her chin. I asked her, "When I met the Bats at church on Sunday, they seemed put off that I live in the new house next door. Are you sure it's okay for me to be here?"

She sipped at the coffee. "I hope you have a good friend back in Ouray, Birdie."

"My best friend is Josie," I said, stammering a bit. "I love and envy her at the same time. She's an amazing artist. I have so much to tell her, but she'll only talk on the telephone if her hair is on fire. I've tried and tried to convince her that short calls won't hurt her, but she won't budge on this point. If I want to talk to her, I walk the three blocks to her house, but I'm not complaining. She loves me like a sister. She'd do anything for me as long as I don't ask her to hold a phone to her ear."

"I think I told you about Helen. She lived in the house your family razed to build their home. The older I get, the more sentimental I become. We do tend to see the past through a veil of half-truth and wishful thinking, don't we?"

"Oh, yes."

"I'm not saying this to make you feel bad, only to help you understand the Bats a bit better. The four of us stood at this window and watched the bulldozer tear Helen's house down. I don't know what came over me. I tend to be an optimistic and reasonable person, but that day I cried like a baby."

"I'm so sorry, Ruth."

"You have nothing to be sorry for. Things change, and it's a good thing they do or we'd all be living in soddies. Besides, Helen hadn't lived there in years." Ruth scratched her chin. "Let's see, there were the Clantons. They moved in when Helen's children sold the place back in '78. They had three adorable children. The middle girl sold me pot holders as fast as she could make them. Everyone on my Christmas list received pot holders that year, and oh, the colors she put together! I still have one in the back of my linen drawer. I can't bear to part with it. The next year she made tooled leather bookmarks with yarn tassels. She nearly cleaned out my bank account when she discovered I belonged to a literary club. 'Oh, Mrs. Spencer, these will make lovely gifts for all of your reading friends,' she said as wide-eyed as an owl. I couldn't resist her brown eyes and auburn curls, and she knew it. She was a cunning little thing. Let's see, they sold the house when Clark got a job in Indiana. I'll never forget the day he came over to say good-bye. The dear had shoveled my walks from the day he moved in, and that was a winter to remember. This strapping man had tears in his eyes as he told me Mark Patton would be shoveling my walks from then on. 'And if he doesn't, call me in Indiana. I'll make sure it gets done right.' Mark shoveled my walks the rest of that winter, but, well, life gets busy, doesn't it?

"When the Clantons moved out, the Stones bought the place. Linda, the mother, sang like a meadowlark. Each of her three daughters delighted me in her own way, called me Grandma along with my own grandchildren, and I loved them the same. How they did squeal as they ran through the sprinklers on a summer day! Linda had a knack of knowing just when I needed a dinner invitation. They moved some years ago to be near Linda's ailing parents. That's the kind of people they were. I still hear from Linda at Christmastime. Her husband, Vick, passed away last summer. It's been tough for her.

"Then a real estate investor bought the place as a rental. Renters came and went more often than the seasons. At first, I baked a cake and trotted over there, secretly hoping another Helen might move in. One woman threatened to call the police if I showed up again. In no uncertain terms, she let me know she wasn't interested in getting to know her neighbors. She worked hard, and she didn't need touchy-feely neighbors knocking at her door. Can you imagine?"

Although I wasn't sure I wanted to know the answer, I asked, "Did you approach Andy and Suzanne?"

"I did."

"And they welcomed you?" I said, hoping.

"More than anything they seemed surprised by my sudden appearance at their door. They weren't sure they should accept my offering of muffins. It dawned on me much later they were afraid I'd laced the muffins with poison, but I supposed that's the kind of suspicion that helps this generation survive. It's all so terribly sad."

"Andy knows better. We relied on our neighbors all through his growing-up years." I set my coffee on the table. "I don't know what to say. I'd give my eye teeth to have a neighbor like you."

"For the time being, you do. I don't hold a grudge against your son or his family. They've built a lovely home, and they're nice and quiet. The Bats are protective even when they have no need to be." The doorbell rang. "Just promise me you'll give them a fair chance. They're lovely and the best entertainment a girl could ask for."

"I can always use another friend," I said, lonesome for Josie, the Super Seniors, and the Round Robins. And Emory.

Ruth led me to a round table she'd set up at the far end of the living room and pulled out a chair. "Sit here, Birdie, on the right side of Betty. Then you won't have to repeat everything seven times."

Betty patted the chair to her left. "Sit here," she said. "My hearing isn't so good on my right side."

Ruth kissed Betty's cheek. "It's worse on your left side, dear."

Although Betty may have suffered hearing loss, no one had trouble hearing her. "I've got retinitis pigmentosa, but these macular degenerates let me come anyway!"

When I met new people, I concentrated on connecting a name, not with a face but with hair color and style or other distinguishing feature. Betty's pewter hair rose like a mist over her scalp. Shifting the fog revealed welder-grade sunglasses. Distinctive. I wouldn't forget Betty.

Ruth put her hand on my shoulder. "Birdie, I'm going to the kitchen to slice your pie."

Her touch and words expressed the consideration low-vision people extended to one another, a way to fill in the visual blanks. Otherwise, being the chatty kind of gal I was, I would have continued talking like she was still in the room. She deserved a kindness returned.

"I can help," I said, rising.

She put her hands on my shoulders. "Not on your first visit. We'll make you supply the flowers, set the table, and wash out the coffeepot next time . . . but only if your ankle is better."

"No, we won't," bellowed Betty too close to my ear. "She's just joshing you!"

The door opened and a new voice sang out. "A newbie! Hallelujah! Thank you, Jesus! One more week with these degenerates, and I was going to explode with boredom." She introduced herself as Ruby, a fitting name for her pile of paprika curls. "Are you the gal who lives next door?"

"You'll have to watch out for that one." As Betty spoke, I leaned against my ear as if deep in concentration. In truth, I hoped to save what hearing remained. "Ruby comes off all sweetness and light, but don't try to drive with her. As sure as I'm sitting here, you'll end up in a ditch somewhere."

Ruth called from the kitchen. "That was me, Betty. Don't you remember the fella at the gas station? He told us to turn right when we should have turned left."

"Don't listen to Ruth. She takes credit for everything, good or bad. Ruby dumped us in the ditch as sure as I'm sitting here."

"You're right, Betty. It was me," Ruby admitted unconvincingly. "Do you travel, Birdie?"

Finally, a topic I loved. "I take a couple trips a year, although I have to live like a pauper to do so, but there's nothing better than traveling with friends. Unless, of course, it's eating with friends."

Ruby patted my shoulder before she sat down across from me. "You're going to fit in with this group just fine."

Betty's voice trembled with irritation. "Don't tell us another word until Margie gets here. Otherwise, she'll needle us for every last detail."

"Pie in front of you, Birdie. Fork on the right." Ruth served generous wedges of pie, not the half slivers we'd agreed upon before the Bats showed up. Ruth's place remained empty of pie. I'd often seen my mother make the same sacrifice for a guest, saying she was too full to indulge. My admiration for Ruth grew. As for the other Bats, they were hard of hearing, generous, and a touch crotchety. And they tussled like sisters. The Bats suited me fine.

"Did Margie call anyone? She's not usually this late." Ruby lowered her voice. "Let's pray before she gets here. I'm terribly concerned about her."

Ruth sat beside me. "We also need to bless this beautiful pie Birdie baked for us, so why don't you do that, Ruby. I'll keep my good eye on the door."

Ruby's prayer ushered us into a holy place. The prayer could have been for me, as it was all about restoring Margie's joy and unifying her family. Finally she thanked the Lord for my skillful fingers and generous heart. I squirmed in my chair, knowing I'd brought leftovers.

Ruth clanked her coffee cup with her spoon. "Okay, girls, I'm setting the timer. You have ten minutes to talk about your vision issues and not a minute more, but visitors first. Birdie, we're just dying to know. What kind of degenerate are you?"

The timer ticked insistently. I explained about the fog and the gift of sharp peripheral vision. "At least, for now, that is. I'm end-stage."

"My life's a blur," said Betty. "When I look at you, all I see is white fuzz on top of a featureless face." She moved close enough that I felt her breath on my face. I wished she'd done a better job brushing her teeth that morning. "There, now you have eyes."

Ruby said, "I had a Lucentis treatment Monday. It felt like the doctor emptied his sand pail into my eye, and it felt that way until yesterday afternoon. My eye leaked like a spigot, and I'm not exaggerating. I slept with a towel over my pillow. The doctor warned me, but I always think they're covering their hineys with their doom-and-gloom warnings. All in all, I'm praising God that my eyesight is remaining stable."

"When's your next treatment?"

"In four weeks—the usual—unless I notice a change. But you have to hear this: I walked around the hospital yesterday with a coffee stain that practically covered my bosom. I didn't have a clue until my husband pointed it out to me at dinner. I like to think my stained blouse provided a little levity for a patient or two."

Betty leaned into me to whisper loudly enough for everyone to hear. "Ruby's our Holy Roller. She goes to the Pentecostal church downtown."

Ruby added. "And I've stopped driving."

When I'd parked the Volkswagen in the garage for what I knew was the last time, I'd mourned the loss of my freedom as if both my feet had been amputated. Ouray was too small for public transportation, but then everything was within walking distance, albeit with steep hills to descend and climb back up again. Without the car, flights of fancy—like lunch in Ridgway for a buffalo burger—became organized field trips with my sighted friends. I traveled around the world and to Wal-Mart every other week with the Round Robins. Without them, I'd be forced to move to a bigger town, maybe even Denver. I took a breath to offer my condolences to Ruby, but an unknown voice announced her arrival.

"Hey, everyone, is there any coffee left?"

"Margie, you're just in time," Ruth said. "The timer's about to go off."

Margie's voice sagged. "I'm done with treatments. And I'm done with pushing myself to go places, excepting here, of course. I'm tired of embarrassing myself."

"Done with treatments?" Ruby asked.

"I can't put myself through those shots one more time. The results aren't that great, and I get so worked up the week before the appointment. It's not worth—"

Ding!

"Ignore the timer, Margie. Tell us what's really going on," Ruth urged.

"There's nothing to tell. I'm tired. I don't want to live recuperating from one shot, just to anticipate the next."

Ruth moved around the table to embrace Margie. The other gals reached out to touch her. Like hens cooing over a returned chick, the Bats offered their encouragement.

"You've been very brave."

"You've shouldered plenty of disappointment."

"I'm awfully glad you told us."

"I'm relieved, really," Margie said. "Bart and I want to focus on the grandchildren. As for my vision, it's one day at a time, just as it is for Bart's diabetes and my blood pressure. God will see us through. He always has. I'd rather live day to day than live under the tyranny of the treatment schedule. I must seem like a weakling to—"

"You're a gladiator in my book."

"I've always admired your strength."

"Your faith encourages me."

The room went silent. An expectation to add an exhortation nudged me. Before I could think of anything to say, Margie asked, "Now, is that Myrtle back from the dead, or do we have a new member?"

The group enjoyed a good laugh over my mistaken identity. I jumped in with the universal topic of delight. "How many grandchildren do you have, Margie?"

"Three, but if I don't play by the rules, my daughter-in-law stops taking my calls. Don't ask me why. I can offend her by stepping into the room. I don't dare complain. The last time I did, I didn't see the grandkids for six months. Sophie, the youngest one, didn't know me. She screamed and clutched her mother's legs when I reached for her. I tell you, seeing how I'd frightened that dear one was like dying from the inside out."

Betty chimed in. "My kids live so far away, and the grandkids are in college. I never hear a word from any of them. And 'thank you' notes? I'm lucky if anyone makes it home for Christmas."

"Birdie, you're in a tough situation, aren't you?" Ruth said.

"I think things are getting better, as long as I keep Bee—that's my dog—in the bedroom with me."

Ruby jumped in. "Listen, honey, this is a support group, and as such, we're your personal counselors and prayer warriors. We're here to help you live as a degenerate in a seeing world. Our lips are sealed."

I never meant to tell the story all the way back to Andy and Suzanne's engagement. I blame my verbosity on the fog. The ladies around the table could have been comatose with boredom, and yet I prattled on.

"That Suzanne is a controlling little thing, isn't she?" Betty asked.

"She sounds just like my daughter-in-law," Ruby added. "Are they churning these crazy women out at a factory somewhere?"

"Suzanne's a cosmetic surgeon, but all she really wants is to be a mother," I offered, surprised by my desire to defend her.

"I don't care if she's president of the United States of America." Betty pounded the table hard enough to clank the silverware. "Who does she think she is? Can you imagine warning your mother-in-law to keep her dog off your floors?"

I'd only seen my mother-in-law when we traveled to North Dakota. Frankly, Mother Wainwright had spent too many winters listening to the mice in her pantry, but I loved her dearly and the kids adored her, even the mismatched socks she knitted every Christmas. She tipped the sherry bottle after dinner, told sentimental stories of growing up with her grandparents, and cuddled the closest child to her chest. I never thought to forbid her contact with the children. Even with all of her eccentricities, she'd generously displayed her approval, for the children and for me. For that, I remembered her fondly.

This conversation never should have happened. I tried to backpedal. "My son and his wife are trying very hard to balance their sense of duty with the demands of their daily lives. I'm so grateful. We all have our foibles. I know that better than anyone." After all, I visited with an imaginary boy. What would the Bats think about that?

Ruth laid her hand over mine. "You're right, Birdie. We should be talking to the One who can actually see into the hearts of our children. I have a daughter who's old enough to retire next year. Her name is Jane. From the day she was born she owned my heart, even though I went on to have three more children. I guess I'm a terrible mother, but Jane was such a sweet, tender child."

"She was all that and more," Margie added.

"Speak up, Ruth. I can barely hear you!" Betty said.

"I remember Jane climbing into my lap and begging me to tell her another story about Jesus. She especially enjoyed the story about his healing the paralytic lowered through the roof by his friends."

"I always wondered who got to clean up the mess from them digging through the roof tiles. You know it was a woman. It's always a woman!"

Ruby said, "Healing the man was a small thing compared to forgiving his sins. At least, that's what I always thought about the story, and Jesus did so because of his friends' faith, not the paralytic's."

Ruth squeezed my hand. "I think you're right, Ruby. That's why it's so ironic that Jane loved this story. The Bats know Jane's story well enough, Birdie. I'll just give you the highlights: Jane just married for the fifth time. She's an alcoholic and a con artist. Every few years, once she's depleted a husband's bank account, Jane will divorce him and take him for whatever he has left. In between rich husbands, she scams senior citizens of their life savings. She's been in prison twice.

"I can't pull Jane onto my lap anymore to tell her stories about Jesus or sing her songs of his love and mercy. I barely hear from her at all, so I pray. I lower her into his presence on a mat, just like the friends of the paralytic. There's no better place for her. In his presence is grace and forgiveness, healing and hope, rest for the weary."

"That's a beautiful picture of prayer."

"But Jane isn't a paralytic, and she isn't a child at rest in my lap. I may lower her through the roof to Jesus' presence, but chances are she hops off the mat and elbows through the crowd toward the door."

Ruby raised her arms. "And sisters, that's where the Holy Ghost comes in."

"Yes, the Holy Ghost. I believe there will be a time when Jane stays on the mat long enough to look into the eyes of Jesus. Finally, she'll behold his love. Knowing her, she'll challenge him to offer her more than what a bottle of gin can offer, and he will. Until then, I'll keep praying."

Chapter 13

"Don't come in!" Lupe rushed me at the door. "The floor, it's not so dry yet."

I slumped down to sit on the top step that led from the garage to the kitchen.

"No, don't go sitting in the garage like a bad dog. Go around. The patio door, it's not locked."

I should have elevated my foot while at Ruth's. Now my ankle burned. I pumped the boot tighter. The pressure smoldered the heat, if only moderately. "You're usually done with the floors by now." I regretted my whiny tone immediately.

"Your room is ready. I did it first, before I watched *The People's Court*."

"I thought you'd sworn off that show."

Lupe held the mop across her chest. "You think I'll feel guilty and let you in? You can forget about it."

"I'm tired. I don't have anywhere to go. I'm happy sitting here." Ruth had percolated the coffee, a rarity to be savored. I'd had three cups, and yet lead ran through my veins.

"You want something to drink?"

I squeezed my legs together. "I'm fine, Lupe. I just want to rest."

She leaned the mop against the wall with a huff. "Fine. Take your shoe off and leave the walker in the garage—"

"Doctor's orders. Weight as tolerated, and I've overdone already. I've got plenty to keep me occupied." Ruth's story about lowering her daughter to Jesus had really hit home. I longed to dig through this roof until my fingers bled.

"You want I should turn on the television loud so you can hear the crazy people on Jerry Springer? They have big, fat girls who love their mother's boyfriends on today."

"Pass." I pulled the door closed. From the soothing darkness of the garage, I yelled through the door. "I'm not here! Proceed as planned."

The door opened. Lupe stood over me, hands on hips. "Take the shoe off, or I'll clobber you with the mop. I'll hold you up."

"I'll mark the floor."

"Not so much. I'm stronger than I look."

I looked up in time to watch Huck march toward the bedroom, leaving a trail of muddy footprints.

"You win. Take me to my room."

Once inside the room, I pushed back the recliner and let the upholstery envelope me. Huck sat at the end of the bed, his legs dangling over the footboard. Although his feet were muddy, he wore a clean coarse shirt and trousers that he'd rolled up almost to his knees. And a belt. The outfit looked new except for a brown stain near the collar.

I leaned forward to whisper. "This isn't a good time, Huck. Lupe's in the house. She's liable to hear me talking to you."

Huck shrugged.

"That's fine for you. No one will think you're a loon."

He hopped off the bed to stand over Bee who twitched and mewed in her sleep.

"She's fine. Go ahead and pet her. I'm just going to watch you. Mum's the word."

The boy squatted next to Bee. He held his hand just above her shoulder.

"Go on," I said too loudly. I covered my mouth.

Huck stood, shaking his head at Bee.

"She won't bite, boy. Her ears are like silk. There's nothing she likes better than a good scratching behind her ears."

He hiked up his trousers to kneel beside Bee. Again, he held his outstretched hand over Bee for a long while. Finally, his hand fell to his thigh. "I can't," he said.

"What? You can't what? Talk to me, boy. What is it you can't do?"

Lupe knocked and opened the door. Huck jumped up to stand on the bed. He smiled broad enough to show a crooked incisor and hopped tentatively until he gained his sea legs, so to speak. He reached for the ceiling with each jump. The springs groaned under his weight. I didn't dare scowl or say anything, not with Lupe there.

"I think maybe some ice would be good for your foot." Lupe laid the ice pack on my ankle. "It's funny, but I think I heard you talking to someone. My sister, she talks to herself all the time. Long time ago, when they were still in grade school, my brother talked her into catching pitches for him. One pitch hit her smack in the middle of her forehead. She still has a dent. She never seemed quite right after that. She lives with my mother's sister. Otherwise, she wouldn't know to take a bath, and boy, she can stink."

Huck landed on his hiney and slid off the bed. He walked backwards toward the door, waving and grinning. I sighed and my shoulders lowered past my ears. I needed to change the subject. "Do you believe in prayer, Lupe?"

"I have to believe in prayer. One of my sisters, she's a nun."

"I thought I believed in prayer until—"

"No good will come of finishing that sentence, Miz Birdie." She crossed herself.

"Yes, of course, you're right, but I've been thinking about this more than usual. Mostly it seems God answers prayers for other people. I've seen people healed. The head usher at my church lived with debilitating back pain for years, could barely get out of bed on a winter morning. The elders anointed him and laid hands on him, and then they prayed. Nothing happened just then, but a strange popping along his spine woke him up in the middle of the night. He lay there, he told us later, breathing heavy, afraid to move lest his spine shatter into a million pieces. And then, a peace settled on him. Jim's quite a fisherman, so he explained the peace like standing in the middle of a mountain stream unfurling his line in a graceful arc over and over again, never disappointed that the fly hadn't attracted a hungry trout. Finally, he threw the covers back, which made Martha, his wife, grouse at him, and he took a few gingerly steps. No pain. He stretched his arms over his head. No pain. He bent to touch his toes. No pain. Martha says he pulled her out of bed to dance around the bedroom. The pain had plum vanished.

"I've seen people battered by life find the courage to live another day and another. I've seen relationships rekindled. Hope restored. People set free from terrible addictions. I guess I'm a bit jealous. I'm feeling like a second-class citizen in the family of God." I reached out my hand to Lupe. "Will you pray with me?"

"Now?"

"Is there a toilet you're dying to clean?"

"Nothing like that. Dr. Phil is coming on. I like him on the big screen. It's like he's sitting right in the living room with me. Some women don't like bald men, but he is very strong, don't you think? I like that. Besides, he has some catty sisters on today. I saw the previews. One of them looks like my third youngest sister."

I moved to the bed and patted a place for Lupe to sit down. "This won't take long."

"Shouldn't we kneel?"

"Jesus prayed standing up."

"How do you know that?"

"It's in the Bible."

"With all those funny words in the Bible, how can you be so sure?"

"It gets worse. At the Last Supper, he prayed reclining at the table."

"You better watch what you say. Everyone knows he sat on a fancy chair at a long, long table for the Last Supper."

Part of me wanted to pull my Bible out to prove how very wrong she was. Instead, I slid my aching ankle over the side of the bed to kneel as I'd done all through my growing-up years. To my utter amazement, Lupe knelt beside me, shoulder to shoulder. She smelled of bleach and Jean Naté and sweat.

"What are we praying about, anyway?" she asked.

"The Bible says: 'For where two or three are gathered together in my name, there am I in the midst of them.'"

"*With* us? Who you talking about?"

"Jesus."

Lupe shot to her feet. "I should clear this with Sister Corazon Barbara first." She started for the door.

I grabbed the back of her pant leg. "Wait!"

"Miz Birdie, I like you and everything, but I don't think this is a good idea."

"Lupe, before you go, give me a hand up."

She knelt beside me. "I guess kneeling here is okay, if I don't say anything."

I patted her hand and bowed my head. "Lord, I'm lowering my family through the roof to you because I believe you love them and want them to experience how wide, how high, and how very, very deep your love is for them."

Lupe whispered, "I have arthritis in my knees."

"Oh. Okay. Lord, I surrender my family to you. Amen."

Lupe grunted as she pushed against the bed to stand. "I think Jesus had the right idea when he prayed standing up."

"Next time."

Chapter 14

"Dad's going to kill me."

"Your father complained about not having time to drive with you. I have tons of time. Now, adjust the mirrors and start the engine."

Fletcher tapped the rearview mirror. "All I see is Bee's face."

I turned and swatted Bee's rump. "For goodness' sake, you sorry excuse for a hound dog. Lay down!"

"Is she still on the towel?"

"You worry about driving. I'll worry about the *la-tee-dah* interior of your father's truck."

"You don't know how Dad—"

"Any man who buys a Cadillac and calls the thing a truck . . . well, never mind. Let's see what you can do."

Fletcher pushed a button, and the seat hummed away from the dashboard, toggled a switch to adjust the mirrors, and laid his forehead against the steering wheel.

"Do you want to pray?"

"I'm gonna spew. If anything happens to Dad's truck, I'm toast."

"To learn how to drive, you have to actually drive a car. True, this is more like an ocean liner, but it all works the same—gas pedal, brake, steering wheel." I placed my hand on his shoulder. His shirt was damp. "You can do this, Fletcher. If I didn't think so, I surely wouldn't be sitting here or let Bee go along for the ride."

"Once a guy tapped the truck's bumper on Speer. You should have seen Dad. I thought he was going to kill that guy."

Fletcher needed historical perspective. "Your dad ripped the bumper off our truck, pulling five of his friends along a snowy road in an inner tube."

"Really?"

"Trucks are meant to work, and anything that works is bound to get tapped a time or two."

Fletcher paused with his hand on the ignition key. "Grandma, I don't mean to be rude, but you *do* have a driver's license, don't you? I mean, how much can you see, exactly? If you're going to be teaching me . . ."

I missed most traffic lights, and stop signs flitted in and out of my field of vision. Other than that, a stream of houses and trees and lights floated by. "I think you're stalling. Put your seat belt on and let's go." As for the driver's license, what the Department of Motor Vehicles didn't know wouldn't hurt them.

"I don't wanna go too far," he said, his voice pinched like an air hose.

"How far is the park?"

"Pretty far, Grandma."

"More than a couple blocks?"

"Maybe five . . . or six. I think five."

"Since this is our first lesson, let's go around the block, shall we?"

Lupe directed Fletcher as he backed the behemoth truck out

of the garage. Fletcher pointed to the rearview mirror. "Grandma, Bee's drooling."

I put my hand over his. He gripped the steering wheel like a lifeline. "Fletcher, you're a smart boy, nearly a man. You're going to be the best driver on the streets today. Just step on the gas nice and easy and off we go."

Fletcher nearly touched the windshield with his nose.

"Relax," I said. "Imagine there's an egg under the pedal. Press down nice and easy."

Fletcher followed my instructions perfectly, only I'd forgotten to tell him to shift into drive. We backed toward the house. He stomped the brake pedal, which sent Bee onto the floor, a good test of Fletcher's reflexes.

"Happens all the time," I said. "That's why you always start out nice and easy. Besides, you knew exactly what to do. Slide her into drive and don't forget the egg under the gas pedal."

It took us half an hour to drive around the block. We never topped fifteen miles per hour. The narrow streets, lined with parked cars on both sides, intimidated Fletcher terribly. Driving the Titanic down Broadway, quite frankly, would have been roomier.

"Someone might open a door or something," he said when I told him to press the accelerator.

Teaching my children to drive on service roads inside Yellowstone had been very different. Our biggest concern was watching for deer and potholes, although Diane delayed getting her license a whole year after she'd hit a marmot.

"Sweetie, car doors don't just fly open. Someone has to be sitting in the car for that to happen, so let your gaze glide from the street to the parked cars occasionally," I said in my best flight-attendant voice.

"And steer too?"

"That may overwhelm you now, but with practice, driving will become one smooth movement."

Once we were back at the house, safe and sound, Lupe served us pie and milk. "What happened?" she asked Fletcher. "You look like you seen a big ol' ugly ghost."

"I did. My own." Fletcher pushed the pie away. "I can't eat anything, not now."

"Every day will get easier," I said, rubbing the ridge of spine between his shoulder blades. That boy needed some meat on his bones.

"I'm never driving again," he mumbled.

"You'll thank me someday. You can drive to Ouray for a visit. Bee would love that."

"I'll take the bus."

"Buses are filled with bums and drug addicts. You want to arrive in style, don't you?"

Fletcher pushed away from the counter. "I want to arrive alive, Grandma." He rubbed his eyes with the heels of his hands. "We'll listen to *Huck* later. I have a quiz on the assigned chapters tomorrow, plus I have a project proposal to write." He recited baseball stats for Frank Selee as he climbed the stairs: "Boston Beaneaters. Field Manager 1890 to 1905. Died in Denver, just like me." His door slammed shut.

"Lupe, I need an ice pack," I said, heading for the bedroom. "What's a Boston Beaneater? Is that some kind of dog?"

I OPENED THE DOOR just enough to scan the living area. It was long past midnight and no light shone at the top of the stairs. I pulled the door closed, climbed back into bed, and stared into the darkness.

"I heard you, darling boy. There's not a doubt in my mind. You said something. Not much of something, that's true, but something."

A siren droned in the distance.

"The house is asleep, Huck. Come on out." I threw back the covers and worked myself off the bed to stand behind the walker. "Jump on the bed all you like."

A truck rumbled past the house.

"I listened to more of your story tonight. Buck gave you those pants and the shirt. He's a fine friend for you, from such a nice family. A regular woodsman he is, catching that young rabbit and the blue jay. I like the idea of you eating proper and having a family to look after you. Yes, the Shepherdsons turned out to be a lucky find. Now come on out here. You have to tell me what a 'roundabout' is."

The darkness was silent as a grave. I crawled back into bed, pulled the covers to my chin, and waited. My snores woke me around five.

Chapter 15

Fletcher stopped the truck a good thirty feet from the intersection.

"You can't see a thing from back here. Inch your way on up to the white line."

The idle of the engine propelled the truck to the intersection. Fletcher flipped on his blinker to turn right, our usual route around the block.

"Is that restaurant with the shu mai near here?"

He looked up and down the street repeatedly for approaching traffic. "Why?"

"I'm feeling a little hungry."

Bee pressed her head between the seat and the window to drool on my arm. Not wanting to distract Fletcher, I used a tissue from my bra to dry my arm and pushed Bee away from the window. In a wink, she was back, resting her muzzle on my shoulder.

"Grandma, I'm perfectly happy going around the block."

"That may have been true yesterday, but today you have a destination, and nothing sweetens a journey like a destination."

Fletcher kneaded the steering wheel. "You want to go to the Snappy Dragon? Now? I don't know . . . and what will we do with Bee? She can't stay in the truck."

"How far?"

Fletcher rested his forehead on the steering wheel. "Straight ahead five blocks with nothing but parallel parking along Glaser Street."

"You're excellent at straight ahead. I say we go for it."

"And the parking?"

"Have a little faith. I've prayed myself into more than one parking space in my time."

Fletcher fell back against the seat. "Grand*ma*."

Looking back now, I realize I shouldn't have pushed the boy, but I longed to hear Huck's voice again, see the tilt of his head when I asked him a question and the way his face contorted over issues of Providence. Heartburn from the shu mai seemed to open one door for him to appear. "You have a suggestion?" I said, my voice laced with annoyance.

"There are diagonal parking spaces on 14th Street but just a few. You'll have to walk over a block. But I say, no diagonal parking, no Snappy Dragon. Are you cool with that?"

"Is there a loading zone in front of the restaurant?"

"No."

Surely he would have changed his tune if he knew our snack ushered me into the presence of a literary character the likes of Huckleberry Finn. Who was I kidding? My fickle appetite and questionable company would end our driving lessons forever or worse. "Fletcher, honey, courage doesn't mean we aren't afraid. It means we choose not to let our fear control us."

Not one car was visible in either direction when Fletcher finally pressed the gas pedal with a tad too much enthusiasm. He stomped on the brake. I fought the urge to yell at him for stopping in the middle of the intersection. "Sweetie, let's ease on out of the intersection before you take a break. Remember that egg under the gas pedal."

In the middle of the next block, a horn sounded behind us. I turned to see a splash of brilliant red, low to the ground, rumbling. Bee barked a reply.

"What should I do?" Fletcher asked, his voice climbing an octave.

"How fast are you going?"

"Almost twenty."

"If you're comfortable, increase your speed. If not, you're well within range. Stay the course."

The horn sounded again, only more heavy-handed this time. Bee enjoyed the game and answered the horn enthusiastically. Fletcher eased up on the gas.

"Keep your speed up. You'll have to deal with distractions when driving. Consistency means safety." Bless his heart, Fletcher got the truck moving. "There will always be people trying to tell you how to drive, and they won't be saying 'please' and 'thank you.'"

"He's shaking his fist out the window."

"Ignore him. Keep your eyes on what's ahead of you. If he wants to go faster, he can pass."

"Maybe I should pull over."

"Bad idea. Keep going. You have as much right to the street as anyone." Cross traffic whizzed by at the next intersection. "But since we don't want Mr. Ants-in-His-Pants to go ballistic, you must cross the intersection even if you can see cars in the distance. I'm not saying take a crazy chance. Don't floor the pedal, but don't dillydally either."

"I'd rather not."

"You're a smart boy. You can do this."

"I'm happy waiting."

"Do you want to meet the man in the red car?"

The truck's acceleration pushed me into the upholstery. Bee whimpered. I waited for the sound of crunching metal.

"Open your eyes, Grandma. We made it."

A SMALL-TOWN SHOPPING DISTRICT was the last thing I'd expected in the middle of Denver. The Snappy Dragon stood between an antique shop and a bike store. Although I couldn't be sure, I think we passed an art gallery or two. A quilt shop set my heart racing, but my piecing days were long over. I figured that out when a sewing machine needle punched through my thumbnail. Besides the Snappy Dragon, a fancy eatery they called a *brew haus* sat on one corner, and a coffee shop lined the sidewalk with tables and rainbow umbrellas. Emory would definitely like the coffee shop.

I bit into the shu mai and chewed the doughy shell adoringly to release the heat inside my mouth. "Should we get a pastry from the coffee shop for Lupe?"

"We should go home."

"Not so soon. It's lovely to be out of the house, Fletcher. Thanks for driving me."

Bee, leashed to a light pole, whined for attention and a handout. A couple dressed in Colorado chic—sleeveless vests, river pants, and sandals—indulged her with a scratch under her chin. She rolled onto her back to offer her pink belly. They walked on. True dog lovers understood a fuzzy belly offered friendship. Imposters. Completely unperturbed by their aloofness, Bee stretched in the sun. How I envied her lack of self-consciousness.

"So, Fletcher, did you see your friend from church in school today?"

He leaned back and wiped his mouth with a deliberation I'd not seen in him. I didn't raise a son through puberty without learning a thing or two. Fletcher's friend was definitely female.

"What's her name?" I asked.

"What makes you think she's a girl?"

"Well?"

"Grandma . . ."

"She has a name."

"We're only friends."

"I thought you were laying low until graduation."

"This isn't anything like that."

"She has a name?"

He took a long swig off his soda.

"Fletcher!"

"Mi Sun."

"She's Chinese?"

"Korean. Her family adopted her."

"You're going to think I'm daft, but I'd once dreamed of being Korean. One of the boys who attended my high school, Gene was his name, he lied about his age to join the army and headed off to Korea. His brashness made him incredibly romantic, although I couldn't say I'd ever noticed him before he enlisted. I was as dumb as a turtle. I had no idea what those boys faced over there. They didn't talk much when they got home, always changed the subject when someone asked them a question, but Gene came back with an exotic Korean bride. He called her Honey. I'd never seen anyone more beautiful."

Fletcher rested his head on his folded arms, and if I could have seen his face, no doubt he rolled his eyes. Once you have seven decades under your belt, you have something to say about everything. I needed to learn how to keep my mouth shut. But not yet.

"Have you learned about the Korean War in school?"

"American History is next year."

"Don't think I've forgotten about . . ."

"Mi Sun?"

"Tell me about her."

"What?" he said with exasperation in his voice.

I marched on. "You left your beloved box scores to attend a church service with your grandmother. Something tells me there's more to this story."

"She's pretty."

"Of course. What else?"

"I guess she's smart."

"How smart?"

"She gets good grades, and she has common sense. She doesn't go for all the stupid stuff other girls do."

I didn't want to know what he meant by that. "And?"

"She plays first-chair flute, a position usually held by a senior. She's a junior."

"An older woman?"

Fletcher sucked in a sharp breath.

"Don't worry, sweetie. Mum's the word."

"Huh?"

"Your secret is safe with me."

The fortitude required to milk information out of an adolescent male wearied me. However, once I got warmed up, the thrill of the hunt propelled me on. To let him think the hounds had been rested, I slipped in an unrelated question. "We should go see the Rockies play. When's the next home game?"

Fletcher crushed his soda can. Did he sigh? "The Rockies suck. Besides, Dad's too busy."

"They need a rooting section. If your dad can't go, we'll go. Invite a friend." Mi Sun?

"I'm not driving."

"We'll take a taxi."

"I appreciate your asking, but their pitching stinks. It's hardly worth watching a game."

The conversational diversion proved more turbulent than expected. Oh well, I was the grandma. Old women were expected to stir the waters. Onward. "Do you see Mi Sun outside of class?"

"Her locker's near mine."

"How about lunch?"

"She sits with her friends outside the library."

"Who do you sit with?"

"I read in the library."

"You don't eat?"

"The cafeteria is brutal. The food sucks, and . . . there's no place to sit. It's better to grab something when I get home."

That explained his mad dash for the refrigerator every afternoon. "If I fixed you breakfast, would you eat it?"

He shrugged.

Later, at the house, Fletcher taught me how to order groceries on the Internet, not so different than calling in my order to the It's-All-Here Market in Ouray, except they didn't carry grits at the newfangled grocery store. Once Fletcher showed me how to log in to the Wainwright account and enlarge the font to megasize, I excused him to do his studies.

His tennis shoes squeaked to a stop on the hardwood floors. "Are you up for a few chapters of *Huck* tonight? It'll be pretty late."

"I wouldn't miss it."

Chapter 16

I poured out a dose of Mylanta and waited for Huck to appear. It had been several days since his last visit, and I was counting on a mild case of heartburn to invite him back. The clock announced midnight had come and gone.

"Phooey on you, Huck Finn. An old woman has no business staying up half the night to yammer at a boy." I downed the Mylanta, aiming for the back of my throat to avoid the nauseating sweetness of the concoction. Emory would just be getting home from a night of dancing at the Moose Lodge. I called him.

"Who'd you dance with?" I asked.

"Every woman in the room. You've spoiled me rotten, Birdie. Leading some of those gals was like dancing with a sheet of plywood in the wind." He groaned. "What are you doing up so late?"

I hadn't thought this through. If I told him I had heartburn again, he may have hopped in his car to deliver an antacid to Denver personally. On the other hand, telling him I was waiting for Huckleberry Finn to show up—well, I couldn't do that, either.

"Thinking of you," I said. "I know you're tired, and you have work early tomorrow, so good night. I'll talk to you soon." And I hung up. I lay in bed, my hand over my pounding heart. Once the rhythm eased to an easy fox-trot, I adjusted the bed for sleep and said my prayers, remembering to lower everyone in my family—including Emory—through the roof and into Jesus' presence.

IIIIIIIIIIIIIIIIIIIIIIIIIIIIIII

MY SNORES WOKE ME and there was Huck, pacing back and forth at the foot of the bed. Bee whimpered in her sleep and set to galloping like she was herding rabbits. I stroked her shoulder, and gradually her spasms slowed. Huck paused his pacing to watch her. I withdrew my hand, remembering his interest in Bee.

"She's all right," I said. "She's dreaming. If I wake her, she'll know she didn't catch whatever she was chasing. I'd hate to disappoint her."

Huck rubbed his face with the palms of his hands.

"You seem agitated, boy."

He frowned. Something he'd eaten had dried on his chin.

"You know—tangle headed?"

He sighed. The sound of his breath sent a shiver through my body.

"Did you bring your pipe?"

He patted his pockets but came up empty.

"I guess you like a good cigar too."

He sat down, head in hands.

"I only know that because you enjoyed the cigars you found on the sinking steamer." I slapped my forehead. "What am I saying? You shouldn't smoke cigars. Honey, they're real bad for you." And not wanting him to think I was a complete ninny, I said, "I wish I'd gotten after Chuck about his smoking. All those years of sucking on cigarettes hardened his arteries. The pressure of his own blood got to be too much, and one of those arteries burst. He bled to death right in our bed. It took me a long time before I slept in that bed again."

Huck shoved his hands deep into his pockets. "I've been peacefuler, that's for sure, and I guess you know what I'm talking about, seeing how you seen your dead husband and all. But that dratted night, if I'd a knowed . . . my heart's swimmin' with my lungs and liver and things. I hain't never been so sick at the sight of nothing."

"What night was that, Huck?"

"Generly, I like to let things play out as they will. That's one thing worth remembering I learned from Pap: Keep your mouth shut and your head low. It warn't right that I gived that note to Miss Sophia. I should've told the old man. He'd put an end to such frivolishness, locked her up or sent her to visit an aunt. Then that awful peck of trouble never would have happened. Buck would still be alive, or at least I think he would. We was exactly the same age, only he was a spite bigger than me." Huck slumped into the recliner. "That gives a boy something to think about."

My heart pounded out a reverie. Fletcher and I had listened about the bloody feud between the Grangerfords and the Shepherdsons that night. Huck watched from a tree as the Sheperdsons killed his friend Buck.

Huck bent over, hugging his middle. "When I found Buck, his face was as white as a fish belly in the moonlight."

"You had nothing to do with his death, Huck. The Grangerfords and Shepherdsons had been feuding for—what, thirty years? Buck couldn't even remember who'd taken the first shot. You can't blame yourself."

"I hain't never experienced nothing like it."

"Hate can make a good man crazy." And as soon as I said it, Chuck's face came to mind. I shook the vision off.

Huck rubbed his hands together. "No one treated me better than Colonel Grangerford. I had my own *valley*, only he didn't have much to do 'cause I'd ruther do for myself. Buck was mighty good to me too—the closest thing, except for Tom, I reckon, I've ever had to a brother. Only Buck never made me attack a Sunday school picnic like Tom done.

"I wish I ain't never come ashore that night the steamboat split the raft into flinders. I thought Jim was dead, and I'd gone and landed myself in a jug of honey, but it warn't like that, no how." Huck squinted down. "It all came from touching them rattlesnake skins. I'm shore of it. I dream about Buck and his cousin, though I won't say nothing more. It would make a body sick."

"I'm very sorry for your loss, Huck."

"I put my mind to this long and hard. Them Grangerfords and the Shepherdsons, they went to church together that very day, got all combed up with their roundabouts snug, and carried their rifles fully loaded, they did. Held them betwixt their legs or leaned them against the wall so as to grab them if needed. All the while the preacher is sermonizing on brotherly love like he could holler the deviltry right out of them. I can't think of a good reason why a man would shackle himself to a woman, but nobody should have died because Sophia and Harney got married. I wonder if Miss Sophia knowed that her pap and brothers died on her wedding day?"

Huck ran his fingers through his hair, leaving deep furrows to reveal a dirty scalp. When Bee got that dirty, I took a hose to her. If I scrubbed all that dirt away and gave him a fresh haircut, Huck would still stand apart from the boys of my time. Even in his anguish, he moved looser and with more confidence. Scrambling on his own had given him that. But still, he was just a boy, and a hurting boy at that. Every century suffered under the foolishness of offense.

I tried to console him. "Huck, Miss Sophia knew marrying Haney would cause trouble. That's why they met on the sly. If you hadn't delivered the note, someone else would have. You believed Sophia was sweet and gentle as a dove. You had no cause to believe she meant mischief."

Huck's voice went wistful. "It was the prettiest house I'd ever seen."

"A pretty house doesn't make a family."

He stretched. "I reckon I better skedaddle."

"Will you come back?"

"You won't make me wear no shoes, will you?"

"I hate shoes." I slid my foot out from under the blankets and wiggled my toes for him.

"I reckon you wouldn't." He stood, looked down on Bee. "I ain't never had a dog before. Yourn looks like a good one."

"She's always here. You can visit anytime."

He sat in the recliner, let his head fall back. "If you don't mind, I think I'll rest here a minute before I move on. I'm powerful tired."

"I'll turn off the light."

In the dark Bee and Huck snored. I felt bad for the boy. He believed he'd landed himself in an upright family at last, one that allowed him a measure of freedom and a pleasant place to gather by the fire, a place to belong. He learned in the most painful way possible that the Grangerfords lived as if hate and breathing meant the same thing.

The pastor's question popped into my head: *To whom will you show the full extent of his love?*

I looked to Huck, but he was gone.

To whom will you *show the full extent of his love?*

"First thing tomorrow morning, Lord."

Chapter 17

"What's going on in here?" Suzanne said, lifting the skillet from the burner and pouring the bacon and grease into the trash. I sidled to stand in front of the oven light, evidence that more bacon kept warm inside.

"Well, I was cooking breakfast," I said, struggling to control my anger. Cooking on a broken ankle had seemed like a grand notion. Who would deny such a noble gesture?

Suzanne squirted cleaner on the cooktop. "It smells like a truck stop in here."

The full extent of his love. "How would you like your eggs, Suzanne?"

"You're kidding, right? I don't eat breakfast." She huffed and set the cleaner on the counter. "I don't have time for this. I have rounds." Before the door to the garage slammed, she yelled, "Get that putrid smell out of the house before I get home."

The door opened again. "And Birdie, get that dog off the wood floors, *now*."

Oops. I enticed Bee through the bedroom to the back door with the bacon Suzanne had thrown in the trash. On the way back to the kitchen, I punched a silky pillow and seriously considered sliding under the coverlet.

He demonstrated the full extent of his love . . .

I met Andy at the coffeemaker. "Scrambled or fried?" I asked, waving a spatula.

"I'm sorry, Ma, I can't." He poured coffee into a travel mug. "There's a meeting, too much to do."

"It takes a minute to fry an egg, less to eat one." I lowered bread into the toaster. "You have to eat."

Andy slipped into his suit jacket. He threw his wallet and keys into his briefcase and closed it with a *snap-snap* and kissed my cheek. "I'm glad you're feeling better, Ma." He started for the door. "Fletcher! We're out of here!"

I followed him, hop scooting as fast as I could without the walker. "Wait a minute," I said to his back. "Fletcher needs to eat something."

Andy worked his fingers into leather gloves. "I give him money."

"He hates the cafeteria. He doesn't eat until he comes home."

"He hasn't said anything to me." Andy yelled up the stairs. "Fletcher, get your—!"

I fought to keep my voice even, pleasant, nonjudgmental. "When, exactly, would he have the chance to do that? You're never here. He orders take-out food every night. A growing boy—"

The bite of Andy's tone let me know I'd failed on all points. "Ma . . ."

. . . the full extent of his love . . .

"Let me scramble an egg and slap it on some toast. He can take the sandwich with him. At least he'll have something."

Fletcher thumped down the stairs.

"How many times do I have to tell you?" Andy yelled at him.

"Sorry."

"Andy?" I pleaded.

He looked at his watch. "I'm already late."

LUPE AND I ATE our breakfast on the patio, our backs to the sun like lizards. She mopped egg yolk off her plate with a bagel and gestured with it as she talked. "These people, they are like those big yellow butterflies that never land. I chased a pair of them butterflies around the yard, trying to take their picture with my cell phone to show my granddaughter. Those crazy butterflies never did land, except for on the very top of a bush. I wasn't about to stand on no ladder to take a picture of a butterfly."

"I need your help, Lupe. You know my family better than I do. What do they need?"

Her palms flew up in surrender. "Nothing. If they need something, and I mean like a truck that isn't over a year old, they go Miz Doctor Lady couldn't find her camera. She looked everywhere, blamed everyone—and I mean everyone—for moving it from its place in the drawer. My nephews don't swear so bad as her sometimes. The mister and the boy huddled by the front door afraid to say nothing. Finally, she stomped past them and said, 'We'll stop at Best Buy. There's one on Federal.'" Lupe spread cream cheese on a second bagel. "The good cameras cost more than I make in a week, and she didn't even check the newspaper for sales."

The camera Suzanne had dutifully pulled out during my Christmas visit easily cost four times that much. If I meant to demonstrate the full extent of his love to my family, I would have to do so at no charge, exactly like a servant. "If the family had a servant—"

"I'm no servant. I'm a housekeeping manager, but I do everything they don't want to do. The cleanest toilets in all of America are in this house. About a week after I started working for them, Miz Doctor Lady took samples of water from the toilet to a lab." Lupe crossed herself. "Thank the Lord I used extra bleach that day."

I wasn't ready to give up. "Down deep, they must need something. Everybody does."

Lupe's chair scraped across the tile. "I do the best I can."

I grabbed her hand. The tips of her fingers were cracked and rough. "I know you do. You should feel very good about what you do here. You make this house sparkle." I tugged on her hand. "Please sit with me."

"You want to pray again, don't you? I talked to Sister Corazon Barbara about you."

"She backed me up, didn't she?"

"She wants to know if you belong to a cult."

"Tell her I'm a Baptist."

Lupe rubbed at a spot, real or imagined, on the tabletop. "Maybe you should pray for an immaculate conception."

"That's already been done."

"No, really. Miz Doctor Lady has an appointment with a . . . a doctor who helps you get pregnant. I never needed no help from a doctor. If Ernesto looked at me from across the room, I started throwing up the next day."

"How do you know about the fertility doctor?"

"I'm invisible—*poof!*—like I don't exist to Miz Doctor Lady. She made the appointment while I was cleaning the bathroom. She talked about her temperature and how the mister would be at the appointment with her to provide a fresh—what do you call it?"

"Specimen?"

"That's it. I never heard her so worked up. I peeked around the corner, but her hair covered her face. She talked to the mister too. I turned the water on in the sink, so she would talk louder."

I should have told Lupe to keep the gossip to herself, but I didn't.

"She told the mister that he better make a way to be at the doctor's no later than three. Success depended on a fresh . . ."

"*Specimen*," I said, my mind tumbling. Specimen and procedures meant Suzanne and Andy were more serious about parenthood than I thought.

"Pray with me, Lupe."

"I'm not kneeling on the rock."

"We'll pray Leonardo da Vinci-style, sitting in these cushy chairs."

"I had an Uncle Leandro, he mumbled like an old woman after a few beers, but I don't think he prayed much. Maybe when he bet money on his *fútbol* team, but he didn't dare tell *Tía* Rosalina. She carried a knife in her girdle."

I extended my hand to her. "Let's hold hands then."

"I don't think so." She bowed her head.

I withdrew my hand. "Lupe?"

"I still have three toilets to clean."

"Fine."

"Fine."

I prayed. "Lord, we know something we shouldn't know about Suzanne and Andy, so we come to you on their behalf to ask that your good will happens in their lives today."

Lupe looked up. "Shouldn't we be praying for a baby to happen?"

"Go ahead."

"Out loud?"

"Whatever's comfortable for you, Lupe."

Roger, the gardener, started a lawn mower in the front yard. Bee ran to the gate to bark at him. Trash cans thundered against the waste pickup truck in the alley. I was about to prod Lupe on when she prayed: *"Padre nuestro, que estás en el cielo. Santificado sea tu nombre. Venga tu reino. Hágase tu voluntad en la tierra como en el cielo. Danos hoy nuestro pan de cada día. Perdona nuestras ofensas, como también nosotros perdonamos a los que nos ofenden. No nos dejes caer en tentación y líbranos del mal."*

Bee nuzzled my pocket for a liver treat. Roger revved the lawn trimmer. Lupe kept her head lowered.

"I don't think I heard anything about a baby," I said.

"I'm getting to that."

"Take your time." Bee nibbled at my pocket, so I slipped a few liver treats her way as I waited.

"También, nuestro Padre, ayude a la señora a tener a un bebé. Tal vez entonces ella no sera así excéntrico."

Be-bee? Ex-SEN-tree-ko?

"Amén."

"Amen."

Lupe's chair scraped against the stone, and she gathered the plates and cups. "It's time to get to work."

||||||||||||||||||||||||||||||||

FLETCHER STARTED THE TRUCK. "Where to, Grandma?" He thrummed the steering wheel with his fingers.

"My, my, aren't we getting confident?"

"Shu mai sound good?"

"Are we listening to *Huckleberry Finn* tonight?"

"I have a French quiz and a chem lab due tomorrow."

"Let's save a trip to Snappy Dragon for another day then." I tapped my chin, making like I had no idea where I wanted to go. A bristly poke to my finger reminded me to get the tweezers out. Back home Josie let me know when my whiskers got too distracting for conversation. That's friendship. "Where does Mi Sun live?"

He straightened. "Why?"

"Just a drive-by, Fletcher."

"We're not stopping."

Bee pushed my arm from the window to bark at something. "Sit down, Bee!" I raised the window with a hum. And to Fletcher, I said, "Of course not."

"She lives across from the park."

"Bee loves parks. It's a lovely day, the first warm day in a week. I think the park is the place, don't you?"

At a stop sign, Fletcher rested his chin on the steering wheel.

"What are you thinking about?"

"There's diagonal parking on the south side of the park."

"Excellent. We'll stop by the pet store on the way."

"I'm not completely comfortable with that, Grandma."

"Everything will be fine. I'm on a mission from God."

"WE'RE ALMOST THERE," FLETCHER said between clenched teeth. He slowed slightly. "She lives on the right. There it is, her house. On the corner. Don't look at it."

Opposite Mi Sun's house, a most accommodating length of curb presented itself. "Stop! Park there," I said, pointing at the curb.

He slowed. "I don't know about this."

"We'll only stop for a minute. To see her house I have to concentrate."

Fletcher sidled the truck along the curb. Across the street, a brick bungalow, a hobbit sort of house with its rounded door and stoic façade, winked in the afternoon light. A splash of red along the walkway hinted at a border of tulips. Huck sat on the curb, waving.

I patted Fletcher's shoulder. "See? Nothing terrible happened. You're safe behind the tinted windows." I looked back to Mi Sun's house. "I like her house. It's sensible and tidy."

Bee stepped over the console to join us in the front. Clipping her leash on, I said, "Unless you want puddles of dog drool all over the seats, I think we better get Bee out of the truck."

Fletcher tied Bee to a bench while I unfolded the walker at the curb. We'd decided on a short walk to the lake and back when Huck crossed the street to join us, and Mi Sun called from the porch. "Fletcher! Don't go anywhere! I have to get my shoes on."

"Oh man, oh man. I'm busted," Fletcher said, covering his head with his arms.

"What? She's happy to see you. Couldn't you hear that?"

"She'll think I hunted her down."

"She'll think you're a nice boy who isn't above taking your grandma to the park. Besides, I'm sure she saw you driving."

"Yeah? Cool."

Huck mocked, gagging himself with a finger down his throat. I turned from him to look at the rose bushes, afraid I'd give his presence away. The roses sported burgundy leaves, and with a cautious touch, I found teardrop buds. Blooms were still a couple weeks off. Mi Sun took the roses' lack of performance personally. "This is terrible. You came to the park to see flowers. We can walk to the annual garden. Something has to be blooming there."

I doubted the gardeners had even planted the annual garden yet. What do young girls know of frost warnings? From her enthusiasm I wasn't sure Mi Sun had noticed the walker or the enormous black boot on my foot. Her confidence ignited a spark in me, nevertheless. "Which way?"

Mi Sun, as talkative as a parakeet, only more melodious, wore a hooded sweatshirt and red Converse tennis shoes. Her black hair, held out of her face by a broad yellow headband, shimmered in the sunlight. Best of all, she answered my questions about school and her family with complete sentences. And she asked about living in

Ouray and my painting, meaning I'd been a subject of conversation for her and Fletcher while beakers warmed. I liked her.

My good leg felt like rubber by the time we reached the annual garden. "Can we sit for a few minutes?"

Mi Sun and I sat on a low concrete wall while Fletcher and Huck sat on the grass with Bee between them. Beyond, geometric plots of earth stood out from the greening grass, most likely the annual garden awaiting longer days and warmer nights to receive seedlings.

Huck reached out a skeptical finger to touch the top of Bee's head and withdrew it quickly. With two fingers he stroked the length of her back. Bee lay down and rolled onto her back, exposing her pale belly. He looked to me, a question etched in his face. I nodded ever so slightly. Huck rubbed small circles on Bee's belly. She stretched to luxuriate in his attention. Huck obliged her with a vigorous massage. I startled when Mi Sun asked me a question.

"Do you miss Ouray? It's so beautiful there."

Fletcher hugged his long legs to his chest. "You've been there?"

"Every winter. My brother ice climbs. We *all* have to go. My mom wants to be there to tell the ambulance driver ice climbing was *not* her idea." She laughed. "That's *not* going to work this year. Mom's been working out at the climbing gym. She learned how to belay for my stupid brother. She doesn't trust anyone else to keep him from falling. I think she's crazy."

"Next time you go to Ouray, let Fletcher know you're coming. You must stop by. I make the best pie in town."

Fletcher spoke like I'd twirled my underwear over my head. "Grandma, she hardly knows you."

"It's different in the mountains," Mi Sun said. "There you're friends with *everybody*. People look you in the eye. It's so *not* Denver."

"So, you come to Ouray every winter?"

"Three or four times. We *love* the hot springs, and we stay at a place with a vapor cave. It feels so good in there after standing in the snow all day."

"You come that often? No kidding? Is there room in your car for Fletcher? It's been forever since he visited."

Mi Sun shook a finger at Fletcher. "You don't visit your grandma?"

"I want to. It's . . . complicated."

"You *have* to come with us," she said. "It's *deadly* boring to watch Ty climb. We could go to the hot springs pool and the skating rink. You'd love it."

"Yeah . . . well . . . maybe."

Fletcher and Mi Sun walked ahead of me. Bee stayed at Fletcher's knee, looking up at him for approval and a liver treat, but Fletcher was preoccupied. Huck walked with his hand on Bee's back. I toddled behind, concentrating on the uneven path and praying that the Good Father would use Mi Sun to bless Fletcher. Who among us hasn't benefited from the approval of someone like her? For me, it was Darrel Sichel. That boy had dimples as deep as canyons. He carried my books home one day. I floated on air and treated Evelyn kindly for a month afterward. Grace comes to us in the most unexpected ways.

Back at the truck, Mi Sun knelt face-to-face with Bee and massaged her shoulders. Huck leaned against the truck, studying the scene like he expected a genie to appear.

"What a well-behaved dog," she said. "I can't take Tootsie anywhere. He nearly pulls my arm off."

Breathless from the trek across the park, I said, "Fletcher helped train Bee. You should have him work with Tootsie."

As we drove away, I looked back to see Huck shinnying up a tree.

FLETCHER DROVE WITH HIS elbow resting on the window. "Maybe we should go to the park tomorrow."

"You get those hands back to ten and two and we'll discuss it."

He sat up, gripped the steering wheel. He flashed the turn signal, slowed, and took the turn like a champ. "Thanks, Grandma."

My ankle pressed against the inside of the boot. Ice. I needed ice.

"Let's try out Bee's new booties when we get home." That's what I said, but what tickled my brain was this: If Bee could feel Huck's touch, could I?

Chapter 18

Bee slunk under the dining room table. Her head thudded against an oaken post, but she snaked deeper into the tangle of table and chair legs. She lay there, panting, probably believing herself invisible. Not the smartest of the litter, but she sure had a hard head. Like owner, like dog?

Suzanne followed Bee into the dining room, moving silently in her stocking feet. "What is that dog doing in the house? Get it out of here now."

The intensity of Suzanne's anger surprised me. I fumbled over my words. "I bought her booties. They have rubber soles. They're meant for hiking, but she won't scratch the floors. I wanted to . . ." *Express the full extent of his love.* It had taken Fletcher and me nearly an hour to fit Bee with the booties, and then she'd spent the next half hour chewing at the Velcro fasteners. I figured they'd last another five minutes, tops. "I only wanted to protect your floors."

Suzanne rubbed her temples and blew out hard breaths. "I had an especially difficult day. Nothing went as planned. I don't need this kind of aggravation." She bent to look under the table.

Each word punched the air. "She's drooling all over my Kelmscott rug!" Suzanne pulled out a chair and reached for Bee. "We had an agreement, Birdie. The dog stays out of the living area."

"Let me get her," I said, reaching from the walker for a chair. "She's frightened."

Suzanne ignored me. "Lupe, call the number I left in the desk drawer."

Lupe's slippers shuffled toward the back door. "I'm off the clock."

Fletcher bounded down the stairs until I pointed to Suzanne under the table. He took the final steps one at a time. "Hey, what's going on?" he asked evenly.

I started to answer, but Suzanne jerked on Bee's collar with each word of her command. "Get out, you miserable piece of flea-bitten hide." True to form, Bee made like a statue. Suzanne persisted, yanking Bee's collar with surprising force. My mouth went dry and my hands trembled. I pushed the walker aside to kneel beside Suzanne and felt my way past her to Bee. I caught a glimpse of Fletcher's feet behind us.

"That's enough," I said to Suzanne as if talking someone off the ledge. "Let me handle this."

Suzanne ignored me, pulling Bee millimeter by millimeter across the rug.

Fletcher shouted, "Leave her alone, Suzanne."

I startled and hit my head on the table. Bee growled deep in her throat.

Uh-oh.

"Why you—!" Suzanne swung her arm to strike Bee, but Fletcher grabbed Suzanne around the waist and pulled her from under the table. He held her as she swore, all the while kicking and swinging her fists.

Bee no longer considered the dining room a safe place, so she trotted toward the bedroom, pausing to shake a booted foot every step or so. Fletcher released Suzanne the second Bee crossed the threshold into my room. She turned on Fletcher, her fists thudding against his chest. Fletcher collapsed into a ball on the floor.

She screamed at him, "Never. Touch. Me. Do you hear me?" Struggling to pull myself up with the walker, I heard a smack of flesh. "Answer me, you little—"

I pushed my walker toward her, missing my mark by a wide mile. Still, it skidded across Suzanne's beloved hardwood floors with enough screeching and clanking to distract her. "That's enough! Get away from him." I reached for Fletcher. Under his T-shirt, he trembled. "Fletcher, go on upstairs—"

"You crossed the line, big time." Suzanne spoke to Fletcher as if spitting poison. "Don't expect your granny to save you. You're out of here. Which will it be? Parading in the hot sun of Virginia or shivering in the wilds of Alaska?"

Fletcher's fists shook at his side. "Fine!" he yelled into her face. "The farther the better." He took the stairs three at a time. "I hate this place!" His door slammed.

Suzanne stood with her arms crossed and her head down. Without the walker, I was anchored in place. "I don't know what to say. I've never seen a child treated—"

Suzanne's head swung up. "No, but you knew what your husband did to Andrew."

"What are you talking about? Chuck loved Andy. There wasn't a kinder, gentler man on the planet."

"Then why did Andrew run away?"

"Your days of bullying Fletcher are over," I said, feeling small and ineffectual and hating myself for it.

She returned the chair to its place at the table and flipped her hair over her shoulder. "I'd ask Andrew about the kindness of his father, if you have any doubts." And she walked toward the stairs without so much as stirring the air.

Back in the bedroom, I flipped through the pages of my Bible until I came to the story of Jesus washing the disciples' feet. I skimmed the story under a magnifying glass, looking for the very moment Judas left the Upper Room to betray the Lord. Once I discovered Jesus had washed Judas's feet long before Judas rose to betray him, I closed the pages to curl around Bee on the bed.

Lord, this isn't working. I cannot love that woman to the full extent of anything, not now. I'd just as soon drop her through a hole in a roof. No more pussyfooting around. Unless you want me to wash her feet with lye, you've got some work to do. My heart's empty.

WHEN ANDY AND SUZANNE left for the evening, I scooted up the stairs on my hind end and sat on the floor at Fletcher's closed door. I tapped lightly. "Fletcher? Honey? Are you okay?"

Silence.

I knocked harder, spoke louder. "Are you all right in there?" I jiggled the doorknob.

"I'm okay, Grandma."

"Open the door, Fletcher. Did she hurt you?"

"I'd rather not, not now."

I spoke through the crack of the door. "You did the right thing. I'm so proud of you. You protected the innocent. You kept your cool. You treated Suzanne respectfully." I tapped on the door again. "Did you hear all that?"

"Yeah."

"Do you believe it?"

"Listen, Grandma, I have a lot to do tonight."

I rested my forehead against the door.

Oh, Lord, what have I done? The boy is so dear, and I've mucked things up for him something awful. Bless him in a big way in spite of me, won't you? I lower him into your presence. I rubbed my hands, feeling the burn of the rope. *Oh, Savior, accomplish your good will for him.*

WHEN I HEARD EMORY'S voice on the other end of the line, I swallowed hard to loosen my throat. I spewed the story about Fletcher and Suzanne and idiotic ol' me.

"Remember what Jesus said about brushing the dust from your feet?" he said.

"I can't do that. Who would be here for Fletcher? What a dope I've been! As if I could serve this family. They don't even wash their own underwear."

"Andy's the one to talk to."

Yes, I had to talk to Andy about Suzanne and Fletcher, but the conversation that scared me more was talking to Andy about Chuck. The months leading up to Andy's "adventure," as Chuck and I referred to his running away, had been tough. I read books about personality disorders, thinking a flood of testosterone had flipped a switch in his brain. Overnight he'd gone from being a pleasant, compliant boy to surly and cantankerous. Elsa Nagel insisted I leave laxatives in his bathroom, but that was back when an enema solved all our problems. I'd had my suspicions that something more than cross words had been exchanged between Chuck and Andy up on the meadow, but, well, I'd never asked. And now I regretted my silence.

"Andy's never home to talk. And when he is, he's working on reports in front of the TV. And Suzanne is never out of sight."

"Can you catch him before he goes to work?"

I'd already ordered the rhubarb and strawberries. Breakfast pie had worked once.

Emory said, "If you won't come home, let me get Bee. She can dig and drool to her heart's content at my house."

"Too many coyotes around your place."

"Josie will watch her while I'm at work."

I needed Bee. She kept me warm at night and snored to cover the traffic sounds. "She's doing just fine outside. Fletcher's taking her for walks. She's good for him. Her approval means more to him than mine."

"Don't underestimate yourself, Birdie. He's a lucky young man to have someone like you on his side."

A brooding presence settled on the house in the days that followed. We moved around each other as if we walked on tight-ropes—one false move meant a headlong fall. No one wanted to know what waited for us on the ground. I no longer dreamed of my quiet cabin. For the rest of my stay, I promised myself to never leave Suzanne and Fletcher alone together, which wasn't so hard. I stopped resenting the time she and Andy stayed away and focused my attention fully on Fletcher. I made him breakfast sandwiches every morning and packed a lunch that I slipped into his book bag without Andy knowing.

Chapter 19

Andy huffed, an echo of years gone by. "I don't have time for pie this morning."

"It's rhubarb and strawberry, your favorite," I cooed.

He paused. "Is this about Fletcher and Suzanne?"

I gave up on corralling my anger. "The boy protected Bee, and he did so in the safest, most respectful manner possible, given Suzanne's irrational anger."

He snapped his briefcase closed. "This is an extremely tough time for Suzanne. You need to cut her some slack."

I lowered my voice, scooted closer. "She pounded Fletcher's chest with her fists and slapped him."

Andy tucked the briefcase under his arm and turned. "I'll talk to her, I promise."

I followed. "Is there anything I need to know?"

He stopped, lowered his head and put a hand on the doorjamb. "We're both under a lot of pressure. We'll sit down with him and get this straightened out." He turned to face me. His shoulders sagged. "I'm sorry I can't stop for pie, Ma. I have a breakfast meeting I still need to prepare for."

"How will Fletcher get to school?"

"I've made arrangements with my secretary."

"Can I pray for you, son?"

"I'm already late. Maybe later." And he was gone.

Later *schmater.* I leaned against the door, listened to the garage door grind open and closed. "I'm loading the whole Wainwright family onto the mat, Lord. By your strength, I lower them into your presence. Could you whistle a happy tune to get their attention? Part the traffic on I-25 like the Red Sea? Better yet, offer them an espresso, a grande something or other from one of the bistros in LoDo. If they could just see the love in your eyes. Is that too much to ask?"

Chapter 20

Fletcher sat next to me on a park bench across from Mi Sun's house.

"She won't be here today. She has an orthodontist appointment."

"Mi Sun has a beautiful smile."

"She wears the invisible kind."

"I had no idea." Diane had hated me for putting her in braces, claimed I ruined her life. All I remembered was wishing I'd kept her in braces through college. Her life needed ruining those seven years.

Huck lay in the grass with Bee, stroking her belly and grinning like a boy who had found the key to the candy store. Seeing him there, without a care to shackle his thoughts, I blurted, "Fletcher, something wondrous has happened to me."

"Huh?"

"How are you at keeping secrets?"

"Pretty good, I guess."

"Well, I need you to promise not to tell a soul what I'm going to tell you."

"You aren't in love with some old guy, are you?"

"Something much better. Bigger. Much more mysterious. Even magical."

"You won the lottery?"

"Better than winning the lottery."

Huck sat up, narrowed his gaze at me.

Fletcher shifted in his seat. "Are you sure I'm the one to tell?"

"There's no one else. This will do you good."

He surrendered to the inevitable by leaning back and stretching his legs. "Shoot."

I patted his leg. "Not good for you like a vitamin or reading some tiresome textbook. Good for you like discovering a portal to the fifth dimension or a wormhole to another time and place." I smiled. "I watch the Sci-Fi channel too."

"Grandma, the chances of aliens living in our galaxy or universe are nearly nil . . . or less than nil. If you're seeing aliens—"

"I'm not sure what I'm seeing, but that's what's so fascinating."

Huck rose to a knee and leaned forward.

"I'll leave it up to you. I'm content keeping my secret. I'll wait for you to decide if you want in or not." I rose.

Fletcher grabbed my wrist. "I want to know, Grandma. I really want to know."

I skipped the part about the mountainside on the staircase and the purple flowers popping up in unlikely places—pretty boring stuff for a young man. I told him instead about Huck's coming after I'd awakened with heartburn, how he'd winked at me before he left.

"He winked? Did he come back?"

"Oh yes, several times. I enjoy his visits very much, although he never shows up when I want him to. You know what kind of boy that Huck is—more feral than tame. That he's interested in the likes of me is the best part of the mystery."

"Cool."

"There's more." I told him about Huck mimicking Suzanne and his fascination with Bee.

"Does that mean I'm off the hook walking the dog?"

"He just pets her."

Huck stepped closer, cocked his head. Had I said too much? Broken some kind of cosmic rule? Would speaking about our visits drive Huck from my life? He said, "The boy's in a sweat to find out all about me. I reckon a body that ups and tells the truth when he is in a tight place is taking considerable many risks, though I ain't had no experience and can't say for certain."

"Then it's okay to tell him?" I asked.

"The boy is mild as goose milk. He won't be no trouble."

Fletcher's voice broke. "Is he here, Grandma? Is he here, now?"

Huck sashayed, kicked up his heels, and bowed deeply. He stood only a few feet away, with hands on hips and one foot crossed over the other.

"You mustn't be afraid, Fletcher. Huck is a good-hearted fellow." I pointed to the place in the grass where Huck stood. "He's right there."

Fletcher jumped up to stand behind the bench. "What do the two of you talk about?"

Huck rolled on the grass guffawing at Fletcher. I shot him a stern look that sobered him up quick.

"He's like any boy," I said. "It took him a long while to open up. We talked about Buck's death the other night."

Fletcher eased around the bench to sit next to me. "Why can't I see him?"

"I wish I knew, but I thought you might like to hear about our adventures."

"Your secret's safe with me."

Chapter 21

I dreamed I walked down a long corridor lined with doors, each one a different color and shape. A woman's wails compelled me to pound on each door and jiggle the doorknob. Door after door resisted my efforts, and the wailing grew louder. I doubled my efforts. I rubbed my knuckles and knocked harder at the doors. Then I came to a red door with a tiny window just above my head. I was certain the cries came from within. I jerked the knob. Locked. And this is the annoying thing about dreams: Each one repeats a thousand times, like the brain is practicing how to solve a confounding problem from its wakeful time, so when I raised my fist to knock on the door, I already knew my efforts were useless, but I knocked anyway. When no one answered, I kicked the door. Still no answer, only the heaving sobs of the woman. I stood on tiptoes to look through the window. A lone candle burned inside to illuminate a woman, her face draped by her dark hair. From deep within her soul, a grievous moan pierced my heart.

I sat bolt up in bed, blinking in the darkness. Outside the bedroom door, the weeping continued. Suzanne? Light seeped into the room from under the door.

"This was only our first try with this procedure." Andy shushed her. "You'll wake the house."

"I don't care."

I lay back down and closed my eyes. This wasn't a conversation for my ears.

Andy said, "We have two more cycles for success. We're far from defeated. If this doesn't work, there's still in vitro. Baby. Sweetie. We'll try again."

"Why is this so hard? I get it. I mean, I understand what's going on, but I'm a mess. Heather brought her baby to the office yesterday. I almost said something. Oh God, I'm so glad I didn't. I don't know how much more of this I can take. The waiting, the disappointment." More crying, only muffled this time. I pictured Andy holding Suzanne's head to his shoulder, and the image comforted me.

Heels tapped on the kitchen floor. "I have to shake this off. I have patients to see in twenty minutes." The tapping stopped. "Oh, my eyes! I look like I've been on a bender."

"Sit down. A cool cloth will help."

Their voices softened. I rose to my elbows to listen.

Suzanne said, "My mother keeps asking about a grandbaby. I never should have told her."

"You were excited. Don't blame yourself."

"I waited too long, that's the problem. I thought I had forever. Residency. Chief surgeon. A practice. I'd trade it all for a baby. The woman I beat out for the residency at Women's Hospital? She has three kids. How could I have been so stupid?"

"Hey, you had responsibilities, obligations. You can't blame yourself."

"Oh no? Watch me."

"Suzanne, stop. I won't let you drive like this."

They were quiet again. Rock her, Andy.

"I have an idea," Andy said. "I'll see if the Vail house is

available in a couple weeks. Fletcher can stay here with my mother. We'll get a fire going, play some jazz. We'll order in from Chez Marilyn. We'll be relaxed. No cell phones. No beepers. We'll put a do-not-disturb sign on the door. The doc said to minimize stress. How about it?"

When Suzanne spoke again, her voice was throaty but pliable. "Sounds good."

"I'll arrange everything. Nothing will interfere, I promise."

For goodness' sake, Andy, this is no time to bring up past mistakes.

"You've said that before."

See?

"This will be different."

Tell her.

"Forget about the Vail house. We'll go someplace else, where no one knows how to get hold of us. You can't tell your mother either."

That's better.

"The world won't fall apart in two days. We'll leave right after work on Friday and come home late Sunday."

Suzanne's voice was butter melting in a pan. "Sounds wonderful."

"I wish we had time now."

"Are you suggesting . . . ?"

"When have you ever been late for rounds?"

"Never."

"Must keep the sperm count up."

"So this is doctor's orders?"

"None other."

I never thought to be embarrassed when they ran up the stairs toward their bedroom. When the door clicked shut, I tapped my clock. "Five-thirty-eight a.m." Then I popped in the earplugs of my older-than-dirt Walkman to listen to instrumental hymns. To the swelling strings of "Holy, Holy, Holy" I turned to John 15. The words tickled my imagination. I closed my eyes to imagine Jesus and his disciples walking over the spongy earth of the vineyard, the broad leaves like palms reflecting the Passover moon. During this intimate, befuddling moment, Jesus did what all true friends do when they must say good-bye: He tells his friends how to stay in touch.

"Lord of the vineyard," I prayed, "let's keep in touch. Empower me to love as you have loved."

Bee pushed her nose under the Bible to rest her head in my lap. "You're a pushy old dog. You're not the center of the world. You know that, don't you?"

The Lord's voice, like the stirring of a tree in a spring breeze or the tender kisses of snowflakes, beckoned me to love as he loved. It was the fastest answer to prayer I could ever remember.

"MIZ BIRDIE, YOU'RE FLINGING big gobs of dough all over the place," Lupe said.

I felt around the counter to wrangle the lost clump of cookie dough back into the bowl and grunted with the strain of pushing the spoon through the batter. And I hadn't added the chocolate chips or nuts yet.

Lupe sipped coffee on the other side of the island. "If I was making cookies—and I'm not saying that I ever would. That's what the Keebler elves are for, you know what I mean? Anyway, I would use a mixer like they do on those cooking shows you watch."

I'd spent a half hour poking through the kitchen cupboards looking for a mixer. "Trust me, Lupe, if this kitchen had a mixer, I would have used it."

"Did you look in the garage? There's a bunch of wedding gifts out there still in boxes. I think I saw a mixer, one of the fancy kind with a bowl that raises and lowers, just like Martha Stewart's got. You like Martha Stewart, I know you do."

I dabbed the perspiration off my face with the hem of my T-shirt.

Lupe set her coffee down. "You aren't thinking I should carry a big, heavy mixer in here. You didn't see Martha Stewart carrying one of those things when they interviewed her in front of the courthouse. She has people to do that for her. Besides, my back's not so good."

"I'll ask Andy when he gets home."

"You better get that batter off the counter."

Such attentiveness was unusual for Lupe. I dropped the spoon to the counter. "Lupe, is there something you want to tell me?"

"I know you don't like to gossip about your family."

"No, I don't."

"But I think I should warn you that things won't be so pleasant around here for a few days."

I picked up the spoon. "Thank you. I'll make sure I clean up my mess."

"They need me to work a weekend this month, said they'd pay me overtime. That's a first."

"Actually, that won't be necessary. Fletcher and I have plans."

Chapter 22

Fletcher dropped his book bag on the floor with a thud and opened the refrigerator.

I asked him how his day had been and received the usual noncommittal grunt in reply. "That's good. By the way, Mi Sun called about ten minutes ago, asked if you were available to help her with Tootsie. Do you want a snack before we go? I baked some cookies."

You would have thought I'd asked him to donate a kidney. "What?! I'm not going. I don't know anything about dogs."

"Of course you do. You've done a wonderful job with Bee. And anything you don't know, I can teach you on the drive to Mi Sun's house."

"When is she expecting us?"

I felt my Braille watch. "Fifteen minutes. At the park."

"No way. You have to call her back. I'll look like an idiot."

"Nonsense. The first lesson is all about the *sit* and *stay* commands, a piece of cake. Would you like a sandwich? Your father loved peanut-butter-and-banana sandwiches after school."

Fletcher slumped onto the sofa. "I couldn't."

In the driveway I demonstrated a sleight of hand using a liver treat with Bee. I held the liver treat between my fingers in front of Bee's nose. As she licked and nibbled at my fingers, I raised the treat up and over her head as I told her to sit, which she performed perfectly. "When a dog's nose goes up, its tail goes down. Works like a charm every time. You always start with the sit command because if a dog is sitting, it's under control.

Fletcher's voice was flat. "Is the licking mandatory?"

"Absolutely. If Tootsie doesn't believe the treat is accessible, he'll lose interest."

Fletcher looked at his watch. "This isn't going to work. We're late already."

"Rule number one: Never keep a pretty girl waiting." I moved toward the truck.

Fletcher climbed in beside me. "And *stay*? What about *stay*?"

"We'll work as a team. I'll demonstrate with Bee. You and Mi Sun follow along with Tootsie."

The truck jumped the curb and came to a stop. A flash of red sweater and the swing of ebony hair caught my eye. A low-slung bundle of amber and white fur pulled her toward us.

"This was a huge mistake," Fletcher mumbled.

Tootsie turned out to be a Welsh corgi, eager to please and perpetually smiling. While Fletcher made himself friendly with Tootsie as I'd suggested, I sat with Bee and prayed fervently: *Jesus, you rode a donkey colt that had never been ridden. You directed ravens to feed Elijah. You made ants wise, and I don't even think they have what you'd call a brain, but that's something else entirely, isn't it? Let's see, you care when a sparrow falls to the ground. Seems to me that making Bee and Tootsie good dogs should be a piece of cake for you, as well as a benefit to Fletcher's cause. Only you can make so much out of so little. Amen.*

Bee sat with ears pricked forward, leaning into her collar so hard she coughed. I used my no-nonsense voice in her ear.

"You're going to sit right here until you're needed, do you hear me?"

She mouthed a complaint, so I fed her a liver treat.

"Today, you're a tool in God's hands."

MI SUN BACKED AWAY from Tootsie, who sat still as a stone waiting for his mistress to release him from the *stay* command.

Fletcher said, "Go ahead and release him."

"Okay!" The corgi paddled through the grass toward Mi Sun. "This is *so* cool. What's next?"

"That's enough for his first lesson," Fletcher said, sounding like Mrs. Wilson, my eighth-grade PE teacher.

Fletcher and Mi Sun joined me under a tree. The lacey parasol of leaves overhead became denser with each visit to the park.

"I can't *believe* how much you know about dogs," Mi Sun said, and I almost thanked her. Her breathless awe was reserved for young men, not grandmas. "You're *so* good with them," she gushed.

"Grandma taught me."

Obviously he didn't get that humility from me. "Practice the sit and stay," I told Mi Sun. "We'll get together next week to work on his pulling problem."

Fletcher couldn't hide the panic in his voice. "Tootsie's such a fast learner, Grandma. Do you suppose he's ready to move on today?"

I felt my watch. "It's almost five o'clock."

Fletcher pulled me up from the bench as we'd practiced and set the walker in front of me. "Yeah, we gotta go."

Mi Sun and Fletcher walked ahead of me, like everyone these days. She said, "You should think about going to youth group. We meet on Wednesday nights at the church."

"I don't know. My . . . it's probably not a good idea."

"You'd love it. The kids are *great.* You complained about not knowing anyone."

Please note for posterity's sake that I kept my mouth shut and prayed.

"It's not my thing. I'm pretty busy."

"How do you know if it's your thing if you haven't tried it?"

I liked her tenacity.

Fletcher opened the truck door for me. "I'll let you know," he said in his most noncommittal voice.

"You are *so* going." Mi Sun laughed. "You'll love the kids. They're great. And I don't give up, *ever.*"

"Maybe." Fletcher bent over Bee to unhook her leash, and before I had the chance to warn him, Bee bolted for freedom. Fletcher ran after her, screaming her name.

"Stop!" I called after him. "Fletcher! Don't run! Stop!"

He obeyed to turn, openhanded. "Grandma, she's across the park already."

I swallowed down bitter panic. Cars. Vicious dogs. Bee was a country dog. "If you chase her, she thinks you're playing a game. Trust me. She'll look back eventually, and when she does, we have to be doing something to arouse her curiosity."

"Like?" I heard the threat of tears in Fletcher's voice.

"Whoop as loud as you can and walk away from her."

Fletcher moved closer, whispered his panic. "We have to get home or else."

"We can't leave Bee behind. This is the quickest way." Mi Sun moved closer. "You have to trust me about this. Mi Sun will help, won't you?"

"What do you want me to do?"

"Run toward the lake with Tootsie." I handed Fletcher the leash. "Don't look at Bee. Give Tootsie lots of attention. Feed her liver treats. When Bee gets closer, fall to the ground—she'll move in to give you a bath—and grab her. Go! Run! Make lots of noise!"

Mi Sun let out a war whoop and took off with Tootsie.

Fletcher stood like a mailbox in front of me. His voice trembled. "If Dad finds out . . ."

I pushed him in the direction of Mi Sun and Tootsie.

"The sooner you start whooping . . ."

FLETCHER AND I SAT at the kitchen counter, breathing hard from the rushed trip home. "So," he said, taking a bite out of a cookie, "was Huck at the park?"

"I haven't seen him for a couple days. He's like that. He shows up when it suits him."

"The next time you see him, ask what's on the lit final."

"I guarantee he knows nothing about it. If you remember, school isn't exactly his favorite hangout."

The door from the garage opened and the authoritative click of Suzanne's heels announced her arrival. She paused inside the door with a rustle of packages. Fletcher stiffened beside me. To distract her from his anxiety, I greeted her with the friendliness of Mickey Mouse at the gates of Disney World. With age, sadly, came the ability to camouflage one's true feelings.

. . . love one another . . .

"Welcome home! How was your day?" I all but chirped.

Although she spoke to Fletcher, I shivered with the chill of her voice. "Shouldn't you be doing homework?"

Fletcher expelled a sigh of relief. "Totally." He left me alone with Suzanne.

This was the moment I'd prayed for. I'd rehearsed an apology for my self-serving attempt at saving her floors with doggie booties. Before I started my preamble, Suzanne said, "Andrew asked me to do a little research, see if there is anything new to help your AMD."

Huck stepped out of the bedroom, yawning and stretching liked he'd just woken from a nap.

"That's lovely of you," I said to Suzanne, "but I'm sorry you went to so much trouble. I have a retinal specialist who monitors my condition."

Huck leaned against the doorjamb and rubbed at his eyes with the palms of his hands.

"Am I keeping you from something, Birdie?"

I snapped to, giving Suzanne my full attention, and who wouldn't? She wore a red dress no bigger than my sleeve. "No. Nothing. Sometimes I get lazy about focusing my attention visually." That was true.

"My assistant read through all the reports and came up with some recommendations. For instance, there are some experimental procedures that look promising, most having to do with stem cell technology, but those are some years off. Although there is another procedure they're already doing on a limited basis in the UK, a telescopic—"

"—intraocular lens? That's a treatment for folks with dry AMD. I have wet."

"I told Annemarie that." She shuffled papers before dropping them on the counter. "Anyway, I stopped by the health-food store on the way home." A tumble of plastic bottles rattled across the granite. "Let's see, Omega-3 helps with inflammation and has been shown in studies to benefit the retina. And chocolate has more antioxidant power than wine or green tea, so here's some Godiva chocolate. I didn't know if you liked your chocolate with or without nuts, so I bought both."

Huck moved closer, eyeing the chocolate. I turned my back to him ever so slightly. "Suzanne, that's very—"

"Here's a bottle of lutein, vitamin A, and high-potency C, E, and zinc are supposed to be helpful. Chronic inflammation arose as a recurring theme in the research, so I bought zeaxanthin, beta-carotene, beta-cryptoxanthin, and lycopene. Simply follow the RDAs on the labels."

Huck walked behind Suzanne, opening and closing cabinet doors, making a terrible ruckus, looking like a boy with an appetite after a day at school. He still wore the coarse shirt Buck had given him. He'd snagged something to cut a flap of fabric at the shoulder, and the hem had gone rusty like he'd been swimming in the river. More than anything, I wanted to feel the texture of that homespun shirt.

"Do you have any questions?" Suzanne asked.

At some point I'd taken all these supplements and more—most faithfully, the chocolate. Perhaps Godiva outperformed a Snickers bar; I was willing to experiment. When the utter inevitability of my condition had sunk in, I simplified my life by tossing the boatload of bottles in the trash. My vitamin of choice became good ol' One-A-Day, along with a daily piece of fruit pie. But I had no intention of telling Suzanne of my loss of enthusiasm for swallowing pills, especially since this was the most she'd said to me since the incident in the dining room.

"Suzanne, you're a fabulous doctor. Thank you, thank you."

Huck frowned at me.

"We want you to have everything you need."

Huck opened the refrigerator. I sucked in a breath. The light illuminated his face—every pore, every freckle, the peach fuzz growing down his cheeks. I scrambled for something to say to Suzanne to justify my gasp. "I could never do what you do. I've watched those television shows where they peel back a person's face like they're removing skin from a chicken." Huck closed the door, totally enthralled with talk of peeling faces. "I change the channel every time."

"I'm surprised you can see the television at all."

"I wear telescoping glasses at home. I'm sure I look like a clown, but I wouldn't want to miss *Meerkat Manor*."

Suzanne slipped out of her heels before she sat beside me. "We visited the Tswalu Reserve in South Africa where we watched the meerkats for hours. An amazing experience."

Keep the conversation moving, Birdie.

"I don't know how to thank you for your kindness, Suzanne. I know this stuff cost a fortune."

Huck sauntered back to the bedroom and disappeared. Too much politeness tended to repel him. I stifled a sigh. He was terribly distracting and impossible to explain, except to open-minded grandsons, and I wanted to talk to Suzanne.

"It really was Andrew's idea." She left her stool and moved toward the stairs.

"I baked cookies today," I said to her back.

She stopped and turned. "What kind?"

"Is there another kind? Chocolate chip, of course."

"Soft or crunchy?"

"Thick and chewy."

"Nuts?"

"Doubled." When she didn't move, I asked, "Milk or coffee?"

"Milk. Definitely milk."

SUZANNE LICKED HER FINGERS. "I haven't had a cookie like this since . . . before my parents divorced."

"I didn't know. That must have been difficult for you."

"Not really. My parents fought all the time. Dad had issues. My mother found a wonderful man almost immediately, and he opened the world to us."

"How old were you?"

"Six. I was in first grade. I remember because I had to change schools, and I loved Miss Baker with all my heart."

"How fortunate your mother found a man who loved you. My parents didn't divorce, but my ma died. Two months later Pa brought home Flora Blumgaurd. If he had looked the world over for the one woman who got under my craw and stayed there, he found her. Needless, to say, she wasn't anything like Ma."

"How did your mother die?" Suzanne asked with an unfamiliar softness.

"She died of sepsis. Her appendix burst. Pa tried to get a doctor to the station. He rode for two days through the snow, but the doctor got there too late. He was on the other side of the valley delivering a baby."

"Who cared for your mother while your father went for a doctor?"

"I did. I was thirteen. My sister, Evelyn, she didn't handle illness well. I tried to lower the fever with cool cloths, just like Ma had done for me. Evelyn brought in buckets of snow to melt." Ma's face, twisted in pain, came to mind unbeckoned. No matter how many quilts I had piled on her, she shook with chills. Her skin had yellowed like an old newspaper with a bloodred rash dotting her skin. "I couldn't do anything for her pain."

"You were so young. I can't imagine."

The tenderness of Suzanne's words slit my defenses. "I've never told this to a soul, but I whispered a prayer of thanksgiving when she finally slipped away."

"Your father had no business leaving you like that."

"I don't blame him. He was the only one strong enough to go. It nearly killed him to leave us; I saw it in his eyes." I rubbed my temples where a headache threatened. I rubbed harder. "By default, I became the woman of the house, or queen of the house, if you'd asked Evelyn. Flora stepped into an impossible situation.

More than anything I wish I'd swallowed all the hateful words I slung at her. I considered her nothing less than demonic for taking Ma's place. And my pa, we'd been so close. He became a stranger to me, so I hated him too. Oh, the pain I inflicted on my poor, grieving father, trying to do his best to provide for his daughters. As a ranger, he traveled for weeks at a time into the back country doing wildlife studies, patrolling for poachers, rescuing lost hikers. I thought I could take care of myself and Evelyn, but he did the right thing bringing Flora to us."

Suzanne laid her head on the counter. "Being a stepmother is the hardest thing I've ever done. I never dreamed . . . I've never failed at anything, but this . . ."

"Something changed between Flora and me when my father died. Death brings startling clarity. We owned a common pain, there was no doubt about that. Looking back over the years she'd been with us, I saw breakfast spread out on the table on a winter's morning, steaming from the chill inside the station, and Flora dishing the last of the scramble onto Pa's plate. She hadn't set a place for herself. Pa died when I was fifty-seven years old, and Flora had just turned eighty. His death knitted us together about as close as two women could be. During those three years the Lord gave us, I learned her first husband and two children had died in a fire just six months before Pa brought her home as his bride. She had no family to take her in and only the clothes the church had gathered to her name."

Suzanne leaned closer. "What could she have done to make things better?"

"As a girl I wished Pa had never brought her home in the first place, but Pa and Flora were only human. They had their needs, and I don't begrudge them, not now, for coming together to smother their loneliness. Times were different then. We didn't read books about our dysfunctional childhoods. We had the self-awareness of tree stumps, but knowing her story may have helped."

"Did he even know Flora? I mean, two months?"

I sat straighter. "He needed a mother for his daughters. I loved him for that—eventually."

"She was awfully brave to go with him."

"Braver than you know."

Suzanne wrapped a cookie in a napkin and excused herself.

I moved to a bench in the backyard to play fetch with Bee, all the while running my words over and over in my head. Nothing I'd said resembled the speech I had rehearsed. Something else had taken place between Suzanne and me, something I couldn't quite name. I now held a robin's egg in my hand, its weight barely noticeable, and yet the burden nearly toppled me.

"Come on, Bee. Ready for dinner?"

Bee trotted toward the patio door and our bedroom within. The click of her toenails on the stone patio birthed an idea.

Chapter 23

Bee leapt into the cargo area of Emory's orange and white Bronco, a relic of the seventies and a testament to his unfaltering if misguided devotion to the Denver Broncos football team. He closed the gate, and Bee barked in protest.

"Do you think she'll be all right back there?" I asked. "She's used to the front seat."

Emory held me by the shoulders. "Let me help you pack. It would take no time at all. If we left within the hour, I could have you home in Ouray by nine, even if we stopped for enchiladas in Edwards or a hamburger in Glenwood Springs. I can call Elsie. She'll turn up your heat, make it nice and cozy for you." He wrapped his arms around me, and to my utter amazement, my shoulders shuddered and the tears finally fell. There's nothing more pitiful than a weepy old woman, but I couldn't stop. His warmth, the pure humanness of his presence pulling me closer disarmed me. Besides, his jacket smelled of smoke and pine sap. Home.

"I sure do miss you, Birdie."

"I miss you too." And because I'd already saturated his shoulder with tears, I released him, lowering my head to gather my emotions like shells off the sand before I dared to speak. "Things are complicated here. I thought I knew my family. I don't, and that's nobody's fault but mine. I don't believe God pushed me down the stairs, but he's not above using a broken ankle to change me."

"I think you're perfect just the way you are."

Bee had stopped barking. Some faithful companion.

"I've known from the beginning that Bee's my top competition for your affection," he said, taking my hand. "It's no small thing that you're sending her away."

"Don't make me out to be a saint. I'm having second thoughts; Fletcher and Bee have become bosom buddies. But sending Bee home just seems like the right thing to do." I rested my forehead on Emory's chest again. I sure liked the sound of his heartbeat. "Promise me you'll take Bee out to Carver meadow to chase rabbits."

"And Josie will keep her in town while I'm working."

"You've talked to Josie?"

"I see her now and again. She stops by the pharmacy."

"Is she all right? It's not like Josie to take a pill, unless you count those grass clippings she mixes in her orange juice."

"She misses you. She asks for news."

"She *could* call."

"You and I both know that won't happen."

If this good-bye took any longer, I would jump in the cargo area with Bee. I said to Emory, in my best good-soldier voice, "You better get going."

"Will you be okay?"

"That old dog snores like a freight train."

"I snore a little."

My heart fluttered. "Everybody does."

"Birdie . . . ?"

"Lord willing, I'll be walking without restrictions in three weeks. We'll have all the time in the world to talk about the future."

"When you get home, I have a surprise for you. But first I'll grill you a steak with a touch of pink, just the way you like it, and I'll sauté some mushrooms for the top with lots of butter and garlic. And I'll trade a bottle of Elsie's blood-pressure medication for a loaf of her sourdough bread. If she balks, I'll throw in a can of Gold Bond. She goes through that stuff like water."

Tears threatened again. "I'll bring a pie."

"Elderberry?"

"I thought you liked my apple best."

"I like your apple pie fine. But your elderberry pie makes my toes curl."

Talk of curling toes warmed my face. "You better get going," I said with more authority than I felt. "That storm's supposed to hit the mountains before midnight."

"I've driven through lots of storms. In fact, I'd drive to hell and back to see you."

"Thanks for answering my distress call. I wouldn't trust Bee with anyone else. I'm awfully glad you came."

"How glad?"

"Glad enough to tell you I don't deserve your kindness, but selfish enough to want it all the more."

Emory got quiet, and I feared I'd played my hand too boldly.

"There's a woman watching us from a window," he said.

"To the south?"

"About two hundred years old?"

"That's Ruth, and she's watching out for me, so you better mind your manners."

"I don't think I will." He hooked my chin with a finger and covered my lips with a hungry kiss. A flood of warmth weakened my knees. "I'll be seeing you," he said. I stood at the curb, leaning hard on my walker until the grind of his motor accelerated into traffic at the corner.

"Is there room in your life for a misbehavin' dog and Huckleberry Finn, Sir Emory?"

❘❘❘❘❘❘❘❘❘❘❘❘❘❘❘❘❘❘❘❘❘❘❘❘❘❘❘❘❘❘

"YOU SENT BEE HOME? Why? You said I was doing a good job with her."

"Sit down," I said, patting the bed, but Fletcher remained at the door. "This has nothing to do with you. You were great with Bee. She loves you. You're not so bad with old women either. This one loves you."

He turned to look out the door. "Did you send Bee away to make Suzanne happy?"

Yes. No. It's not that simple. "Bee needs room to run. She's a mountain dog. If she doesn't chase a rabbit every now and then, she gets herself in trouble, or worse yet, I get her in trouble thinking booties will turn her into a lapdog."

"This is about Suzanne," he said, collapsing into the recliner.

"Fletcher, come visit us when school's out. We'll go for hikes. Bee will be awfully happy to see you, and so will I."

Fletcher held his head in his hands. He whispered, "Joe DiMaggio. Center field. New York Yankees from 1936 to 1942 and 1946 to 1951. Played in ten World Series."

"Fletcher?"

He looked up. "Joe had a 56-consecutive-game hitting streak in 1941. Some say that's the most accomplished statistic in baseball. I'm not so sure."

"When I feel overwhelmed, I remember a Bible verse my pa taught me."

"Huh?"

"When life gets out of control, I say this to myself: 'Some trust in chariots, and some in horses: but I will remember the name of the Lord my God.'"

I didn't have to see Fletcher's face to know I'd completely confounded the fellow. "Have you seen *Ben Hur*? It's a movie, kind of old but very dramatic. There's a chariot race. Terribly bloody. I think you'd like it."

"It's not one of those musical things, is it?"

"Heaven's no. The story takes place when Rome ruled the known world. Four-horse teams pulled chariots at a full gallop around a huge racetrack, with the drivers snapping whips over the horses' heads. One of the chariots is rigged with blades to shred his opponents' wheels. Oh, it's quite the nail-biter. Evelyn spent that whole scene in the bathroom. Not me. I cheered on Charlton Heston."

"Who?"

"You don't know Charlton Heston?"

"Did he ever play James Bond?"

For the sake of the story, I overlooked Fletcher's ignorance, however heartbreaking. "You'll have to check him out on the Internet."

"What happened in the chariot race?"

At least he was paying attention. "The pounding of the horses' hooves rattled my rib cage. The race was thrilling and terrifying at the same time. I watched a lot of it through my fingers. Charlton Heston wins, of course, but his childhood friend is trampled to death by horses.

"But that was just a race. The chariots and their mighty horses represented the strength of the Roman Empire. I can only imagine how their enemies trembled when teams of chariots thundered toward them and their puny swords. Surely the ground shook. The point is, to this day, when things go bad, people reach for their most powerful weapons. The Egyptians and the Romans brought out their chariots. Today we fling hateful words about. Sadly, some resort to violence. When I'm threatened, sarcasm is my weapon of choice. But when I stop to remember the name of the Lord my God, I know he is faithful to look after me. No sarcasm needed."

"I don't get—"

"Fletcher, bringing Bee here was a big mistake, selfish on my part. I knew Suzanne wouldn't like it, even though your father finally relented to bring her along. You did a great job exercising her and keeping her out of trouble, but her presence caused more problems than she solved. You mustn't worry about her. She's staying with a good friend of mine who lives above Ouray. She'll have the run of the mountain."

Fletcher fumed, then bolted for the door, slamming the wall as he walked out of the room. "I hate her! I *hate* her!"

I lowered the bed to stare at the ceiling, now covered with a constellation of purple flowers. "Go away," I said. But if anything, more flowers bloomed.

No wonder I'd botched everything. I was nuts. Crazy nuts. Mixed nuts. Spiced nuts. I promised myself to talk to a psychiatrist when I got back to Ouray. Surely they had a pill for people who grew flowers on the ceilings, fell down imaginary mountainsides, and carried on conversations with literary characters.

The bigger the pill, the better.

HUCK SAT CROSS-LEGGED ON the floor by the bed, his shoulders rounded, his head bent low. He traced the shape of an oak leaf in the rug. "I sure miss that hound of yourn's."

"The lady of this house isn't crazy about dogs," I said. "Bee made her nervous. And to be fair, Bee did rip the skirt off her sofa. A very expensive sofa."

He met my gaze. "I heard your humbug talky-talk with her, all polite as pie. All I can say is ladies is ladies, and you got to make allowances, but yourn dog was a sockdolager."

"A sockdolager? Is that a good thing?"

"If I'd a-wanted a dog, there warn't one better." He drew deep furrows in the rug. "That is, if I'd a-wanted one, which I don't."

"There's no better companion than a dog if it's approval you're looking for. Of course, they can be a lot of trouble too. Bee nearly eats me out of house and home."

"That ain't no matter, not if a hound will eat catfish."

I watched Huck rub away the furrows like swiping writing in clear sand. "I couldn't help noticing that you touched Bee and she responded."

"Geewhillikins, I 'bout swallowed my tongue when she showed her belly. I warn't sure at all if I should touch her. But then I put a hard think on it. I can touch this here rug, and I can feel the coolness of the grass through my pants at the park. But I ain't never touched nothing breathing—at least not that I can tell."

"Huck, is this your first time out of the story? Do you mean to tell me you've never visited anyone before me?"

"No ma'am, I ain't never been out of the story a-fore, although I'd like to light out for the territory. There's injuns out there, and space for a body to do as he pleases. But I always end up where I started, back with the Widow Douglas, trying my best to be respectable."

"Let me get this straight. As far as you know, you're always living the story. You run away to Jackson Island, find Jim, float down the river, come across con men and pirates, but you have never ever stepped out of the story to explore the real world? If I was pulled out of my world to visit another, I'm afraid I wouldn't be as calm as you."

"Afeard of you? You're a gentle lady, 'wellborn' as the saying is, and that's worth as much in a woman as it is in a horse. Besides, I could shinny through the dark and you'd never find me nohow."

"That's all well and good, but how did you get here, Huck? Did you walk into a wardrobe? Drink a mysterious brew? Eat a poisoned apple?"

"I reckoned it was you who called me out with the magic of a hair-ball oracle or some such thing. Tom would know. He reads books about magical and romantical things all the time."

"If I called you, I don't know what I did, but I'm awfully glad you came. At the very least, you've made a difficult time quite interesting. Beyond that, you've filled an old woman's life with wonderment and a breathless expectation that anything's possible." I swung my feet over the bed. "Huck, you must tell me if I'm asking too much, but I would very much like to touch your shirt. That may seem like an odd request, but I haven't seen a homespun shirt since I was a young girl in Tennessee."

Huck drew his hands into his lap. "After I touched the hound, I had a long think about this. Do you suppose there's rules about what a body should do in t'nother world? It pulls on me pretty tight that I could end up in an awful peck of trouble."

"I would never hurt you. You believe that, don't you?"

He stood and paced the length of the bed. "I touched a rattlesnake skin once and that fetched me some powerful bad luck."

"Look at me, Huck. I'm not a rattlesnake; I'm a grandmother. And I wouldn't be touching your skin. Quite frankly I'm not sure I should do that either, but I would very much like to touch your shirt. My pa wore a homespun shirt when we read in front of the fire. I spent many nights sitting on his lap, leaning into his chest, feeling the pebbliness of his shirt against my cheek. He read us Bible stories that puzzled me something awful back then. Of course, Evelyn felt all superior whenever I asked a question, but Pa didn't mind.

"He read about a talking donkey, a woman turned into a pillar of salt, and a Levite who chopped his concubine into twelve pieces. Pa would never let me read a story like that from the library, but there it was, right in the Bible. He said some stories are meant to teach us what not to do."

Huck yawned and stretched. "Aunt Peggy only told me about loaves and fishes, and I knowed plenty about fish already."

I swallowed hard. "What do you think, Huck? Should we chance it?"

He raised his arm to me, cocked at the elbow. I reached out like he was a snake until my finger lit on his cuff. His eyes opened wide.

"Do you feel that?" I asked.

"Yup. Do you?"

I traced small circles on the fabric. Saddle leather. Wet wool. Tobacco. *Pa.* "Oh my."

Huck withdrew his arm like he'd touched a hot iron.

I reached for him. "No, don't."

"Your eyes went somewheres else. I seen mesmerizers and phrenologists do that. Gave me the willies, it did."

"I can't hypnotize you, Huck. But when I touched your sleeve, I smelled my pa." I reached out my hand. "Please, may I touch your shirt again?"

"This ain't no deviltry, is it?"

Was it? Surely not! "I'm a good Christian woman. I don't give the devil any credit for all that God the Father delivers through his beloved Son."

He lifted his arm again. I rubbed the fabric between my fingers. And then Huck did the most surprising thing of all. He rested his fingers, as light as a sparrow, on my hand. I felt the calloused tips of his fingers and the pulse of blood under his skin. He pulled away and jumped up.

Huck clutched his shirt over his heart and scooted away. "My heart jumped up amongst my lungs. I reckon we tested preforeordestination as best as we ought."

"I didn't mean to scare you."

"I ain't afeard, not worth bothring about. But I'd druther not be a tangle-headed fool. I reckon it's best I skedaddle." And he rose and walked to the patio door. With his hand on the knob, his shoulders drooped. "I'm all tuckered out."

"You can sleep in the chair like you did before."

"I won't a-turn in. Me and Jim a-going to boom along down the river tonight. I'll see the moon go off watch. That's the splendist sight, unless a storm's a-brewing."

He opened the door.

"Huck! Thanks for . . . well, thanks for sharing your time with me."

"Talking donkeys? I'm gonna have to get me one of them Bibles you have a fondness for."

Chapter 24

"Okay, Bats, the timer's set," announced Ruth. "Who's first?"

"Praise the Lord, all's stable for me," Ruby said.

"Me, too," added Ruth. "Just counting down the days until the great-grandkids come. Betty?"

She sniffed loudly. She did everything loudly. "I suppose you want to hear about my latest hallucination?"

I set my coffee cup down and held my trembling hands in my lap. "Hallucinations?"

"Did Cary Grant show up at the foot of your bed again?" Ruby asked, breathy and eager.

"That's a little pedestrian, Ruby. I'm on to smaller things."

"Don't toy with us, Betty," Margie said.

"If you insist." She wagged her fork at Margie. "You know I listen to Fox News every morning. Yesterday, during my second cup of coffee, I wasn't thinking about anything in particular, and clowns certainly never came to mind—but there they were. Very strange."

"Clowns? You had clowns in your kitchen? How many?"

"I never thought to count them, but at least half a dozen of them, right on my table. They stood no more than five or six inches tall, moved just like people . . . or clowns. Some sat at a picnic table, eating a dinner of fried chicken and mashed potatoes. Teeny-tiny cobs of corn, stripped down to the husks. One clown sat in front of a mirror—the kind movie stars use, you know, with all the lights—touching up his makeup. Another scratched his head under a purple wig. A clown wearing oversized shoes smoked a cigarette, which didn't seem very funny to me at all."

I thought of Huck's pipe. "Could you smell the cigarette?"

"Oh no, I didn't smell a thing. But my schnozz doesn't work too well anyway, not since I had chemotherapy a few years back."

Margie said, "This is your craziest hallucination yet. Had you been thinking about clowns?"

"I said I hadn't. Don't you listen? I've never even been to a circus my whole life, and if I had, I would have gone for popcorn when the clowns showed up. Back when the kids were small, I saw clowns on *The Ed Sullivan Show*. All that falling and hitting didn't sit well with me."

Ruby pounded the table. "Your doctor said every memory is stored away just waiting for a chance to pop out. I'll wager cold, hard cash that your parents took you to a circus when you were too young to remember."

Ruth laid her hand over mine. "Birdie, you look white as a ghost. You don't have to worry. Betty isn't crazy. She's experiencing Charles Bonnet Syndrome. Some folks who've lost their sight have vivid hallucinations. Betty's the lucky one of us. She's had Cary Grant come to call."

"Stepped straight out of *To Catch a Thief*. I must have watched that movie a hundred times after he showed up, but he never came back. Now I'm seeing miniature clowns on my breakfast table. What kind of trade-off is that?"

My heart raced so that I had to gulp air to talk. "And this is perfectly normal?"

Betty leaned closer. I eased away as much as I dared. "The doctor," she said, "when I finally got the nerve to ask him, told me the brain gets tired of blank spots, or so they think." Her voice got low as to add to the mystery. "The brain pulls pictures out of the deep coves of the mind. But honestly, nobody's sure how the mind really works."

Ding!

"Ignore the timer," Ruth said. "This is fascinating. Betty, tell Birdie about the stone wall."

I laid my fork down.

"Most of the things I see are quite pleasant. Flowers where no flowers have business growing. Children playing in the yard. And Cary Grant. For obvious reasons, Cary's my favorite. But every once in a while, a stone wall appears. The stones fit so closely together, there's no need for mortar. A real craftsman built the wall, that's for sure. Moss covers the rocks, so if I've ever seen a wall like that, it wasn't in Colorado."

"Betty, tell her about the time you went to the zoo," prompted Ruby.

"The wall never fails to show up at the most inappropriate times. The first time it happened, I was visiting the zoo with my son's family. We were on the way to the elephants, munching on cotton candy as we walked. All of a sudden, the stone wall appeared."

Ruby said, "Tell her how tall it was."

"Do you want to tell this story?"

"You leave out the interesting details."

"Fine. The wall was about chest high, so I stopped cold. My family kept walking. All of a sudden I was on one side of the wall and they were on the other. I looked up and down the wall. No gate anywhere. I knew the wall wasn't real, even though the stones looked as solid as any I'd ever seen. My son returned to find me gaping at nothing. I struggled over what to tell him. I didn't know a thing about Charles Bonnet Syndrome. I thought the only reasonable thing a woman in my situation could think: I was losing my mind. And I certainly wasn't going to announce that I'd lost my marbles at the zoo, of all places. Next thing I knew, I'd be living with the penguins."

"It was wide too, wasn't it?"

"That wall reached the full width of the walkway. Everything in me said to climb over it to rejoin my family. Wouldn't that have been a pretty picture? Somehow, I knew better. I looked in my son's eyes and walked toward him. I fully expected to crash into the stones, but I didn't. When the wall appears now, I can't help but take a moment to admire its workmanship, enjoy the flecks of color in the stones, admire the cushiony softness of the moss. I welcome its arrival. It's the clearest thing I see, except for the flowers and the clowns."

"And Cary Grant."

"His eyes were the color of caramels, not the kind you buy in the bag, the kind you get at the candy store—rich and buttery."

"Cary brings out the poet in you, Betty."

Charles Bonnet Syndrome? My hallucinations had a name, a French name. I wished I'd taken French in high school like Evelyn. I took German, but still my heart said, *Frohe Weihnachter*—the only celebratory phrase I remembered. Knowing my brain caused the visions made the moment as happy as any Christmas I'd remembered.

"Did Cary speak to you?" I asked.

"Oh no, the doctor spoke quite adamantly about that. The hallucinations do not talk, and I was to report to him if they ever did. That's an entirely different part of the brain. And if you don't think I longed to hear something out of Cary's mouth, especially with Harry snoring like a chain saw right next to me, you girls are older than I thought. As a matter of fact, Cary looked completely self-absorbed, as if thinking about a pleasant memory, maybe something about Audrey Hepburn. They were gorgeous together in *Charade*. I love that movie."

Ruby said, "If he was thinking about anyone, it was Deborah Kerr from *An Affair to Remember*. Now they had an explosive chemistry. I get goose bumps just thinking about it."

"*I Was a Male War Bride* was on TCM the other night," Ruth added. "Maybe Cary was thinking about how to get out of his garter belt."

The ladies around the table laughed. My stomach soured, and I pushed Margie's lemon pudding away. If Josie or Emory had seen me refuse a dessert, one of them surely would have called 9-1-1. The Bats jabbered on about Cary Grant movies. I squirmed, my thoughts a jumble.

One speculation after another bounced around my cranium. Maybe Huck's appearances weren't Charles Bonnet Syndrome after all. Maybe another syndrome, something equally benign, allowed me to talk to and touch Huck. Besides, I'd known more than one doctor who talked out of the top of his head. Think of all the recent medical discoveries, especially involving the brain. Perhaps Betty's doctor was behind in his reading. Better still, maybe I'd dreamed Huck's visits. I'd heard that anesthesia remained in a body long after surgery. Surely something as sedative as anesthesia would affect dreams.

Who was I kidding?

Huck and I shared a conversation—many conversations—and he touched the back of my hand with his fingertips. Life doesn't get stranger than that.

Just for clarification, I asked Betty, "Are you absolutely, positively sure you didn't hear one word from those clowns? Or a honking horn? A whoopee cushion? Laughing? Anything?"

"If I had, mum's the word. I'm not looking for a short trip to the funny farm."

ııııııııııııııııııııııııııııııııı

THAT NIGHT I BEGGED off listening to the end of *Huck Finn* with Fletcher. He asked if I was feeling okay, and he seemed genuinely concerned, but my thoughts were too tangled to follow a story. He left me a plate of shu mai that I dumped in the trash. I heated a can of tofu soup that tasted like soggy cardboard, then I sat in the dark, hoping Huck would be too caught up in his adventures with Tom to bother with the likes of me. It wasn't that I didn't want to see him. Far from it. He provided color where grayness reigned. I just didn't want to explain him, especially not to myself, and that was getting tougher by the day.

Chapter 25

This grandmother's heart swelled when Fletcher swung behind the truck's steering wheel and brought the engine to life without gulping for air. He even waved off Lupe from directing him out of the garage. At the corner where we usually went straight to go to the Snappy Dragon, Fletcher flipped his turn signal on. "Might I suggest a diner in the Fremont District?" he offered. "They have the best hamburgers in Denver."

"You don't have to ask me twice."

The spring afternoons had settled into a congenial pattern of sunshine and a playful breeze, so we chose to sit under a broad umbrella. I sat with my back to the sun. The breeze fluttered the hem of the umbrella. I closed my eyes and I was overlooking Ouray. The town looked toyish from the top of Box Canyon falls. And then a car drove by with the resonance of a drum.

The waitress brought hamburgers she assured us were organic and antibiotic-free. One less thing to worry about.

Beef as pure as the driven snow didn't improve Fletcher's table manners. He talked around a hunk of beef and whole wheat bun. "So, Grandma, what's Huck been up to lately?"

"Can we talk about something else?"

"Sure. I guess."

I swirled a French fry in catsup. "Okay. I talked to him for an hour the other day." I told Fletcher that Huck had never left his story before to meet with people in the real world. "I'm honored, but I don't know why he chose me, although he says he didn't. It all gets rather complicated."

Fletcher waited for a motorcycle to pass. "He hasn't tried to hurt you, has he?"

"Absolutely not. Far from it. He allowed me to touch his shirt the other night. It brought back such wonderful memories of my father."

Fletcher lowered his hamburger to his plate and wiped his hands clean with three napkins. "Let me get this straight. You *touched* Huckleberry Finn."

"Just his shirt," I said with a flip of a hand, but my heart was beating wildly. "And I only touched him once." I pushed my plate away. "You don't think I'm crazy, do you?"

Fletcher swirled the ice in his drink.

"Fletch?" I pleaded.

"No, Grandma. No. You're not crazy. It's just that I walk around on a certain plane of reality that's full of jocks, dorks, and cranky teachers. I've dreamed of traveling through time and meeting people from history, but I never dreamed it would happen. So, like, this is kinda weird, is all."

"It's weirder than that when you consider Huck isn't a historical figure. He's the figment of Mark Twain's imagination." The breeze delivered a waft of hamburger to my nose. I pulled the plate back. "Besides, I like Huck's visits. I like the unpredictability and the mystery of his appearances, but I'd be lying to you if I didn't admit to worrying about the state of my mind. You haven't told anyone, have you?"

"No way."

"Not even Mi Sun?"

Fletcher leaned back in his chair. "She asked me to the prom."

"And you're going?"

"I don't dance. She's asking another guy from chemistry."

"Finish your hamburger. You're going to call Mi Sun the minute we get home to beg her forgiveness and accept her invitation. You're a Wainwright, Fletcher, my boy. Dancing's in your blood."

"I think that gene must be recessive in me."

"Not at all, not with your grandmother on the job. Lessons begin the moment you convince Mi Sun you're her escort."

Fletcher covered his face.

I scooted closer and leaned in to whisper in his ear. "You want to hold that girl in your arms, don't you?"

"Do you know how to waltz?"

"I was born waltzing."

FLETCHER DROVE SLOWLY THROUGH the business district, but then, he drove slowly everywhere. "I ate too much," he said.

"You ate that whole order of—"

Fletcher braked hard. The seat belt pinned me to the seat.

"Why are you stopping?" I said, aggravated.

Fletcher leaned over the steering wheel. "There's a pigeon crossing the street."

"I'll pay you fifty bucks if you can hit him."

"Oh man, he sat down."

"Offer still stands. For goodness' sake, Fletcher, get the lead out." Little did he know the Phillips Milk of Magnesia I'd taken the night before had finally kicked in. "I need to get home sometime today."

Fletcher waited at the next intersection as a bevy of cars whizzed past. "Okay, okay."

"I appreciate your caution, but keep in mind that you're going straight across the intersection. You don't need as much time as you think you do to get—"

Fletcher floored the accelerator.

The force pressed me into the seat. A flash of metallic blue. The screech of tires. The back end of the truck lurched. A shotgun? The world went white around the fog, and then trees, houses, and cars blurred. The world fell silent and still.

I tasted blood.

The air bag puckered and sagged like a spent balloon.

Fletcher moaned beside me.

"Fletcher!" I reached out, cursing the fog. *Concentrate! Look!* Blood ran through his fingers tented over his nose.

His palm came up, red with blood. "Don't touch! My nose, it's broken."

"Are you hurt anywhere else? Don't move."

A rap of knuckles on the window. The man wore a big watch and sunshine reflected off the dome of his head. He shouted through the glass, "Are you all right in there?"

I lowered the window. "We need help. My grandson's hurt." I pulled up on the handle to open the door, which the man pressed closed.

"You shouldn't move until the EMTs get here."

"Is the other driver okay?" I asked.

"That would be me. I'm fine. Now sit still. Help is on the way."

Someone yelled, "I hear a siren!"

A WOMAN WEARING A lab coat over navy scrubs shuffled through papers on a clipboard. Cinnamon hair spiked wildly around her face. "You were lucky, Mrs. Wainwright. Besides the bruising on your chest from the seat belt and the cut to your lip from the air bag, you're in good shape. The cough is from talcum powder they use to coat the air bags. That will clear up in a few days. Drink plenty of fluids."

Each breath burned.

She continued. Don't people introduce themselves anymore? "A staff orthopedist looked at your x-rays. Your ankle held perfectly. No damage to the incision sites or to the hardware inside. You're good to go. Do you have someone to take you home?"

Good question. After a cursory visit, I hadn't seen Andy in hours. "My grandson was driving. I haven't seen him since we got here. I'm sick with worry. No one will tell me anything."

The woman moved closer. I caught MD on her name tag as she leaned in. She lowered her voice. "I'm a grandmother myself. As far as I'm concerned, HIPAA doesn't apply to us. That kid's gone through every test we have to offer, thanks to his mom."

"Suzanne? She's a plastic—I mean, cosmetic surgeon here."

She straightened. "He's had an MRI, x-rays, and ultrasounds. To his credit, he refused the rhinoscopy. Makes me cringe just to think about a hose snaking up a broken nose. There's not enough Xylocaine in the world."

"How is he?"

"Sore. But he'll be fine. If he were my son, I'd send him home with an ice pack and Tylenol."

"But Suzanne is overseeing his case," I guessed.

"If his nose is the least bit off, he'll have surgery." She patted my leg. "Now, should I have the nurse call a taxi?"

I deserved to be banished from the family forever. Not only had I encouraged Fletcher to drive around the neighborhood at my bidding, I'd harangued him into rushing into traffic. The accident never would have happened if I'd done what common sense dictated and just sat in front of the television for six to eight weeks. On the other hand, Fletcher had developed confidence with his driving, and he'd helped a friend, who happened to be a beautiful and brilliant girl. That counted for something.

Besides, screwup or not, I was still his grandmother.

"Which way to pediatrics?"

IIIIIIIIIIIIIIIIIIIIIIIIIIIIII

I FOUND ANDY SITTING outside Fletcher's room, head in hands. He looked up when I said his name. "Ma, I'm sorry. I should have been down to check on you. Your lip looks sore."

"I deserve worse. How's Fletcher doing?"

"They've been trying to get an IV in his vein for nearly an hour."

"Who's in there with him?"

"Just the nurses. Suzanne went to—"

"He's in there alone?"

"I've never been good with—"

"Nobody is, Son, but this is your job." I shooed him toward the door. "I'll be in the waiting room when he's ready for visitors."

I nearly ran over an expectant mother, but I wheeled myself away from Andy and toward the waiting room. The doors of the elevator opened, and a woman rushed out in a flurry of chiffon. "Birdie!"

I recognized Ruth's voice.

"Are you all right?" she said, bending to wrap an arm around my shoulders and kiss my forehead. Her kindness threatened to unleash the emotion I struggled to contain.

I swallowed hard before answering. "Fine, but how did you know?"

She crouched beside the wheelchair. "I still have my sources."

"I'm just a stupid old woman. I don't deserve the time of day."

"What are you talking about? You're precious in his sight. You know that. Now, what's this all about?"

"I had no business taking the boy out to drive."

"You stepped in to help your grandson. So he had an accident. Happens every day. No one was seriously hurt. We don't know how the Lord will use this event in Fletcher's life."

"You don't understand. I nagged him to be more assertive."

"He'll be more judicious about listening to backseat drivers from now on."

"I should be taken out and horsewhipped."

"It's a wonder our children survive us at all, isn't it?"

She rose and pushed me to a waiting room and parked me in front of a rocker. Big Bird and Mr. Snuffleupagus filled an entire wall. Across the room, a cluster of people hunched over coffee cups and talked on cell phones.

Lord, bring healing to their little one.

Ruth sat in the rocker. "There. That's better. Would you like a cup of coffee?"

I knew better than to accept hospital coffee. "No, as soon as I see Fletcher, I'm going home to pack."

"Pack? You're not ready to go home."

"I won't hurt anyone in Ouray."

"Birdie, you experienced a lapse in judgment, but your heart was in the right place. There's a new lightness in Fletcher's step as he walks by. I can see it. Besides, you don't seem like the sort of woman who sidesteps difficult situations."

Hurting my grandson undermined everything I'd believed about myself.

Ruth stood. "How's our boy doing?"

"I haven't seen him yet."

Ruth pushed the wheelchair toward Fletcher's room. "That will never do for a devoted grandmother like you."

ANDY STOOD IN THE corner of Fletcher's room, talking on his cell phone, head down, his other hand deep in his pocket. Ruth pushed me to the bedside and whispered in my ear, "He adores you. Call me when you're finished. I'll be outside the door."

I wanted to argue with her, tell her to go on home, but I needed her. Nothing surprised me more. I felt for Fletcher's hand and sandwiched it between mine. His fingers hung out of my hands.

"Hey, Grandma," he said, sleepily.

"Oh, Fletcher, I'm sorry I woke you. Go back to sleep."

His speech was soft and slow. "They gave me something for the pain."

"Good." I dared not say more, or I'd blubber like a schoolgirl.

"Nice fat lip, Grandma. Does it hurt?"

"The lip's fine. My chest feels like I've been kicked by a mule."

"Yeah, me too."

I squeezed his hand. "Fletcher, I am so sorry. I never should have urged you to take a chance."

"Grandma, I was the driver. We're cool."

Andy stood over me. "I just got off the phone with the police. Fletcher won't be getting his license for six to twelve months beyond his sixteenth birthday, thanks to this fiasco."

"It's no big deal. Grandma, I won't need to drive anyway where they're sending me."

"What's he talking about?" I asked Andy.

"Crashing my truck earned Fletcher enrollment in boarding school. Obviously, he has a good deal to learn about discipline and responsibility, something he's been unwilling to learn at home. All that's about to change."

"We need to talk," I said.

As we passed Ruth in the hall, I put my palms together for the international signal to pray. I directed Andy to the waiting room with Big Bird. The family that had occupied the corner had left, hopefully to a happy ending. Andy pushed me to a sofa and sat down. "I'm not in much of a mood to talk about Fletcher's future."

"I don't imagine you are, not with a sorry excuse of a mother like me. Andy, I never should have taken the boy driving. I know that now."

He stood. "We'll talk tomorrow."

"Tomorrow? I'd love to, but twenty-four hours provides too many opportunities to say or do something stupid. Or worse yet, say nothing at all."

"I'm not a kid anymore. I think—"

"That's why I'll talk to you as a friend, not a son." I took his silence as permission to continue. "You love your son. That's very clear."

"But not enough to make good decisions about his future, according to you."

"If this is going to work, you have to listen like a friend—no looking for hidden insults and no interruptions. Does that work for you?"

He sat back down.

"You want the best for Fletcher. That's love, Andy. You've provided a beautiful home, fabulous opportunities to see the world, a computer he dearly loves—he wants for nothing."

"Except the good sense to say no to his grandmother."

"That will come with time."

"What is this leading to?"

"Children don't always interpret our best intentions as adults do."

"Ma . . ."

"Call me Birdie if it helps."

He stood again. "This is craziness. I have a son facing surgery, reports to study, résumés to review. I've hardly slept for a week."

"I'm almost done." I patted the sofa and he plopped down. "From your point of view, sending Fletcher to boarding school will toughen him up. He'll learn self-discipline and apply himself to his studies. I can't argue with those goals, but Andy, darling, that's not how Fletcher sees a boarding school. To him, he's being sent to Elba. This is exile, plain and simple."

Andy started to rise, and I touched his knee.

"His mother left him," I continued, not sure where I was headed. "Some would argue her departure worked out for the best. Jeannine had her issues, but Fletcher knew her only as Mommy. As irrational and unwarranted as that title applies to Jeannine, that's who she is to Fletcher. And she left. Mommies don't leave. It's counterintuitive. It's written on every child's heart that mommies are ever present, especially when you don't want them anywhere near."

Andy ran his hands over his face.

I kept talking. "Despite your best attempts to be everything to him—and you did a wonderful job—he felt like a puppy kicked out the door on a cold winter's night. It's not fair that he felt that way, given how hard you worked to make things right. It's just the way things work."

"He never said a word."

"Maybe he was too ashamed."

"That's crazy. He had nothing to do with Jeannine leaving. She . . . she was just Jeannine."

"Like I said, children don't see things like adults do. Andy, I fear sending Fletcher away will make him feel like that rejected puppy again."

Andy's voice was flint. "There must be consequences for his actions."

"Fletcher's a smart kid. He knows he messed up, but sending him two thousand miles away will be received as a completely different message. Be sure it's the message you want to send."

"Suzanne says he wants to leave. That this is no big deal to him."

"Yes, I suppose he did say that. But do you always say what you mean?"

"Yes. I'm quite deliberate that way. My success is built on the integrity of my word."

"Then all I have left to say is this: Extend the same mercy you received."

A clock ticked. A bubble glugged in the water cooler. Someone opened and closed the door.

"Mercy? Like when Dad found me in Tuolumne Meadows, when he took his belt off—?"

"He never!"

Andy stood in front of me, pulling his shirttail out of his pants.

"What is this about?" I said.

He grabbed my hand. "Feel that."

Under my fingers, a jagged rise of skin interrupted the smoothness of his back. "How did this happen?"

"Belt buckle, I imagine. It all happened pretty fast."

Chapter 26

I lay in the suffocating darkness, pulling memories out of dusty files. I'd already tried drowning the memories with the last chapters of *Huckleberry Finn*, but with Fletcher contemplating an uncertain future, for me, facing the past head-on seemed the most honest thing to do.

Andy, my firstborn, the tender one, had been the apple of my eye. Nine months out of the year, I waited for his bus to turn the bend along the river and stop at the shelter. We lived in a remote station in Yellowstone during his grade school years. With a new baby and plenty to keep me busy at the station, I relished my time taking Andy to and from school. When he saw me, his furrowed brow loosened and he smiled with teeth as big as movie screens. On the February afternoon I remembered most clearly, he held a paper bag decorated with construction-paper hearts and paper doilies against his chest, a formidable treasure for an eight-year-old boy. He'd already traveled ten miles on the stubby bus to the north entrance to Yellowstone. I'd left the snowmobile fifteen miles farther up the road where the road crews stopped maintaining the road once the snow piled chest high. We took the last five-mile leg to the station by snowmobile. Diane slept in a bundle of snowsuit and blankets on the seat between us.

One by one Andy pulled the Valentines out of the bag. He read the riddles and rhymes and shared his candy. He asked about my day, if the raccoons had gotten in the trash again. I said, "Not since you came up with the new lock." We listened to the radio and sang along with the cowboy's lament.

I drove clutching the steering wheel, shifting gears as smoothly as possible, and as tempting as the brake pedal proved to be on the tight turns, I resisted the urge to press down, all to avoid plowing into a snowbank. We didn't go anywhere without a walkie-talkie, not in the isolated country we lived in, but I'd used it only once, to call in a fire crew. Sliding into a snowbank would feed the chatter of the airwaves for months, from Chuck and all the other rangers.

"Ma?"

"Yes, Andy," I said, downshifting to climb a hill.

"I made something for you."

"You did?" I'd baked a heart-shaped cake for him and Chuck back at the station. In all the years I'd baked with a wood-burning stove, this cake finally approached perfection. I'd spent most of the morning feeding the hopper with kindling and tempering the heat with cool water poured into the reservoir.

Out of his paper bag came a construction-paper card with macaroni flowers. "I wrote a poem for you."

"I can't wait. Read it to me, Son."

He read:

Some boys got a ma who's lacey and refined.
Mine is so much better, so smart and so kind.
She bakes me oatmeal cookies and reads
me *Treasure Island*.
Long past stupid bedtime until I slip off to dreamland.

Happy Valentine's Day, Ma.
I hope your day is great
and that you will still love me
when I finally shout checkmate.

I pressed the brake pedal too hard, and we spun back toward the way we came.

"Do it again!" he yelled.

"Okay, but don't tell your father."

"Don't worry." His honeyed eyes met mine. "Are you okay?"

"Yeah, I'm okay. Very, very okay." I touched his cheek with my gloved hand. "Thanks for the poem, bud."

A wide grin fattened his cheeks.

By the time Andy graduated from college, Chuck had mellowed and Andy had earned a business degree, *summa cum laude.* He worked for a small manufacturing firm outside of Seattle, just a short drive and a ferry trip across the sound from where Chuck rangered at Olympic National Park. He visited often, sometimes bringing a friend who happened to be female. The undertow of tension had dissipated. Chuck and Andy hunted in Northern Idaho, fished for anything with gills, and when not occupied by such manly pursuits, they harassed me. Their needling confirmed their love as surely as endearments, maybe more so.

How does the saying go? *A daughter is a daughter all of her life. A son is a son till he takes a wife?* Andy married Jeannine, a wild-haired girl he'd met at a pub near his apartment. She was—*is*—a flighty thing, never settling on a branch long enough to make a nest. Determined to draw her into the family, Chuck and I answered the young couple's every beck and call, which meant packing and moving the two of them a hundred times, more or less. At least Jeannine liked the outdoors. We traveled together, exploring natural treasures within a day's drive of the peninsula.

From many years of living in national parks, I'd seen plenty of rivers swollen from snowmelt, foaming and churning over boulders, carrying felled trees like toothpicks. When Fletcher was born, a new kind of love carried me on a raucous ride just like a felled tree on a Class V river. With this precious bundle of humanity in tow, we continued our family excursions. Anticipation threatened to burst my heart as each trip neared. We widened our circle of travel, seeing the world through fresh eyes, thanks to Fletcher. But then Andy begged off from a trip to the Adirondacks, said Fletcher was too young to travel that far, and Jeannine didn't like New York. They accepted and canceled at the last minute a trip to Canyonlands in Utah (too hot), a tour of Civil War battlefields (too violent), and an all-expense-paid trip to Cumberland Island (too humid).

The young family moved to Denver. Calls from Andy grew sporadic. He blamed the demands of his new job. When I packed a bag and hopped a plane to visit Fletcher unannounced, I found Jeannine had moved out to live with her fitness trainer, leaving Andy alone to juggle his job and parenting. I kept my mouth shut and dug in to help. A somber Fletcher and I bonded by taking trips to the park and baking pies together. Andy pinched a fold of flesh at his waist each night, complaining about the weight he was gaining, but he always took a second piece, especially if I'd managed to round up strawberries and rhubarb. Chuck and I came within a breath of taking early retirement to move to Denver to be near Andy and Fletcher.

Then along came Suzanne and everything changed—again. Tears welled in my eyes as I remembered Fletcher's graduation from kindergarten. By that time, Chuck and I had retired to Ouray, close enough to see Fletcher as frequently as we liked, but a fair distance to minimize the disparity of our lifestyles and values. After the ceremony, back at Andy and Suzanne's house, we'd relaxed on the sofa, waiting for Suzanne's parents to arrive from the school. Suzanne insisted that Fletcher change his clothes as we were going out to lunch. This seemed like unnecessary folderol for a kindergartner's graduation. How about some grilled wieners and potato salad?

Andy sat in a wing-backed chair across from me and Chuck. He spoke in a low, apologetic voice. "There's been a misunderstanding. Suzanne's folks reserved the dining room at the club months ago. They forgot you were coming. They've sunk a lot of money into this."

"What are you saying?" I asked, the nearest to tears I'd been in public since I slammed face first into the monkey bars in grade school.

He continued, sounding too much like a snake oil salesman. "The refrigerator is full. On our way home, we'll stop for ice cream to go with that elderberry pie you baked." He rubbed his hands together, the dirty deed done. "Suzanne's folks have tickets for the theater tonight, so it'll just be the five of us for pie. That means bigger pieces all around."

Fletcher looked over his shoulder and waved as he walked out the door with Suzanne's family. In all the years I'd been married to Chuck, I'd never seen his face reduced to rubble. I looked from Chuck to the closed door. From some primal instinct, I stood to follow my grandchild. Chuck pulled me back to the cushions. "Let them go."

I held my camera in front of his nose. "I didn't get any pictures."

"We're leaving."

"Leaving? What do you mean? They'll be back in a couple hours, expecting elderberry pie and ice cream."

"Leave the pie. Andy's made his choice. He prefers his uptown in-laws with their high-society connections. Let's go."

"This isn't Andy's choice. The Bowers reserved the room last fall. You heard him—they forgot we were coming." I said the words, but I didn't believe them.

Chuck said, "The last time I checked, this is still the U.S. of A., where folks are allowed to change their minds, do the right thing, include the ones they love. Our son chose differently."

The reality of his words crushed my heart to smithereens. Walking away meant closing a door—a thick, heavy door. From the guest bedroom, Chuck called, "Are you coming or not?"

Leaving the house that day ripped a gaping wound—a gash, really, with ragged edges, impossible to knit together. Josie's the one who understood I was grieving the loss of my oldest. I never told anyone else about that day, how my son left us like a feral dog on the side of the road, or how Chuck and I had left without leaving so much as a note. The whole thing shamed me.

I pulled the blanket up to my chin. "Enough thinking. Go to sleep, old woman."

"I got me a chance to hog a watermelon." Huck sat on the back of the recliner with a watermelon the size of a basketball in his lap.

I sat up bolt straight, only to regret it. My lip throbbed and my chest ached. "Go away!"

"There's no need t' get skreeky and colicky."

I shook my finger at him. "You're nothing but a hallucination of my own mind's making. If I want you to be quiet, you'll be quiet. Not another word."

Huck thrummed the watermelon. From its hollow tone, the melon sounded good and ripe.

I covered my ears and turned away. "I can't hear you. I won't hear you."

After a few seconds, I peaked through my fingers.

"I see that left-handed look out of the corner of your eye," he said, smiling like he'd sold me an old bridge. Charming. Devilish. Not real.

I sat up. "Look, Huck, I've enjoyed our visits, but this has to stop. This . . . you . . . are some kind of a syndrome. Something French."

"Frenchmen are known for their pearly stretchers, that's for darn sure, but I warn't born French, so you can't pin that on me."

"No, this is the honest truth. You aren't supposed to be talking. You can sit there, looking pleased with yourself for your fine watermelon or chewing on your pipe, and I wouldn't refuse a wink. But, honey, you can't talk. If you talk, chances are I'm a few pennies short of a dollar, if you know what I mean. And stop thumping on that watermelon."

Someone rapped on the door and it opened. I clamped a hand over my mouth. Suzanne's perfume preceded her into the room.

"I couldn't sleep," she said. A flash of minty satin sauntered toward the end of the bed. She held something clublike in her hand. "A concerned employee dropped by a 1993 Marcassin Chardonnay, quite fruity but very smooth. May I pour you a glass?"

Huck set the watermelon between his feet and leaned forward.

"That's a kind offer," I said, "but I can barely keep my eyes open."

Huck let out a long appreciative whistle for my stretcher, no doubt.

A flutter of green. Suzanne moved toward the bathroom. "How are you feeling? Expect those injuries to be troublesome for about a week. Are you taking the supplements I brought home? An optimal immune system will improve healing."

The supplements remained in a bag under the bed, all except the Godiva chocolate, of course. Besides, you can't kid a kidder. She wasn't flouncing around the room looking for supplements. She was like a kid poking an anthill with a stick, and I was the anthill.

"I'll do as you say, doctor," I said, trying to dismiss her with pleasant yet succinct words.

Huck tiptoed behind Suzanne as she walked into the bathroom and turned on the light. I waved him off. He stopped in his tracks. When Suzanne returned, Huck hippity-hopped to his perch on the recliner.

"Birdie," she said, "I thought I heard you talking to someone named Huck. You sounded upset. Is everything all right?"

Huck slapped his hand over his mouth and threw back his head.

Now, don't go lecturing me about the ninth commandment. I was practically there when Moses carried the stone tablets down the mountain. I don't give false witness about my neighbor. But Huckleberry Finn was not my neighbor. He wasn't even real. My mind invented him, so I felt perfectly justified saying what I pleased about him. And seeing as Suzanne had me sweating on the witness stand, I thought it best not to talk about Huck at all. I made up someone else. "Well, actually, I was praying for my friend Huck."

This set Huck into a fit of laughter.

Suzanne said, "You don't hear that name much. In fact, the only Huck I can think of is Huckleberry Finn."

"Huck is short for . . . Huckster . . . Huckster McCallum. He has cancer."

Huck doubled over, holding his stomach and stomping his foot. Tears streamed down his cheeks, and he snorted like a hungry sow.

Suzanne crossed her arms, and although I couldn't see her face, I pictured her drawing me in her sights down her long nose. "Shame on his parents. That's not a very flattering name."

She moved closer. The fog covered the mannerisms I'd learned to read—the tilt of her head when she questioned my intelligence, the twist of her hair that meant I'd confounded her, and the familiar slump of her shoulder that meant I was about to be dismissed.

Suzanne was no dummy. She'd heard enough to know her mother-in-law had been talking to a fictional character, and then invented stories to cover her actions. Something about being found out by Suzanne made me dig in my heels. That meant more stretchers.

With a carelessness I'd learned from Huck, I wound a doozy. "Huck made his fortune in flea markets. He's done pretty well for himself, built a big log house up on Black Lake. Drives a fancy-schmancy car—a Cadillac, I think. He's retired. Volunteers at the homeless shelter three days a week when he's up to it. I sure hope he beats the cancer." I yawned. "I'm exhausted."

"I see," she said as if she'd figured out Professor Plum had been killed in the kitchen with a candlestick.

Huck wiped his tears away, making muddy streaks across his cheeks. How I longed to see Suzanne's face with the same clarity.

She said, "You seem distracted."

If she insisted on grilling me in the middle of the night, we might as well talk about something pertinent. "You're right, I am. I'm worried about Fletcher. Honestly, I thought I was doing him a great favor taking him out to drive. Andy's so busy, and all I have is time. It made sense to help Fletcher and meet a family need all at the same time."

Suzanne's voice went clinical. "Have you had these lapses in judgment before? Perhaps you've noticed a pattern."

"I knowed she was up to no good," Huck said, and I jumped.

Suzanne touched my arm with her cool fingers. "Birdie, are you agitated?"

Yes! "I didn't see you move closer."

"How's your memory these days?"

The more questions she asked, the dumber I looked. I abandoned politeness. "I'm going to sleep now." I lay down. "I'm done answering questions."

Suzanne clicked off the bedside lamp. "True, it's late. Changing sleep schedules can be unsettling, but I think we should chat about this with Andrew as soon as possible."

The door clicked shut, and I turned to give Huck the heave-ho, but the chair was empty. The clean sweetness of the watermelon hung in the air. I lay there a long time, reciting phone numbers of friends and naming every shop owner along Main Street, down the east side and up the west. I stumbled a couple times, forgot that Jim Currier's Gem Stones, Minerals & Fossil Shop came before High Valley Realty, owned by Celeste Detweiler. At home, I wrote lists like some women munched on M&Ms. No one knew but me, but I listed everything I needed to accomplish in a day, even take a shower and walk the dog. Otherwise, without the structure of family or a bona fide job, my day dissolved into a slurry. I constantly came across names and phone numbers written on a sticky note, only to wonder who they were and why I should care. And although I'd lived in my house for eight years, lately I opened two or three cabinets before I found the trash can. What kind of nonsense is that?

Perhaps my hallucinations had nothing to do with Charles What's-his-name after all. Maybe I'd begun a relentless descent into cognitive collapse. Next, I would be wearing my Sunday dresses inside out just like Mrs. Springer.

Lord, help me.

Chapter 27

There's no end to the trouble love and good intentions bring to a person's life. Fletcher spent a full week at home, recuperating from a nose job he didn't want. We made the most of the time, playing some high-spirited cribbage and finishing *The Adventures of Huckleberry Finn*. I'd surrendered the walker around the house, but I used the thing when Fletcher and I walked to the park for lunch a few of those days. Fletcher insisted on making us drippy peanut-butter-and-jelly sandwiches with a thermos of milk and a couple—what else?—organic apples. He always forgot the napkins. And because he slept until eleven, we ate lunch about three, just as Mi Sun arrived home on the bus. Funny how that worked.

A bond of affliction developed between us that week. I taped Fletcher's glasses to his forehead because the swelling and bandage made the bridge too narrow. I called him Rocky the Raccoon for the bruising around his eyes. When he couldn't come up with a name for me, I offered Hopalong Cassidy. He'd never heard of the singing cowboy—a more convincing argument that our culture was dissolving before my eyes could never be made. To do my part in bucking the trend, I taught Fletcher how to waltz. The lessons were short, as much for my ankle as for my patience. The boy moved with the grace of a wounded badger. Could he even count to three? I had my doubts.

We stood at the ready, Fletcher's right hand on my shoulder blade, the other holding my hand. "Flush all that women's lib stuff right out of your brain," I told him. "When you have a lovely lady in your arms, you are king of the dance floor. She's depending on you to navigate her through the obstacle course of other dancers and the punch table. Don't take this responsibility lightly."

"Yes, Grandma."

"Remember, you're the frame. Firm up. Keep your position. When your partner comes against the resistance of your hand on her back, she'll know to step forward. Likewise, when she meets the resistance of your left hand, she'll step back."

"Shouldn't she already know to step back?"

"She does, but you are giving her a sense of safety and freedom, so she can enjoy the swirl of her skirt and the touch of your hands, if you know what I mean."

Fletcher stepped out of the stance to wipe his hands on his pants. "This is supposed to be fun? There's so much to remember."

"Come on, now."

He stepped back into the starting position.

I prompted, "What foot do you always step forward with?"

"The right."

"How many counts in a waltz?"

"Three."

"Start the music."

Fletcher fished a remote out of his pocket and "Moon River" played on the stereo. The guitars strummed and the tenor sax whistled the melody.

"Don't move. Count with me. One, two, three. One, two, three. Step, side, together. Small steps. Keep counting. Ready? Go. Ouch!" Fletcher backed away. I opened my arms to him. "Always start with—"

"The right foot."

"Correct. Again." We counted. This time Fletcher stepped forward with his right foot and I followed his lead. *Sidestep, together. One, two, three.* "Now we're dancing."

"Keep counting, Grandma."

"One, two, three. One, two, three . . ."

"Hey, they said something about Huckleberry!"

"Keep dancing."

Before Suzanne arrived home, we rolled the great-room rug back into place and replaced the furniture. Fletcher returned to his room to catch up on missed homework, and I retreated to my room to listen to a book on tape, but mostly to pray. Quite frankly, I can't remember a time when I'd prayed so much, but then I'd never felt so helpless before. The topic of Fletcher and boarding school seemed to come up regularly.

On a Monday, ten days after the accident, Fletcher returned to school with the skin under his eyes a sickly green and an eye-catching bandage over his nose. He hefted his bag to his shoulder and walked out the door. I admired his courage, especially since he'd announced the night before that he'd be attending youth group with Mi Sun that evening. He'd dismissed Suzanne's arguments handily, saying he had always wanted to learn snake charming. I closed the bedroom door and prayed for him most of the morning, lowering him through the roof to Jesus. I pushed my head through the hole and hollered, "Make him invisible to bullies! Knock on the door of his heart. Harder! Remind him how to waltz! Prepare a loving bride for him! And I wouldn't mind a dozen great-grandchildren either!"

Since it was Lupe's day off, I wandered into the kitchen to throw together a sandwich for lunch. That's when I conceived the worst possible plan of my life, even more ill-fated than painting Grandma Foster's false teeth black.

I made donuts.

Chapter 28

I sat on the patio with my daughter, Diane, freshly arrived from a bridge-building project in Dublin. She sat with her legs splayed out before her. Her hair hung limp over her shoulders, completely platinum as mine had been by her age, only straight as a ruler. I hadn't seen her in five years, even though we had vowed to visit one or the other at least once a year. And here she was on a mission of collusion. A pair of robins I'd come to know from their chittering sounded the alarm. A neighborhood cat on the prowl? A duplicitous daughter?

From inside the house, the whine of power tools and the pounding of hammers thudded against my chest. I promised myself to call Emory once Diane headed back to Ireland. I'd made enough of a mess; it was time to go home.

"Ma, Andy thinks your behavior has been a little . . . erratic. And, well, he's concerned about your safety." Diane's voice, fatigued from hours on jets and in stale airports, made me want to pull her into my arms and sing her a lullaby, but I knew better. Diane, of my two children, was most like me—independent and self-contained.

"Is that Andy talking or Suzanne, the great protector of order and perfection?"

Diane pulled her hair into a ponytail and let it fall down her back. "They say you've been talking to yourself, that you've been agitated."

"It's very sad what passes for a family here, Diane. They never laugh together. Fletcher walks on eggshells constantly."

"You nearly burned the house down."

"I charred some cabinets."

"Perhaps some changes are in order."

"I would have gone home weeks ago, but honestly, Diane, I'm enjoying Fletcher more than I can say." I squinted down, trying to take in my daughter's expression. Her face was a blank. "I think it's Suzanne's idea to put Fletcher in a boarding school, to get him out of the way."

"You can understand why she's upset, can't you? She came home to fire engines parked outside her home." My daughter? My Diane, pleading for me to understand Suzanne?

"No one cooks for the boy. They give him a credit card to order takeout. A boy can't eat that way. How is he supposed to fill out?"

Diane sighed.

"Do you want to hear the story from my point of view?"

"Of course," she said, but her voice packed the emotional punch of a stale dinner roll. I trudged on anyway.

"Do you remember your youth group days? You always had something to do, wonderful friends, adults who cared about you. You acquired a passion for travel on your missionary trips to Central America and Africa. It scared me to death, your going to third-world countries, but you always came back impassioned to make a difference. You refused to buy anything new to wear for a whole year after spending spring break in Guatemala. You sat down with a JCPenney's catalog to list out what you would have spent on clothing and cajoled your father into donating that and more to the orphanage you'd visited."

"What does that have to do with what happened here?"

"I want that for Fletcher too, and this lovely girl has been inviting him to attend her youth group. Only Fletcher wasn't too keen on the idea, mostly for the grief Suzanne dished out. So when he made his stand to go, bandages and all, I was so excited." I would have added that God had answered my prayers, but Diane would have pooh-poohed that.

"And the kitchen?"

"I made donuts for your group every Wednesday. The boys loved them. Remember? Cooking on Suzanne's highfalutin stove is like cooking over a blow torch. The oil got a little hot. Honestly, this could have happened to anyone." I prayed Diane would believe me.

Instead, she buried her face in her hands. "I'm on your side, Ma, but I need to know more than you're telling me." Diane expelled a sharp breath and straightened. I braced myself for what was coming. "Who's Huck, Ma? And don't give me a cock-and-bull story about a reformed huckster."

I rubbed the spot where my glasses dug into my nose. So this was the reason for her visit. I recognized the tone of her voice—she sounded just like me. Had we switched places when I wasn't looking? I'd raised her, so now, I supposed, she felt justified in returning the favor. She needed reminding of who was the mother and who was the daughter.

"Remember when you wanted to go to a concert in Bishop with the Mohawk kid?"

"Jason?"

"I thought his name was Greg. Oh well. We invited him over for dinner. He surprised the dickens out of us with his manners and his appreciation for classical music. If I remember correctly, he brought his flute and played a lovely aria while we ate our dessert."

"He played the cello."

"Are you sure?"

"I held the case on the back of his motorcycle everywhere we went. I was better than a bungee cord."

A bubble of panic bounced in my gut. "He rode a motorcycle."

"Would you have let me go?"

"Never. That boy scared me to death."

"He's a middle school science teacher in Yorba Linda."

"No kidding. I pegged him for an art dealer in New York. Or maybe Santa Fe."

"Your point?"

"I need you to trust me on this Huck thing. He isn't nearly as menacing as Greg—"

"*Jason.*"

"Never mind. When I've got things figured out, I'll tell you everything."

Diane sniffed. I felt my way up her arm to her wet face.

"You're crying! This isn't necessary. I'm fine! I feel great. I'm the same woman who beats you at Scrabble."

She sat at my feet and rested her head in my lap. I stroked her hair away from her face.

"I loved your donuts more than anything, especially the holes," she said, her voice clogged with snot. "You said they tasted better, and they did."

"Of course they did. I rolled them in extra cinnamon and sugar, just for you. It isn't easy being the youngest."

We sat that way until Diane's shoulders stilled. She raised her head to blow her nose. "Have you ever considered living closer to Andy?"

"There was a time when I thought living closer would be

better for my relationship with Andy and Suzanne, and, of course, I miss Fletcher terribly in Ouray."

"Andy says you're still baking pies for the diner, that you fell and broke your ankle hurrying to get the pies out of the oven."

"What are you trying to say, Diane?"

"I'm sorry, Ma. I promised myself to be grown-up and forthright, and here I am blubbering again."

"Diane?"

"I think . . . well, Andy and I think you should consider a living situation that wouldn't require you to cook."

I stood. "A nursing home?"

Diane clutched my hand. "Never! You will never live in a nursing home as long as I'm your daughter. But they have alternatives—assisted living, private cottages with amended services."

I spoke through clenched teeth, "You've done some research."

She stood to face me. "I always believed you were supermom, exempt from the things my friend's parents were going through. Who else had a ma who hiked up vertical cliffs and tripped the light fantastic, all with limited vision? You're a rock—my role model. I'm so proud of you."

"But . . ."

"You're scaring us. First the broken ankle, the accident, and now you're talking to make-believe people and causing house fires. What are we supposed to think? You took amazing care of us. Never once did I feel unloved, even though I may have told you so a time or two. Now, I want—*we* want—to do the same for you. There are some fabulous places near here that are anything but institutional."

I threw up my arms. "You've been checking into places?"

"Only on the Internet."

"And Andy?"

"He talked to a lady at some cottages in Lakewood."

"You two sure have done a good bit of talking about me behind my back."

"You're angry."

I walked to the edge of the patio, anxious for Diane to see how well I moved about. "You want to park me in a padded cell. How would you feel?"

Diane fell to her knees in front of me, took my hands in hers, and smothered them with kisses. "No, Ma, never. This is so hard. I never wanted to hurt you. Please believe that. Think of the cottages as a stepping-stone back to Ouray. Let's see how you do once the boot comes off, and you can return to your normal activities."

She stood, drew me into her arms, and laid her head on my shoulder. I responded the only way this mother's heart knew: I squeezed her to my chest.

"I'm getting too old to kneel on concrete," she said.

"Is that supposed to make me feel better?"

"I hate being so far away."

"You're not responsible for me."

"Not responsible, just invested. I worried about you before all of this. I was sure some crazy tourist wouldn't see you crossing the street. Now . . . maybe I should accept only domestic assignments. Being closer—"

"Don't you—"

"Let me finish, Ma. Being closer would ease my mind."

"Would it ease your mind if I looked at those cottages?"

"Maybe."

"We'll go tomorrow."

DIANE STOOD AT RUTH'S small kitchen table, looking out the window. "It's like living in the shadow of the Great Wall of China. What hubris! My own brother. This room must be as cold as—"

I jumped in, knowing Diane's vocabulary had gained color from working around welders and the like. "Diane, darling, Ruth and her husband were on the building committee of the church I'm attending."

"Building anything by committee is never fun." She turned back to the window. "I imagine this was a lovely place to sit on a winter's day before my brother built that monstrosity."

Ruth joined Diane at the window, looking up at the imposing wall of Andy and Suzanne's home. "This is where I waited for the children to return home from school, especially in the winter. I had a plate of cookies and hot cocoa on the table, but they had to hang up their jackets and pin their wet mittens over the register before they sat down."

"That sounds familiar. Marshmallows?"

"Is it hot cocoa without marshmallows?"

Diane stood behind the chair closest to the window. "Something tells me, Ruth, that you sat right here, warming yourself like a cat on those wintry afternoons."

"You're a clever girl, Diane. I took a good thirty-minute break from my household duties before the children got home. I sat, just as you said, listening to the crooners on the stereo: Frank Sinatra, Dean Martin, and oh, how I loved Tony Bennett." She sang, "*I left my heart . . . in San Francisco . . .*" Ruth ran her hand along the back of the chair. "Those were the days."

"What are the building planners thinking around here?" Diane said, hands on hips, facing her brother's house. "They're ruining a historical neighborhood. Most urban areas are preserving the character of their cities with ultrastrict ordinances. I hate seeing this, and I'm not one bit surprised my brother would build an overblown monument to his self-importance."

"There's no call to talk about your brother like that," I said.

"He should have remodeled the existing home, maintained the profile, or stayed where he was."

"It was a long commute. They hardly saw each other."

I felt Diane's hot gaze. "Then he should have taken his neighbors into consideration. At the very least, if he had to build, he should have built a rancher."

Ruth sat in front of her coffee and stirred thoughtfully. "That may have been his original intent, Diane. He approached me out of the blue one Saturday, came to the door dressed for golf, looking a bit harried, if you ask me. He'd been to the planning department and knew I owned this house and the house to the south. He offered to buy both houses." She laid the spoon on the saucer. "He was very polite, didn't push a bit when I told him I planned on dying in this house and depended on the income from the rental. He excused himself and trotted off to his car."

"Well, short of bulldozing my brother's house to rubble, I can't give you your sunny window back. However, installing a reflective tube shouldn't be a problem. Ma has one in her cabin. It's amazing how much light they bring into an area. And once it's installed, there's no added expense. You wouldn't have to leave your lights on all the time. I'm going to talk to Andy. He owes you that much."

Ruth hardly knew what to do about Diane's zealous championing. "My dear . . . we hardly know one another. I shouldn't think it's up to you to fix . . . I'm fine, really. Birdie? Does the darkness bother you?"

"It's difficult for me to make out much detail."

Diane kneeled by Ruth's chair. "According to years of indoctrination at the hand of my mother, I am definitely my brother's keeper, as well as his conscience. This won't be the first time I've cleaned up after him. Would he listen to me when I told him to leave the soldering gun in the shed? Oh, no. This will be much easier than reupholstering a kitchen chair with a place mat, won't it, Ma?"

Back when Andy had completely lost his mind during puberty,

I'd come home to the scent of burned plastic and a kitchen chair upholstered with a Mickey Mouse place mat. "I'd forgotten all about that."

Diane put an arm around my shoulders and squeezed. "I always knew you liked him best."

"I never!"

"I know, Ma." She touched her cheek to mine. "Ruth, the reflective tubes aren't that expensive, and since my own ma rarely allows me to lend a hand, I'll happily exact a pound of flesh from Andy's scrawny backside." Diane rubbed her hands together. "This is going to be fun."

We walked toward home. Diane's sweater smelled of hot metal and the sea. I promised myself to buy a ticket to Dublin the instant I got home. That meant some serious rehabilitation on my part. Diane hated walking slowly. I toed my way over a rise in the sidewalk. The obstacle snagged my thoughts to Ruth's kitchen.

"Go ahead and say it," Diane said, a little too knowing for my taste.

I stopped. "Whatever do you mean?"

"You're only quiet when you have something you want to say."

"That's not true."

"What's on your mind, Ma?"

"I don't like the way you talked about your brother."

"I don't like the way he feels entitled to all the sunshine in Colorado."

"He's your brother. Once I'm gone, the two of you will hold all the memories of our family. Trust me, sharing those memories—the good, the bad, the mundane—is a powerful antidote to loneliness. I'd give anything to chat with Evelyn again."

"He exploits his outsourced workers."

"You should have seen his face light up when we brought you home from the hospital. You filled a gap in his life then, as different as you were, and as alike as you are."

"I'm nothing like Andy."

"You have the same ma and pa. That's enough to extend him some respect. Will you do that for me?"

Diane embraced me hard. The bruise on my sternum ached, but I squeezed her back with the same ferocity.

"Ma, I'll try. I'll give it a try."

We walked again. "There's something else. If you and Andy have any concerns about me, I want to be included in the conversation. I won't be talked about like the village idiot."

"Ma, I'm so sorry—"

"Promise?"

She hesitated. "I promise."

Chapter 29

The dark green walls of Ms. Something-or-other's small office crowded me. "Welcome to the Grand View Retirement Cottages," she said, her husky voice stretching for enthusiasm. Arms like sausages pulled at the fabric of her lavender suit. She wore her salt-and-pepper hair in soft curls past her shoulders. There was a time when a woman her age would have been considered loose with such a hairdo, if you know what I mean.

"Tell me about your macular degeneration, Mrs. Wainwright. Are you receiving treatments?"

Since agreeing to visit the cottages, Andy's prime contender for assisted living, I'd practiced sounding informed and sane. In truth, I sounded like a Tupperware saleslady who had successfully burped a Fix-n-Mix bowl. "The antiangiogenic treatments that now offer amazing improvement for people like me weren't available ten years ago. At the time, my retinal specialist recommended photodynamic therapy as the safest treatment for my AMD. As you probably know, PDT doesn't stop further blood vessel growth, so the treatments only proved a Band-Aid in my situation. I do see a retinal specialist regularly, but I'm at end-stage. None of the current treatments will improve my eyesight."

"That must be difficult for you. Do you experience limitations due to this condition?"

I wanted to shout at her, *Try living with a gray beach ball glued to the end of your nose!* Everything I did required forethought and happened a good deal slower than satisfied my Annie Oakley temperament. I ate off white plates on a dark table, so the plate and food stood out. I'd given up driving. Bruises covered my body from clipping doorways and counters. And most disturbing of all, I saw and heard things that didn't actually exist. I discovered early on it was best to keep these things to myself.

"I go hiking and dancing and travel whenever I get the chance," I said. "I have a boyfriend who's a pharmacist."

"Fabulous! We have door-to-door van service any time of day, so you'll never feel isolated at Grand View Cottages."

"Once my ankle is healed, I won't have a lick of trouble getting around Ouray either."

She cleared her throat and my stomach tumbled. "Your children are very worried about you, Mrs. Wainwright. Ouray is quite remote. I've been there. It's lovely. My husband and I jeep over Engineer Pass at least once a year, so I'm familiar with the area. The closest hospital is in Montrose, and that really isn't a full-service facility, as I remember." Papers shuffled. "Let's see, after your accident, you were taken by ambulance to Grand Junction for surgery. That's almost two hours north of Ouray, isn't it?"

I shifted in the seat. "Driving two hours doesn't bother me."

"Still, that's a significant distance, especially for issues involving more serious injuries or illnesses. Your children fear another fall, given your limited sight and the number of stairs in your home. And other issues—not always pleasant to discuss or consider—become vital as we age: strokes, heart attacks, chronic illnesses such as cancer, kidney failure, and arthritis. Really, time isn't always our friend now, is it?"

Did she mean arthritis or Alzheimer's?

"The most troubling issue for your family is their inability to meet your needs properly from so great a distance. Your son found out about your injury through a friend. That hurt him deeply."

I leaned forward, hoping to approximate eye contact. "There was no reason to call from the hospital. What could Andy do?"

"Exactly my point. He wants to be helpful, but you're too far away. Your son's peace of mind is the perfect reason to consider Grand View Cottages." She cleared her throat. "He told me about a cooking incident at his home. You must feel terrible."

I did. When I asked Andy about the deductible, he wouldn't talk about it.

She continued. "We understand how important independence is to our residents, so each cottage is equipped with an efficiency kitchen, but most residents enjoy communal meals in our beautiful dining room. No one likes to eat alone. So you see, we've already eliminated a source of concern for your son. Putting his mind at ease feels wonderful, doesn't it?"

"Well . . . I suppose it does make a difference."

"Our children are afraid of hurting our feelings, so they keep too much bottled up inside. Mrs. Wainwright, by accepting your family's invitation to live closer, you are expressing a mother's true love."

I nearly swallowed my partial. "I'm just here to take a look."

"Of course, this is a huge decision." She stood and jingled some keys, my cue to hop-to. "Now, as we ride over to the trial-stay cottage, note the lush lawns and shrub beds. Unlike a private residence, maintenance is never a worry to you or your family. Certified landscape management technicians keep the grounds pristine through all the seasons. We also have twenty-four-hour security. No one enters the grounds unless they're invited by a resident. This really is the perfect balance of independence and support services because in-home health care consultation is always just a phone call away."

I mowed my own lawn with a push mower. "How much does all of this cost?"

She laughed. "Your family knew you'd ask, and they prefer you consider their support a gift."

I rode in a golf cart with the woman while my family followed us to the cottage. Emerald lawns with manicured edges. Boxed hedges. Clusters of red tulips. All a bit fussy for me. I liked my garden impetuous, open to the visitation of a weed or two. After all, dandelions give us opportunities for buttery kisses and far-flung wishes.

Flipping through keys, the woman said, "We've spared no expense to make the cottages beautiful, safe, and welcoming." She unlocked the door and stepped aside for me to enter. Beige entry tile. Beige carpet, low pile, easy on the walker. Beige walls, baseboards, trim, and doors. I supposed neutrality made the coming and going of residents less disruptive but made navigating for degenerates risky. I rubbed a newly acquired bruise. This place promised more of the same. At the cabin, all the woodwork glistened white, and I'd painted each room a saturated color—yellow, blue, red. No sense being shy about something as evocative as color. Besides, the sharp contrasts improved my depth perception. The Grand View cottage made me nostalgic for Pa's vanilla ice cream, with strawberries, of course.

"Check it out, Grandma," Fletcher said, pushing ahead. "There's a guest bedroom. I could stay with you."

The woman took on a cautionary tone. "We do limit overnight guests to one-week stays. Doing so prevents parking problems for the other residents."

Andy said, "Ms. Carlyle, please tell Ma about your twenty-four-hour trial stay."

"Oh yes, the trial-visit cottage is our ace in the hole," Ms. Carlyle said. "Few guests can resist the beauty of this place once they've luxuriated in this cottage for twenty-four hours. My daughter is an interior designer for one of the most prestigious studios in the Denver area; she did the decorating. Besides the jetted tub, fireplace, and efficiency kitchen, every amenity, including all recreation facilities and excursions, will be yours to enjoy during your stay. There's no better way to truly appreciate all that Grand View Cottages offer."

"Ma, if you don't stay, I will. This is lovely," Diane said. "I love the fireplace."

"Do you accept pets?" I asked.

"Yes, we allow small pets."

Fletcher said, "Bee isn't small, Dad."

"I've seen enough," I said and headed for the front door. When I pulled the door open and stepped through the threshold, a cocoon of beige engulfed me. "This closet seems a little small to me," I said, sure I'd solidified my children's misgivings about my mental failings.

"It's a coat closet, Ma," Andy said in an I-told-you-so voice.

I bit down on my quivering lip and honed my words with flint. "I have lots of coats, Andy."

Fletcher, bless his little pea-pickin' heart, took my elbow. "This place sucks." He led me out.

Chapter 30

It's the prerogative of old women to offer unsolicited advice, so pay attention. I'm in no mood to sugarcoat or mince words, but I'm inclined to be redundant: Don't ever mimic the toddling gait of an old person. Don't make your voice quiver when you say, "Happy fortieth birthday, sonny." Do not think for one minute that time will stand still for you. The wrinkles will come. Body parts will head south for the duration, and your blood pressure will almost surely head north.

Women drained of estrogen spontaneously combust with what are euphemistically called hot flashes. Hot is a pie fresh out of the oven, or a sandy beach on a summer day, or the steering wheel of a car parked in the sun: a hot flash is a solar flare that signals every pore of your body to spill fluid. They happen when you are freshly dressed for church, or embarrassed over forgetting a name, or in the middle of the night when your brain, absent your conscious bidding, cries, *Estrogen!* Tote an extra blouse around and never be caught without a bundle of tissues. Consider moving north of the Arctic Circle for the summer. Sleep with the window open all winter.

And never ever brag about your 20-20 vision to anyone.

The reading glasses will come. The holders to keep them around your neck will soon follow. You'll carry a magnifying card in your wallet to read price tags. You'll do so on the sly, cupping the magnifying card in your hand as you read the price tag. The payoff comes when you avoid buying something for $86.00 that you thought cost $36.00. And if you've played and lost the genetic roulette, or you are foolish enough to smoke or avoid green vegetables, the center of your world may slip away.

You will get old. I pray you have the courage to enjoy the sunset years, even if your children think you are going crazy.

Back at Andy's house, the thought of entering squeezed my chest. "I'm going for a walk."

"I'm coming too," Fletcher offered.

Diane pulled me into her side. I fit perfectly under her arm. We used to be the same height. "Ma, I have to be at the airport first thing in the morning."

"I'll be back in ten minutes." And because I sounded dismissive, when all I needed was some quiet to think, I added, "I'll pack you a snack for the plane when I get back. You don't have to worry; I didn't bake anything."

"I could go with you."

"I'll be fine. I need to blow out the pipes. I'll be back by the time you get your suitcase packed. Ask Lupe to brew us some coffee. She makes a mean cup of joe."

Diane laughed nervously and embraced me like a squirming piglet. "I'm sorry," she whispered in my ear.

"I'm okay. I'd put my foot in my mouth if I went into the house. Fletcher, he doesn't talk much."

She laughed again, looser this time. "Like father, like son."

Fletcher recited baseball statistics, barely audible, under his breath. "Don Drysdale. Brooklyn Dodgers, 1956–1957. Los Angeles Dodgers, 1958–1969. Five World Series, including a shutout against the New York Yankees in 1963. Pitched 58 consecutive scoreless innings in 1968. Amazing. Hit 154 batters."

I stopped. "What's up?"

"Did that place smell funny to you?"

"Ms. Carlyle kept potpourri on her desk."

Fletcher turned to continue down the sidewalk. "I hate that stuff."

"Me, too."

Despite my best efforts to discount Ms. Carlyle's comments as fear mongering, my thoughts raced like a hamster on a wheel, faster and faster until the contraption threatened to escape its axis and send my mind tumbling down the sidewalk. No question, seventy-two years qualified me for advanced age. Count the hairs on my chinny-chin-chin, if you have any doubts. This wasn't news. And yes, the likelihood of bad things happening increased with age. If not to me, then to people I loved. How many meals had I delivered to homebound folks that year? How many funerals had I attended? Four funerals, and this was only May. And names of people I met chirped and flitted away like sparrows.

Moving into a hermetically sealed cottage wouldn't fix any of this, but would being closer improve things with Andy? I had my doubts. After all, he'd arranged with Ms. Carlyle to express his love and concern. He claimed to want me nearby, but I barely saw him while living in his own home. Five miles of mind-numbing traffic weren't likely to improve our chances of seeing each other. But refusing their offer would send a message I wasn't sure I wanted to send.

Did I need their protection? True, I'd damaged their magazine-perfect kitchen with a grease fire, all because I'd misplaced my magnifying glass. Without it, I can't read a thermometer. This kind of carelessness was new, or at least more recent, for me. Only months earlier, I never would have turned on a stove without a lighted magnifying glass. I knew better. What had changed?

"Let me catch my breath," I said to Fletcher, leaning hard on the walker.

"Catfish Hunter. Eight-time All-Star. Perfect game, May 8, 1968. Five World Championship teams. American League ERA leader, 1974. Cy Young Award winner, 1974. One toe missing from right foot. Died at age fifty-three from ALS."

Catfish made me think of Huck Finn, and Huck Finn made my stomach hurt. Getting old was one thing. Watching my mind slip-slide into oblivion scared the bejeebies out of me. I shivered.

"Do you need a sweater, Grandma? I'll go get one."

"I'm fine," I said, but he was already running back to the house, leaving me to ponder the future where I hunched in a wheelchair with a bib damp with drool. Would I soon be yelling obscenities at my family and mumbling to myself about Huck Finn?

Lord, help me!

Fletcher arrived with the sweater just as I imagined hefty orderlies strapping me to a bed. "Thanks, darling. That feels good."

"You know, Grandma, I could do a lot of stuff for you."

"What are you talking about?"

"I could shovel your walks when it snows. Chop wood. Go to the store for you. And pretty soon, I can drive you places. If you should get sick in the middle of the night, I'll go to the pharmacy for your medicine or take you to the doctor. And I'm a whiz at computers. I'll set you up with one of those free online phone services. You could talk to Aunt Diane for nothing."

"Fletcher?"

"It's perfect. Living with you would get me out of Dad and Suzanne's hair, and I could help you with stuff."

My heart thumped. "Ouray is a quiet town, Fletcher, honey. Nothing like Denver."

"You want to go home, and I want to leave. And Bee misses you. This is perfect. Please say yes, Grandma."

"Oh, Fletcher, if it were up to me, we'd be sipping tea on the cabin porch right now."

"You can ask Dad tonight."

"Fletcher, I don't think your dad would consider me the best caretaker under the circumstances."

"I wouldn't be any trouble."

"That's not the issue. I'm getting older. Your folks see me as a danger to myself and certainly to you."

"That's stupid."

"I'm not so sure." I stopped to lean on the walker. "Leaving home isn't a step taken lightly. You don't want to burn bridges."

Fletcher threw up his arms. "What's the difference? I'll be out of here by August. Tell me, how is living with you any different?"

"Fletcher, this is a decision with enduring consequences."

I pressed on toward home.

Fletcher walked with me step for step. "If you don't want me—"

"I want you!" I said, grabbing his sleeve. "You're the finest young man I've ever known. This is complicated, and you should know that."

"I guess so."

Oh, to be so blissfully naïve! The longer I lived, the more complicated every decision became. Even simple things, like taking an acid-reflux medication that didn't interfere with an antifungal cream without compromising the effectiveness of a blood-pressure remedy got convoluted. Or a good man came along, eager to love, a fabulous dancer, and he didn't qualify for a senior discount. What's a grandma to do about that? Refining medications was one thing; choices involving family muddied the water. Who else but family owned the opportunity to disappoint, hurt, and betray each other over decades of time? My friends remained comfortably unaware that I'd picked up Andy three hours late from basketball practice, or that I'd mortified Diane by chaperoning her senior prom, or that I kept my mouth shut when Chuck lashed out at Andy.

To live in the cottages would mean surrendering almost everything I enjoyed about life.

Trust in the Lord with all thine heart.

To refuse the cottage meant creating a chasm between me and Andy.

And lean not unto thine own understanding.

And now Fletcher wanted to live with me? That meant trouble.

In all thy ways acknowledge him, and he will direct thy paths.

"Do you trust me, Fletcher?"

"Sure, Grandma."

I heard the doubt in his voice, but I didn't dare indulge him with promises I couldn't keep. "We can't put the cart before the horse. Decisions like this require down-on-the-knees, heart-in-your-hands prayer. God is always faithful, darling boy, to light our path. He only requires that we ask him for directions. I haven't been doing that. Watch and learn from my mistakes. I don't have enough time left to patch all my screwups."

And honestly, neither did he.

FLETCHER SUMMONED ME TO the dining room where the rest of the family already sat around the table. Andy sat at the head with his arms folded; Suzanne examined her nails; Diane hid her face in her hands. Fletcher pulled out a chair for me.

I considered my options. I could waddle pathetically back to my room to call Emory. Or I could collect my dignity and face my family's concerns, accept their help, and surrender to the deterioration of my aging mind and body. I sat down. Fletcher did his best to navigate the heavy chair and heavier me closer to the table. I squared my shoulders.

"Are you close enough, Grandma?" he asked.

"Perfect." I looked toward Andy. Huck leaned against the wall behind him, looking ragged from days and days on the river. Huck's jaw twitched and he stepped toward Andy. I closed my eyes to control any response to what he was about to do. When I opened them again, Huck had made horns of his fingers behind Andy's head.

I smiled despite myself.

"Mother?" Andy asked with consternation.

In my best let's-get-down-to-business voice, I said, "What's up?"

Andy scooted his chair closer to the table and leaned on his elbows. "Diane informed us that you want to be included in any conversations we have about you and your health. Since she's leaving in the morning, we felt that making use of our time together was crucial."

"You have concerns?"

He looked to Suzanne and back to me. "Could you clarify for us any changes you've noticed, either physically or cognitively?"

"I'm happy to report that my bowels remain regular and soft. No straining needed. Honestly, I think you could set the clocks by my—"

"Ma," Diane jumped in, "I think Andy means if you've noticed anything different in the way you perceive the world."

Suzanne laced her finger on the table. Within a hair's breadth of her face, Huck sneered at her. I swallowed down a gasp. "Under times of stress, it's not unusual for underlying conditions to surface." As she spoke, Huck puppeted her words with his hand. *Oh, Huck, please go away.*

"This phenomenon hasn't been fully explained, but we've known for a long time that stress compromises the immune system."

When I spoke, my throat tightened like a knotted rope. "My ankle is getting stronger daily." I coughed and asked Fletcher to get me a glass of water. He trotted to the kitchen, the dear boy. "I'm using the walker less and less. If you've any doubts about my progress, I'll ask Dr. Milner to talk to you."

Lord, help me.

Diane pulled on a strand of hair as she did when she was nervous. "I told them about Huckleberry Finn, Ma."

My mind went blank. I wanted to defend myself, but what was there to defend? Huck mocked surprise and bewilderment.

Fletcher set a glass of water on the table and told me where it was. I loved that boy.

"On the other hand," Suzanne said, crossing her arms, "these sorts of episodes can be aggravated by an underlying medical condition. It wouldn't hurt to have a complete physical; and if that doesn't reveal anything, it's time to call in a neurologist. They've developed some very good medications."

How easy all of this would have been if Huck had remained within the boundaries of Charles Bonnet Syndrome. A simple explanation of the syndrome and collaboration from the Internet would have settled my children's minds. But Huck had strayed way beyond a polite appearance to excite an old woman's senses. Some might argue I should have spilled the beans right there and then, accepted the support and help of my family to uncover the mystery around Huck, but a big part of me feared that making such an admission would mean the end of my hikes in the mountains and the freedom I enjoyed to explore the world. And if Huck happened to stick around, I couldn't see how plodding a trail with Huck was anyone's business but mine.

Instead I said, "You're blowing this out of proportion. I'm quite fine. Really. Never better. I'm tip-top and cheery-o!" I smiled weakly.

Suzanne spoke to Fletcher. "Your father and I can't help noticing how protective you are of your grandmother. That's quite noble of you, but your actions may be hurting her rather than helping, especially if she has an undiagnosed condition. You know, Fletcher, it makes perfect sense to us that some of your behavior lately has been affected by your grandmother. Once we understand better what you've been dealing with, our plans for your schooling could very well change."

Huck leaned close to Suzanne's ear and nearly growled. "I suspicioned you was a meddlesome shrew."

Fletcher hung his head low. "Grandma and me, we've been keeping a secret from you."

Huck jumped back, jaw slack with surprise. Andy and Suzanne leaned toward Fletcher. Diane wrapped a strand of hair around her finger and pulled. Butterflies wearing hiking boots tromped around my gut.

"Grandma's been teaching me how to waltz. I'm really sorry, Suzanne, but we roll back the rug in the great room. We're careful. We dance in our stocking feet, not to scratch anything. I guess I was embarrassed. A girl from school invited me to the prom."

Suzanne sat up straighter. "Do we know this girl? Who are her parents? What do her parents do? When were you going to tell us this?"

Fletcher told them about Mi Sun. "I'm real sorry I didn't tell you. It wasn't until I made it all the way through 'Moon River' without stepping on Grandma that I was sure I was going."

I rubbed my sore toe along the back of my boot.

"When is the prom?" Suzanne said.

"Saturday."

"Saturday?! Have you ordered a corsage? A tux?"

"It's all taken care of. I ordered a corsage online, and I'm going to wear the suit I wore to the surgeon-of-the-year banquet."

Huck raised his clasped hands over his head like a triumphant prizefighter. "He warn't bullyragged. That boy laid a humdinger of an ambuscade."

"You most definitely are not wearing that old thing. Do you know what this means to a girl?"

"Mi Sun isn't your typical girl," I offered.

"You know her?"

"Mi Sun and I have it all figured out," Fletcher said. "We're going to have a good time, not to show off. She borrowed a dress from a friend. We're having dinner with her parents."

Andy finally spoke with a hint of sadness in his voice. "You could have dinner with us, Son."

"Well . . ."

Suzanne flipped her hair over her shoulder. "Then we'll do dessert. I'll call *La Madeleine Patisserie* and ask her to create something out of this world. And the party planner, what was her name? I have her number at work. She'll make the table amazing."

"I'm so proud of you." Diane hugged Fletcher from behind. "You're doing this whole high school thing on your own terms. I congratulate you. You're the man. What sounds good to you, Fletcher?"

Huck waved over his shoulder as he sauntered off toward the bedroom.

"Grandma could bake—" Fletcher started. I assumed every eye at the table sent darts into the poor boy.

"Andrew, get on the phone to the contractor, now," Suzanne said, rising from the table. "The kitchen must be done before Saturday."

Andy reached for his BlackBerry. Fletcher stopped him with a touch. "Hey, everyone, it doesn't matter. It's cool. Mi Sun won't mind a little dust. We'll have sundaes or something. She loves ice cream."

"I have so much to do." Suzanne walked toward the planning desk in the kitchen. "We'll use the Waterford. Everything tastes better in crystal."

I reached out my good foot to tap Fletcher's knee. He returned the gesture. At least for now, Huck had been set aside in Suzanne's mind, which meant Andy wouldn't be thinking about him either. And I had Fletcher to thank.

But what was I to do about Huckleberry Finn?

Chapter 31

Diane leaned into my embrace as we sped toward Denver International Airport in the backseat of Suzanne's sedan. Andy drove. "I'm putting in for a transfer as soon as I get back to Dublin," Diane said.

"Over my dead body."

She probably saw my legs swinging over the edge of my grave. A spark of anger threatened to ignite, but airport good-byes were no place to indulge anger. Diane sucked in a sob.

I pulled her head to my shoulder. "Your willingness to make such a sacrifice honors me," I said, "but sticking with this project until the bridge is finished will honor me more. And that is some bridge you're building. My friend reads me the updates from the Internet. I saw some pictures. There's no more beautiful bridge in the world, darlin'. I'm so proud of you. Now, if you want to make me a happy mama, see that I'm one of the first to ride over that bridge. And I wouldn't mind sailing under it either."

She raised her head, wiped at her eyes. "I can arrange that. When can you come?"

"Let me get this ankle a bit stronger."

"You should bring Emory. We have plenty of room."

At the thought of tramping around Ireland with Emory a warmth settled in my gut. "You're outrageous."

"Don't wait too long. I'll be off to Dubai the first of the year."

I caught a glimpse of the royal blue horse statue at the entrance to the terminal. "Let me pray for you."

"You know I don't—"

"He believes in you, darlin'." I took a deep breath and entered into God's presence. "Bless this girl with all that is good. Keep her healthy. Fill her life with love. Give her a boatload of friends, and give her eyes to see the beauty of your world. Bring us back together real soon, Father. Amen."

"I should be praying for you."

"Promise me you will, Diane. Promise me you will."

Chapter 32

Suzanne had given the construction foreman his marching orders: The kitchen was to be perfect by five o'clock Friday. Whatever she'd said to them certainly upped the activity in the house. To escape the buzz of power tools and paint fumes, Lupe and I took our coffee out to the patio. Already the day was shirt-sleeves and sandals, at least on my healthy foot. I wished I'd packed some shorts. But then, this being Denver, if I waited five minutes, I'd need my down parka too. I preferred to pack light.

Midmorning coffee had become a ritual for Lupe and me, unless Suzanne came home to transcribe her medical reports. Then Lupe sterilized the toilets, and I listened to yet another book Fletcher had downloaded onto his iPod. Listening to *White Fang* made me terribly lonesome for Bee, but I'd asked Fletcher to choose a book he'd read for school, so we could discuss it. I was hoping for *Jane Eyre*, which shows how very close to craziness I hovered. I'd been thinking about all the things Suzanne had said at the family inquisition, trying to reconcile what I knew about Charles Bonnet Syndrome and the dementia she had hinted at. Nothing added up.

I felt a camaraderie with Lupe, and that's not an insult to her. Lupe was transparent as crystal, and I didn't need to see her face to know how she felt about any topic. She blasted her opinion—political, social, or religious—with a ferocity that belied her stature. No one could accuse Lupe of being an enigma, and for that I loved her. Besides, her coffee was heavenly. The swelling of my lip had reduced enough that I didn't dribble it down my chin anymore.

Lupe tossed a Grand View Cottage pamphlet toward me. "Forget that one. No jetted tub, no Lupe. It's all or nothing for this princess."

"Well, this princess has decided there's no harm in staying just one night, jetted tub or not."

"If someone offered me a fancy-dancy cottage with a jetted tub, I would have moved in there yesterday. And then I would invite all of my sisters to come for a visit. While they watched *The Price Is Right,* yelling at the TV, telling the contestants that they're stupid, I would listen to Gilberto Santa Rosa's *El Caballero de la Salsa*, with the jets pounding my back to the salsa beat. And sing? The tiles would all fall down off the walls. *Mi hermanas—*"

"In English, please."

"Let's just say, my sisters wouldn't stay long, not even Sister Corazon Barbara." She fanned herself with the remaining pamphlets. "You got bubble bath?"

I preferred showers. I never saw much sense in sitting around in something I scrubbed off my body. Time was too precious. "Stop by on your way home. Bring your bubble bath and a radio. You can sing all night long if you want to."

Lupe crossed her arms over her ample bosom. "So you are going to let them lock you away, just like that?"

"I thought you said—"

"But you're not me. You are not the kind of woman who sits in a fancy cottage all day."

"The activities director will bus me anywhere I want to go,

and they have a recreation room and classes, like line dancing and yoga." I poured more coffee. "I haven't made a final decision."

"The food probably tastes like—"

"Residents order off a menu, like a restaurant. Ms. Carlyle said the chef was trained at the New England School of Culinary Arts. That's a prestigious school, all right."

"And he's cooking at an old folk's home? It makes you wonder. Maybe he didn't do so good at that school—maybe burned the water, forgot the salt one too many times."

She had a point.

"When *mi esposo* is fishing with his stinky buddies, I don't cook for myself. The food looks too small for the pan, and then I get lonely, so I call one of my sisters and we go out. I always regret asking them, because I end up loaning Dolores money or listening to Pilar gripe about all the rich parents, how they keep their kids up all hours of the night or buy them fancy cell phones to bring to school, and her teachers can't teach them nothing. I didn't have a phone until I married Ernesto, and then we saved for a year for the deposit. Things are so different now. But you know all about that, no?"

I missed my computer terribly, and I depended on my big-buttoned cell phone. "Kids should play outside more."

"You know, Birdie, you're too young to live with those old farts—maybe not so much on the outside, but on the inside you're probably younger than me."

She meant this as a compliment, and that's how I took it. Besides, I'd had some time to wrestle with Ms. Carlyle's scare tactics. Either I believed Jesus when he said he'd always be with me, or I didn't. There were countless "maybes" in my future, some of them good and some of them horrible, but I didn't have to face them alone. And that made all the difference in the world.

"I promised Fletcher I'd pray about the decisions I was facing."

"Good, because I have some things to pray about too. My husband's brother's wife's sister is having a baby. She miscarried lots of times."

I bowed my head. "Let's pray."

"And my sister's husband's mother is having a hernia operation tomorrow."

"Okay."

She gripped my hand fiercely. "Wait. This is really important. My grandson, he is going to Iraq."

"We'd better get started."

FLETCHER UPENDED THE SHOPPING bag, sending its contents clattering, rattling, and thudding onto the workbench. A cool breeze scattered Fletcher's plans, so he closed the garage door and turned on the light. "The hardware store had everything except something that looks like logs for the raft base. Maybe I'll trim some branches off a tree or something. Here's the wood for the planks. It's pretty rough, but I don't think lumber in the 1880s was smooth like it is now. I want the raft to be as authentic as possible, even though it's only a model. I downloaded some pictures from the Internet. None of them look how I pictured the raft after reading the description, but I think this one comes closest."

I leaned into the drawing, using a magnifying glass to sweep the page for details. "If this is what you saw in your mind's eye, that's what your teacher is looking for."

"The guy at the hardware store tried to talk me into dowel rods for the logs, but then I'd have to paint them. That would take too much time."

"Something will show up. When is this due?"

Fletcher sorted his supplies. "Tomorrow."

"Oh."

"Not to worry, Grandma. I got this under control."

"And the poem?"

"It's almost there."

That meant he hadn't started the poem yet either.

"Do you have stones for the fire ring?" I asked.

Pebbles bounced on the workbench. "I picked these up at the park."

"Did Mi Sun help?"

"Tootsie has completely forgotten how to stay."

"You showed him who's boss, right?"

"Absolutely."

"Is Mi Sun excited about the dance?"

He threw up his hands. "We had this all planned. Now the whole thing has taken on a life of its own. She totally changed her mind about borrowing a dress. She went shopping with her mom, and got a purse and shoes to match. She's all excited because she got an appointment to get her hair done."

"You might want to get a haircut."

Fletcher slumped on the stool. "This is getting too complicated."

"Do you know the color of her dress?"

He put up his hands like stop signs. "Tomorrow. I'll have time to do all that tomorrow."

Time lacked meaning to this generation, so I had to ask, "Since you're just starting the raft, and the poem is still in development, will you have time to go to youth group tonight?"

"No problem." Fletcher measured lengths of planking for the raft. "Do they have a youth group in Ouray?"

"Yes. It's not as big. And, of course, Mi Sun wouldn't be there."

Fletcher studied the drawing of the raft. "That's okay. I'm sure I'll like it."

I played with the pebbles, forming a circle, a line, a pile. "I've decided to give the Grand View Cottages a try this Friday."

Fletcher pounded the workbench. "Ouch!" He cradled his hand. "If Dad and Suzanne tell me to jump, I have to jump. I'm not smiling when I do it, but what's with you? You don't have to do anything they tell you."

"Sometimes we do things—" What? To avoid a fight? To leverage a deal? To calm nagging fears? "Your dad is making a generous offer. He's trying to take care of me. I owe it to him to at least try this place out."

Fletcher tightened the vice to hold the wood for cutting. He spoke through his teeth. "Dad gets generous when he wants something."

I didn't know what to say to that, so I did what I could to help Fletcher with the raft model. I distressed and sanded the planks to make them look rough yet well worn, just like me.

Meanwhile Fletcher recited statistics as calming as a lullaby. "James 'Cool Papa' Bell. Played in the Negro leagues from 1922 to 1950. Earned his name at age nineteen striking out slugger Oscar Charleston."

Tapping a handful of planks on the workbench, Fletcher asked, "Now, this staying at the cottage is all about appeasing Dad and Suzanne, right? You'd never actually move in there. We have our plan."

What a sneaky one, my own grandchild, mumbling and sawing, all the while measuring what I'd not-so-casually announced about staying at the cottage. Nothing slipped by this one. Under the Einstein T-shirt, there beat the heart of a man—a young man, yes, but still a thoughtful heart. And way too early in his life, sort of like Huckleberry Finn, he was alert to ways to survive, to find the upper hand, to tame the currents of his life.

Chapter 33

The next morning Fletcher set the raft model on the counter where I was drinking my second cup of coffee. I'd stayed up until eleven to help him before shuffling off to bed. I wasn't sure Fletcher had slept at all. Ah, to be young again.

"I think it turned out good." A lightness lifted his voice.

I ran my hands over the raft. "It turned out great, but did you sleep at all?"

"I'm tough, Grandma."

"Tough or not, you have to eat breakfast. Grab a bagel or something."

As big as an atlas, the raft didn't miss a detail. The tiller balanced on a y-shaped twig; he'd furnished the wigwam with blanket rolls made out of Lupe's dust rags; the firebox he'd finished after I'd gone to bed was filled with sand and circled by stones, including a teepee of twigs ready for a match.

"I can see Huck lazing his feet in the water while Jim manages the tiller. This is just how I imagined it, Fletcher. All that's missing is the Mississippi." I thought about showing the raft to Huck then scolded myself for giving the apparition the time of day. Reality demanded my full attention.

"Did you find the poem I slipped under your door?" Fletcher asked.

I patted the pocket of my jeans, the kind with weathered elastic and huge pockets for all the notes I wrote myself. "I'm waiting for my eyes to wake up."

"The poem's free verse, so it won't rhyme. Just so you know."

"Couldn't find anything to rhyme with *Mississippi*?"

"Sure. *Dippy, hippie, snippy.*"

"You're showing off."

"*Lippy, skippy, yippee, zippy.*"

We were too busy laughing and snorting to notice that Andy had come down the stairs. He took one look at the raft and slammed his briefcase on the counter. I rallied every ounce of self-control I possessed not to scold him for bringing his outdoor behavior inside, so strong is the genetic code of motherhood. But such bumping around had always been Andy's way of flashing a warning flag.

"What the hell is that?" he said with unreasonable anger, flipping the edge of the raft with his finger, spilling sand and pebbles onto the counter. "Is this how you're spending your time? You make toys instead of doing your homework? No wonder your grades are dipping." Andy poured himself a cup of coffee.

Fletcher swept the sand into his palm and poured it back into the fire box, his shoulders rounded, his head down. "This *is* my homework. We read *The Adventures of Huckleberry—*"

"A project for dumb kids? Really, Fletcher, a toy boat? This is unacceptable."

"The teacher—"

"The teacher's an idiot. Making toys won't cut it in college and certainly not in the real world. You will ask your teacher what is required for an *A* and extra credit. No son of mine takes the easy way out. Remember, you're walking in cement now."

I reached for Fletcher's arm, but he moved too quickly. He pushed the raft to the floor and stomped on it, sending pieces of wood and stones skittering across the floor. Andy stood over the carnage. "You need to learn to take criticism like a man. Now, get your stuff together. I'm late."

Instead Fletcher knocked Andy's coffee out of his hand and pointed an accusing finger at his face. He dredged each word from a deep place where, no doubt, they had smoldered for a long, long time. "*I . . . hate . . . you!* I hate the way you live. I hate the way you—"

"Enough!"

"Enough what? Enough Fletcher? Want me to disappear? Maybe you should wave your arm." Fletcher demonstrated with a flourish of his arm. My stomach turned to stone. "Add a little hocus-pocus, Dad. It might help."

"You have five seconds to get in the car."

Fletcher flung his book bag over his shoulder and walked toward the front door. "No thanks." I hadn't put his lunch in the book bag yet.

"This isn't over!" Andy yelled at Fletcher's back.

Fletcher slammed the door behind him.

I sat there like a chameleon being considered by a tree snake. I wanted to pray, but everything I thought to pray involved smiting my very own son. Finally I screamed in my soul, *Be here!*

"Could you help me clean this mess?" Andy said.

"Which mess would that be?"

"The coffee. The toy boat."

"I don't think I will. A puddle of coffee is a good place for you to start. You'll gain confidence to move on to larger tasks, greater priorities." I walked toward the bedroom but stopped and turned.

"And don't you even think of leaving that mess for Lupe, young man."

"I THINK I'D RATHER clean the toilets than watch your face all screwed up like that," Lupe said, her chair scraping the stone patio. "I tell you, the best thing for that boy is to go home with you."

I didn't dare answer her. Somewhere a chain saw made light of a tree branch, and I worried the gardener might get carried away, like the time Chuck made stumps of our beautiful cottonwood. I considered following the sound of the saw. Once a man held a saw and smelled the heat of fresh wood, they couldn't be trusted. A rogue breeze made me plunge my hands into my pockets. When I did, I found a folded piece of paper, probably an old grocery list. Out came the magnifying glass.

Fletcher's poem. I pulled the chair into the sunlight, careful to keep the sun in front of me. The last thing I wanted or needed was another flameout.

A steamer blasts a horn upriver,
The raft totters on the wake
Churned by the clawing paddles.
Waves slap against the logs
And spray my feet with river water
That is life and death—catfish and decay,
Red-eared turtles and bloated fish.
The raft glides down the river where
Crickets chirrup, a white bass leaps for a bug,
And the woo-wah, woo-wah
Of a barred owl slices the night.
I chew my cob to stay a smile.
Who will witness this prudent joy?

The stars that clutter the swallowing sky?
Candles in windows beckon travelers;
Ma and babe escape into sleep.
Hunched willows skim the current
With leafy fingers to catch a dream.
I dream too, but I am not alone.
A shadow man floats with me,
Whistling a familiar song at the tiller.
I bite my cob; my dream floats among the reeds
And rises to the treetops and on to the stars.
"Stir the fire, son," the shadow man says.
"Another cup of joe?
Jaw with me until the moon leaves her post."
Steam moistens my face.
"No other place I'd rather be," he says.
This is my Huckleberry Dream.

||||||||||||||||||||||||||||||||

WITH LUPE BUSY WITH household chores, I called Emory. He listened as I ranted. I pictured him sitting at his desk, cluttered with pharmacological journals and invoices, and a bag torn open with a half-eaten chocolate éclair sitting in a circle of grease.

"I've never heard you so angry," he said with awe in his voice.

"I've never been this angry. The way Andy talked to the boy, belittling his work . . . I'm so disappointed in my son."

"It's time for you to come home, Birdie. How can you get better in an environment like that? I can be there in six hours, maybe five. I'll get William to watch the store. He's been sober nearly a week."

I wanted home and Emory and blissful ignorance more than I cared to admit, but leaving Fletcher to fend for himself was out of the question. "I have a bit of a plan."

"You have a what?"

"A plan," I said, louder.

"I won't have you taking the bus, if that's your plan, not with your ankle. You'll need to stop and move around. Deep-vein thrombosis is a real threat. And, Birdie, there are no strings attached. I won't expect anything in return. Coming to get you is what any friend would do."

Talk about deep-vein thrombosis sent a flush of warmth through my body. "You're much more than a friend."

"I am? Really? I wasn't sure." He sounded like a ten-year-old boy.

"You're a good man, Emory. I've known it since the day I met you. The way you held my hand as you introduced yourself . . . well, I nearly swooned."

The phone went silent, and I feared Emory had inhaled a bite of éclair. I was about to call 9-1-1 when he said, "That surprises me a little."

"You surprised me."

"Are you answering my proposal with a yes?"

A proposal is a fine way to kill a romantic moment. "This is my way of sugaring you up."

"You don't need to do that. Not me. I'm always sweet on you."

I explained about the Grand View Cottages.

Emory spat his words. "I want you away from those people today. You're the last person who belongs in a place like that."

"They mean well."

"They're controlling."

"Just one night, Emory. I want them to see me as being open to ideas and cooperative."

"To what end?"

"So Fletcher can live with me."

"Here? In Ouray?"

"You sound disappointed. And surprised."

"Well, yes, I'm surprised."

"Disappointed?"

"Leery."

"Of Fletcher? He's only a boy and a very good boy. He deserves to be someplace where he can spread his wings without getting them clipped."

"I think I'd like Fletcher just fine, but I may be a little leery of you."

"Me?"

"I think *you* like to control people too. Perhaps it's genetic."

"I called you for support."

"This sort of scheming is beneath you, Birdie. You're a forthright woman. I expect better of you."

"I've met my match in these two. I don't know what made me think I could convince them to be better parents."

"Only the Holy Spirit can do that."

"Then he better get the lead out."

The phone went quiet again. No doubt, Emory prayed for me now.

"Tell me this, Birdie: Have you ever forgiven your son for leaving you and Chuck that day?"

"Of course I have. What kind of mother do you take me for?"

"How do you know you've forgiven him?"

"I won't have you preaching at me Emory McCune."

"Andy is fully aware of your judgment on him."

"Good!"

"Judgment is the Holy Spirit's job."

"I can't help but wonder if the Holy Spirit is sleeping on this job."

Emory coughed to clear his throat. "You've been a student of the Bible much longer than I, so I'm sure you remember the story Jesus told about the debtor who went before the king? He had no chance of paying the king what he owed him. He faced a life of imprisonment away from his family."

"This is sounding like a sermon."

"The man begged the king until he relented and forgave the man his debt. Within hours, however, the forgiven man refused mercy to someone who owed him much less. "

I knew where this was leading. "Emory," I said with just enough warning in my voice that he might change the subject. He didn't. He quoted Scripture at me, for heaven's sake.

"'For if ye forgive men their trespasses . . .'"

"I know the passage."

"'. . . your heavenly Father will also forgive you . . .'"

"Fine! Stay home! I'll take care of this myself."

I hung up, regretting the finality of my words the instant I said them.

Chapter 34

Right in the middle of the day, with Lupe running the vacuum in the bedrooms upstairs, I lay across the bed like the Queen of Sheba. Emory had no way of knowing my history with that verse in Matthew—thanks to my sister, Evelyn, and the movie *Roman Holiday*.

On a supply trip to Bishop, Pa had sprung for tickets to the movies while he and Ma shopped for supplies. We watched *Roman Holiday* twice, and by the time Pa and Ma picked us up in front of the Egyptian Theater, Evelyn had convinced me to cut my bangs just like Audrey Hepburn.

"You have a long neck just like Miss Hepburn," she said. "You'll look like a princess."

I liked the way Audrey Hepburn looked as she scooted around Rome with Gregory Peck, eating ice cream and nervous about losing her hand in the Mouth of Truth, but then she hitched herself into a suit with a hat that looked like an ashtray. She looked mighty uncomfortable to me, and there was no way she would ever shinny up an apple tree in that getup. Still, I fancied the idea of being a princess and lording it over my older sister.

Later, when Pa and Ma sat on the porch talking to the Drakes, Evelyn wrapped my shoulders with a towel and parted my hair straight down the middle and stalled. I should have run. Evelyn grabbed the latest issue of *Star* magazine, with the cover folded back. "See here?" She pointed to a picture of Hepburn. "All I have to do is make another part perpendicular to the first and trim the bangs to the length you want."

I wasn't sure Evelyn knew what perpendicular meant. She'd taken geometry twice. "Maybe we should ask Ma for help," I said, suddenly doubtful of my sister's skills.

"We want to surprise her, don't we? She won't have to braid so much of your hair if you have bangs."

Evelyn gouged a line across my scalp with a comb.

"Ouch!"

"Quiet! Ma will hear."

A veil of hair fell over my eyes. "It's hot under here."

"Hold still or I'm liable to poke your eye out."

Evelyn held a fistful of hair in one hand and Ma's sewing scissors in the other. When the curtain of hair fell, Evelyn looked like she'd seen a ghost.

"What?" I said, rising to look in the mirror.

Evelyn pressed me down into the chair. "Nothing. Your bangs need straightening is all. Aren't you cooler already?"

As a matter of fact, I was. Evelyn snipped and grunted and stood back. "Just a little bit more. You're really starting to look like Miss Hepburn now."

I wore a stocking cap to school the next six months, even in June when temperatures hit the nineties.

I hated my sister, and I took every chance to sock her between the shoulder blades. She got plenty riled over a snake in her bed, although I made sure it was dead first. But it was giving her a mustache with a permanent marker the night before a dance that finally prompted my father to convene a family meeting. I fought not to giggle every time I looked at my sister's puffy red lip.

My father spoke with the solemnity of a judge. "Eloisa Marie," he started, and he could have stopped right there. After all, he'd been the one to nickname me Birdie for all the chirping I did around the house. Calling me Eloisa Marie, well, that was a knife to the gut. "There's no doubt your sister has made life difficult for you, but I think you'd better consider what the Good Book says about the business of forgiveness." He opened his Bible, patiently separating the thin pages until he found the passage he was looking for. "This is what Jesus said to his disciples after he taught them how to pray, so this, my young one, was very important to him . . . and it will be to you." He read, "'For if ye forgive men their trespasses—'"

"Evelyn's a *girl*." The beginning of a smile lifted the corner of Pa's mouth and disappeared.

"I won't be having you interrupt me, young lady. 'For if ye forgive men their trespasses, your heavenly Father will also forgive you: But if ye forgive not men their trespasses, neither will your Father forgive your trespasses.'" Pa's eyebrows collided. "Are you prepared, Eloisa May, to wade into a lake of fire over a bad haircut? If not, I think you'd better forgive Evelyn."

"Pa, she didn't stop cutting when she knew she'd messed up."

"I'm real sorry, Birdie," Evelyn whispered.

"See there, Evelyn admits her mistake," Pa said. "What do you have to say before God and your family?"

I reached for his Bible. "Let me see that verse again."

The words read just as Pa had said them. I handed the Bible back to Pa. He said, "You know what's required of you. Nowhere does Jesus say forgiving those who've wronged you will be easy, but only to follow the Good Lord's example."

I couldn't argue with the words, but I'd already hidden a bucket of tadpoles in the shed, and I had plans for them. Pa took my hesitation as the sign of a rebellious spirit.

"Eloisa May, I'm disappointed, but I can't make you forgive your sister. The apostle Paul says that we must be transformed by the renewing of our minds. Only the Word of God can do that for you." He pulled a brand-new Big Chief tablet from the shelf. "In your neatest hand, you will write Matthew 6:14 and 15 over and over until you fill this tablet. In the meantime, no more pranks on your sister, or you will be confined to quarters for a month."

"I've got that job working in the stables, Pa!"

"Only if I live in a peaceable house." He looked over his heavy glasses at me. "Understood?"

"You know, Pa, I'm feeling generous of spirit toward Evelyn already."

"That's good to know, Eloisa May, but we won't be talking anymore about this topic until that tablet is full of God's Word."

My hand cramped before I reached the bottom of the first page. I rubbed away the soreness, which gave me time to admit forgiveness was important to the Father. That didn't mean I was all that good at forgiving Evelyn or anyone else, but I came close enough that she never mistook tadpoles for raisins in her oatmeal, as I'd planned.

And once we no longer shared a room, we became the best of friends until the day she died. I owed my son and his wife no less.

Soon after I filled that Big Chief pad, Pa informed us we were moving to Yosemite. Evelyn cried all the way from Tennessee to California.

IIIIIIIIIIIIIIIIIIIIIIIIIIIIIII

I PULLED AT THE Velcro straps of the boot since I planned to be on my knees quite awhile. Some prayers came easy: If someone was sick, I prayed for healing. If a friend grieved, I prayed for comfort. If the elders agonized over a scant budget, I prayed for wisdom. I prayed for the things I wanted. But unless I was willing to pray for Andy and Suzanne the blessings that I wanted for myself, I knew I hadn't really forgiven them.

"God, please bless them with health."

And?

"Bless them with prosperity too."

They have everything they need, except . . .

"Bless them with faith that will move mountains. Shepherd them beside still waters. Anoint their heads with healing oil. Be their Alpha and Omega. Satisfy them with Living Water. Be their Rock and shelter them under your everlasting arms."

What do you really want?

"Lord, may Suzanne never have flaps under her arms or gray whiskers on her chin. Prevent liver spots from marring her perfect cheeks. May she never have food poisoning or acid reflux. Give her friends to laugh with and to stand by her when things get rough. May she never find rotten broccoli in her crisper drawer. May she see dandelions as silent kisses and childhood wishes. Keep wads of gum from her path. May Suzanne's stockings never run before an important event."

Does she wear nylons? Does anyone?

"Keep Andy's arteries strong and pliable. Surround him with people who respect him. Provide Suzanne with patients who are wrinkled and flat chested and have the money to remedy the situation. May the two of them always find shoes that make their feet feel great. Bless their marriage with love and respect. Give them strength to endure the disappointments and the good sense to count their blessings."

I stalled. Then I remembered the genetic component of macular degeneration. I prayed earnestly, "Lord, by the authority of Jesus' name and the power of the Resurrection, I pray against any disease in their macula. Keep the blood vessels clear and open. Bless them with vision to see the expressions on their grandchildren's faces." I stopped for a good cry after that one.

"Father, give Andy the time and desire to be a father to Fletcher. Heal the wounds father and son bear from their skirmishes."

"And Lord, create life in the hidden places of Suzanne's womb."

I felt pretty good about my prayer, good enough that I put my boot back on and packed for my stay at the cottage.

Chapter 35

Andy unlocked the bed cover of his brand-new luxury truck, red this time. The cover rose with a hiss, and Andy loaded my overnight bag into the trunk. I told him I could hold it in my lap, but there's no talking sense to a man playing with all the bells and whistles on his new vehicle.

"Is this all you're taking?"

"I thought about taking my beaded chiffon evening gown, but they canceled the prom for tonight."

"*Ma* . . ."

"That was supposed to be funny. I'm looking forward to a night of luxury, honest. I have a schedule of activities all planned out. There's a pastel class this morning."

"Are you still doing art?"

"Never stopped."

"I should have known that."

"If I thought Suzanne would like my work . . ."

"Send me something for my office."

As we passed strip malls and walled communities, I mentally inventoried my work. There was a fall scene from the Silver Jack reservoir area—resplendent aspens against the backdrop of knife-edged cliffs—or maybe Andy would prefer something from the spring, something hopeful and buoyant, like the Fourth of July meadow on the Grand Mesa. I dismissed every canvas in my stack. This called for something new, perhaps a harlequin sunset over Ragged Mountain.

That settled, I pulled Fletcher's poem from my pocket. "Do you remember building the tree house with your pa?"

"At Grandma's?"

"Ma Wainwright and I canned most of the day, and I think we stitched a quilt, but you and your pa ached for something to do out there on the Dakota prairie. We were stretching the quilt in the frame when Pa burst into the kitchen. 'We're on our way to the lumberyard!' he said. Before I had a chance to ask him why, the two of you were nothing but a plume of dust on the horizon. The closest lumberyard was in Rugby—"

"The geographical center of North America," Andy said, tapping the steering wheel.

"That's right! You remember. Ma Wainwright and I speculated until dinner what could be so ding-danged important down at the lumberyard that Pa didn't take the time to explain himself. She was sure you'd starve to death. I don't think she ate at a restaurant her whole life."

"We only built a tree house because Pa said a spaceship would take too long."

"As high as you placed that tree house, you might as well have built a spaceship. Liked to scared me to death watching you up there. I held my breath until you got the siding on."

"We saw a herd of antelope from up there."

"You slept up there too."

"About midnight, Pa regretted not making the tree house bigger."

"I wondered about that. I figured he slept with his legs straight up the wall."

"Just about."

"I hate to admit it now, but I was terribly jealous that he had that time with you while I was stuck in a hot kitchen scrubbing cucumbers and changing Diane's diapers."

"Yeah, but those pickles won a blue ribbon at the fair."

"They were spicy."

"*Very* spicy."

"That night I sat leaning against the tree with one of Ma Wainwright's quilts around me, listening to you and Pa talk."

"What? Listening to man talk? I think there's some kind of universal law against that. I suppose you fell asleep once we got to talking about baseball."

I never thought I'd be thankful for a long wait at an intersection, but I treasured these gifted minutes to reminisce. "I don't remember a lick of what you talked about. What I do remember is how you talked—breathless, like you were on the edge of an adventure, and if you talked fast enough, you would fall right into something spectacular, just like falling into a hole. I was real glad you hadn't decided to build a boat."

I stopped short, worried he'd connected what I'd just said with Fletcher's raft, but he laughed, loose and loud. And so did I, until I snorted, which made us both laugh harder. "I do remember you thanking your pa about a million times for building that tree house as we drove back to Wyoming, saying it was the most fun you'd ever had."

"He taught me how to drive a nail straight."

"A man needs to know how to do that."

Andy turned into a gated community and stopped at the security kiosk to hand the watchman a letter. My stomach puckered. The watchman read the letter from beginning to end before raising the gate for us to enter. "Follow the signs to the trial cottage. You can't miss it. There's a sign out front."

"What time is your class?" Andy asked.

"Not for another hour."

"Do you want me to stay?"

I handed him Fletcher's poem, moist from my sweaty palms. "I want you to go buy yourself a cup of coffee and read this."

He unfolded the paper. "What is this?"

"This is what Fletcher wrote for his English class. It's the second most wonderful poem I've ever read. You wrote the other one, for Valentine's Day, just for me. I set it out in a red frame every Valentine's—that and a pink cupid. So don't get too haughty about being a poet, now."

||||||||||||||||||||||||||||||||

LUPE STOOD AT THE door of the cottage in a cloud of gardenia. "I cleaned the tub real good and left the bubble bath on the ledge. Maybe you should take a bath and call Emory."

"Lupe!"

"Don't Lupe me," she said, flipping her wrist. "I see how you smile like a lovesick Chihuahua after you talk to him."

I turned her by the shoulders and gave her a gentle push. "You better get home to Ernesto."

"Sweet dreams of Emory!" she sang.

I closed the door and the silence clenched me like a new girdle. "Only twelve hours to go," I said to fill the emptiness. I made popcorn in the microwave. The old folks could eat their gourmet dinner without me. The television remote had buttons the size of saucers. When I pushed the on/off button, all of the buttons glowed. Without my goggles, what I watched was pointless. I needed noise, and nothing made noise better than a television. I flipped through the channels, hoping to find TCM. Instead, I heard laugh tracks, a gloomy economic forecast, news of a shooting somewhere near the Capitol, and a perky salesperson pushing the perfect broom.

Click!

I showered, brushed my teeth with exquisite care, flossed all the popcorn hulls out, scrubbed my partial, dried and packed the shampoo and crème rinse into the overnight bag, and rammed my shoulder into the doorjamb when leaving the bathroom. I lay across the bed, massaging my shoulder. As if under water, I listened to traffic groan by. The developers of the cottages had spent a fortune on insulation, but a motorcycle with attitude still rattled the window. Maybe fresh air would lift my spirits, but the locks on the window confounded me. I plopped back on the bed, closed my eyes, and willed sleep to come.

The doorbell rang. If it was Ms. Carlyle, I wouldn't answer. My absence from dinner was nobody's business but mine. I tiptoed to the door. Fog filled the peephole. So much for stealth. "Who is it?" I yelled through the door.

"Get dressed! We're bustin' you out of this joint!"

"Betty?"

The Bats streamed in and scattered. "Turn some lights on," Margie said. "Let me get a look at this place."

"How did you get inside the gate?"

"Are these granite countertops?" Ruby asked.

Betty all but trumpeted from the bathroom, "Come see the tub! Do I smell gardenias?"

Ruth wrapped her arms around me. "Ruby could sweet-talk a tiger out of his stripes." She held me at arm's length. "A jail is a jail no matter how fancy they try to make it. Come on, Birdie. Pick your poison, IHOP or Village Inn? We're going all out."

"The senior breakfast at Denny's is nothing to sneeze at, reasonably priced and generously portioned. They serve it twenty-four hours a day," offered Ruby.

Ruth squeezed my shoulders where a bruise from my run-in with the doorjamb blossomed. "You're choice, Birdie."

"Who's driving?" I said, more cautious than curious.

"You're worried about ending up in a ditch, and I don't blame you," Betty said. "We hired a taxi, so we better be quick with a decision."

The Bats stood waiting, purses in hand and sensible shoes laced. "Denny's makes a scramble I'm quite fond of." I said.

OPINIONS REGARDING ASSISTED LIVING flew around the table. Margie said, "I couldn't walk into a cafeteria three times a day never knowing who I'd run into. It's tough enough going to church where I know lots of people. I thought Jolene Hogart was Mary Beth Campbell last Sunday. I kept saying her name: '*Mary Beth*, do you think the pastor knows what's happening in the mission circles?' 'Oh, *Mary Beth*, I loved that casserole you brought to Sew 'n' Chat last month. Could I get the recipe from you?' Only then did Jolene tell me who she was. I was mortified. I'm afraid I'd stay in that pretty little cottage until I turned to dust."

"Not if the Bats had anything to do with it," Ruby said.

I leaned back as Betty chimed in. "I'm darn tired of cleaning house. Do those places include housekeeping?"

"I didn't even ask."

"It wouldn't hurt my feelings to quit cooking either, what with my doctor telling me to avoid salt and fat and refined sugar. Tell me, why would anyone bother eating without salt? Was the food as good as they'd promised, Birdie?"

"I couldn't tell you. I ate popcorn in the cottage."

Betty plowed on. "How's the lighting? Most new places skimp something awful on lighting. Come to think of it, my apartment isn't so hot. I keep a flashlight in my pocket all day. I never know when I'll need extra light to see something."

"I went to bed before it got dark, but the television remote has illuminated buttons."

Betty slumped back into the booth. "You aren't much help."

"You'd have to drag me into a place like that kicking and screaming," Ruby said, leaning over her plate. Already drips of maple syrup spotted her bosom. "I've lived in my house for forty years. It's not the Taj Mahal, but I know where everything is. The back burner on the left side runs hotter than it should. There's a crack in the basement floor I step over without even thinking. And all of my medications are lined up like soldiers in the medicine cabinet. Roger writes on each bottle with puff paint. It's all there, including my old, lumpy mattress. You may think I'm a turtle, but I'm staying put. I can't see the dust anymore, so why move?"

Margie set down her fork and folded her hands in her lap. "My kids think I should move in with them."

A busboy cleared an adjoining table. Stoneware and glass clanked loudly.

"You're going to have to speak up, if you want to be heard!" Betty said over the din.

Margie expelled a breath and leaned closer to Betty. "My kids want me to move to St. Louis and live in their basement. They've made it into an apartment."

"A basement can be awfully dark," Ruth said.

"It's one of those walk-out kind. I'm considering it. Without my darling, I get awfully lonesome." She tapped the plate with her fork. "Either that, or I'm getting a dog—one of those lapdogs, something I can curl up with on a cold winter's night."

"I'd trade my husband for a dog in a heartbeat," Betty said. "If he tells me to *look at that* one more time, I'm not responsible for my actions. We pulled into the driveway yesterday. He says, 'Look at that, will you?' 'Look at *what*?' 'That!' We've been married for fifty-three years. For twenty of those years, I've been a degenerate. And he can't remember that?"

"I'd take his forgetting as a compliment. You must manage pretty well for him to forget you're not fully sighted," Ruth said without one trace of resentment. Ruth is a good woman.

"You're too nice, Ruth." Betty swiped the air. "I'm going to flatten the side of his head with my iron skillet the next time he tells me to look at something."

"I see the two of you nestling in the pew in front of me," Margie said. "I don't believe a word of it."

The waitress came to divvy up the checks. Had I caught a glimpse of the tattoo on her arm earlier, I may have suggested another restaurant. Wait until she's my age. That tarantula's going to fold like an accordion and swing wildly with every gesture. As the Bats studied their checks with magnifying glasses, I swallowed hard and blurted what I'd wanted to tell them for weeks.

"I have Charles Bonnet Syndrome."

"For heaven's sake, why didn't you tell us before? We love that kind of stuff," Ruby said.

"You let me yammer on and on about my clowns without piping up? Come on, Birdie, spill the beans."

Ruth patted my hand. "I'm sure she had her reasons."

A chatty Huck Finn? There's one reason. "Some of my visions are a little . . . out of the ordinary."

"Nothing will embarrass us, but if you see Brad Pitt naked, we're going to have to ask for details."

"Ruby!"

"What? I'm nearly blind and shriveling up like a prune, but I ain't dead yet."

"Go on, Birdie. No one will interrupt you."

"Feel free to interrupt me anytime. This isn't the easiest thing in the world to say." I waited, hoping one of the Bats would detour the conversation to talk about laxatives or the price of prescription drugs. Conversations buzzed all around us. The cooks yelled to one another in the kitchen. The cash register rattled as it printed a receipt. The Bats sat silently.

I told them about the purple flowers and the mountainside.

"I don't see purple anymore. Everyone at Sew 'n' Chat *oohed* and *ahhed* over a purple suit Lynn Perrizo had made for her son's wedding. It looked like charcoal to me."

"I've been noticing I don't see yellow—"

"Ladies, Birdie has more to say," Ruth interjected.

"You're right, Ruth. I'm sorry. Birdie, the floor is all yours."

"My grandson, Fletcher, eats on his own most nights. Since coming to Denver, I've made a point of eating with him. His tastes are . . . how do I explain? His tastes are exotic. He fancies a *dim sum* restaurant on Glaser Street that makes a spicy shu mai."

"The Snappy Dragon? Are you seeing dragons? That would scare me half to death."

I told them about listening to *The Adventures of Huckleberry Finn* while eating shu mai with spicy mango sauce. "You can bet I woke up with some kind of heartburn. And when I did, Huckleberry Finn was sitting on the recliner at the end of the bed."

"But he's just a made-up character."

"He looked as real as you do. And dirty? That boy needed a bath."

"Why didn't you tell us this before? The fact that your brain conjured up a fictional character makes me believe you're a very creative person. I'm sure if we got on the Internet, we'd find other examples of Charles Bonnet Syndrome involving characters from books. I'd give anything to meet Jo from *Little Women*."

"What about Scarlett O'Hara from *Gone with the Wind*? She wasn't anything like the movie."

"What are you thinking? What about Peter or Mary or, would it be blasphemy to hallucinate Jesus?" asked Ruby.

The Bats thought on the question.

"There's more," I said. "At the end of his visit, Huck winked at me."

"I would have fainted dead away if Cary Grant had winked at me."

Margie spoke breathlessly. "He was communicating with you, wasn't he?"

"That's what I thought, so the next time he showed up, I encouraged him to talk."

"But he didn't, did he?"

"Not until his third visit."

The Bats went silent. I told them how Huck had paced the room, talking about the loss of his friend. I thrummed my fingers on the table. "Say something, girls."

"Well . . ." Ruby started.

"This is highly unusual."

"Have you mentioned this to your doctor?"

"Maybe we should pray."

I LAY ACROSS THE bed of the cottage, still in my clothes, smelling now of burned coffee and grease from the diner. Cars droned by, even at that late hour. My fingers played with the stitched billows of the comforter as I remembered the silence of the Bats. Clearly, one night or a thousand nights in an assisted-living complex wouldn't help my problem: I talked to a literary character, and he talked back to me. Huckleberry Finn. A rogue boy. Mark Twain's alter ego. A quick thinker. Goodwilled. Devoted to his friend. Completely imaginary.

And yet his blood had pulsed under my touch.

Chapter 36

One good thing about being a not-so-little old lady with a booted foot and poor eyesight: The taxi driver took pity on me. He carried my suitcase to the front door and left without putting his hand out for a tip, or if he did, I missed it. The sleepless night had left me muddleheaded with bags under my eyes that rivaled seat cushions. Even I felt sorry for me.

I zipped my suitcase closed and slid it under the bed, only to stand there motionless. Fletcher wouldn't be home for hours. I inventoried the possibilities. Read. File my toenails. Wash my bras. Visit Ruth. Nap. Call Emory. Watch TV. Sit under the maple tree to let the shadow and light dance on my face. The bed repelled me, so many hours had I spent lying there useless to the world. The room and the bed, both were reminders of my decline into madness.

Then again, I could just dig a deep hole and crawl in.

Everything I knew about myself had shifted. My playful encounters with Huck now smacked of delusional tendencies or worse. Hadn't I nearly killed my grandson with my irresponsibility? Somewhere between the newel post of my stairs and the floor,

I'd become a burden. An inconvenience. A rotting piece of flesh. Worthless.

The door to the garage banged open. Heels tapped across the hardwood. Suzanne blew her nose and stifled a sob.

I reached for the suitcase under the bed and flipped it open. I emptied the dresser drawer of my undies. As I scooped my socks out of the drawer, a primal scream from upstairs froze me in place. I counted back the days since Andy and Suzanne had taken their romantic getaway. It hadn't been that long, but rabbits weren't dying to announce pregnancy anymore. Like everything else, I supposed pregnancy tests brought good and bad news with lightning speed. I dropped the socks back in the drawer and moved to the bottom of the stairs. I stood there longer than I like to admit, listening, praying for someone, anyone, to come through the door with the magic words Suzanne needed to hear. My hands trembled over my heart. Every shuddering breath she took, every sob she swallowed, called to me. Clearly she believed I was still safely ensconced at the cottage and she owned the privacy to grieve her loss.

I turned toward the bedroom.

Suzanne called out, "Please, oh please, God. Just one baby. That's all I ask. One baby."

I turned toward the front door. Perhaps a walk would do me good.

"I'm so sorry. Please, *please* forgive me."

With my hand on the doorknob, I stopped. Still uncertain about my ability to climb stairs, I scooted up the risers on my hiney again. I pulled myself up on the newel post and peg legged my way to Suzanne's bedroom door, making as much noise as the deep-piled runner allowed. I scanned the room. Suzanne lay face down on the bed. I tapped on the doorjamb.

"Oh." She stood like a soldier. "What do you want?" She kicked off her shoes. "I'm getting in the shower. Can we talk later?"

I stepped into the room, struggling to see what I could of her face. Strands of black hair clung to her wet cheeks. "You sound upset."

She threw up her arms. "Brilliant!"

"You shouldn't be alone."

"Says who? You? You talk to the walls."

My sister Evelyn had owned a Yorkie who snapped at me in much the same way until I sat down. Then the dog had jumped into my lap and presented her belly for a good rubbing. People aren't so different from dogs. I continued toward the bed. "If you don't mind." I sat down and patted the mattress. "I've lived a long time. Believe me, sorrow only becomes more menacing in the quiet."

"I . . . I'm not used to . . ."

I waited.

"I had a plan," she said.

Metal ticked and the air conditioner purred.

I patted the bed again. "Your cries nearly ripped my heart open. I miscarried at five months. A little girl between Andy and Diane. It felt like someone had skinned me alive, but no one wanted to talk about it, least of all Chuck. It was me and the big, black universe, or so I'd thought."

Suzanne fell onto the bed, the mattress shimmying with her jagged breaths. Her cries rubbed at my memories like clearing frost from a windshield. I was back at St. Francis Hospital, the maternity ward.

"I shared a labor room with another woman," I said. "She smoked one cigarette after another. Long before my contractions grew strong enough to deliver the baby, she delivered a healthy boy. I felt cheated, betrayed. It took me a long time to feel whole again. Not even Diane . . . well, you don't substitute one life for another, now, do you?" I blotted hot tears with my sleeve. "We named her Evangeline, like the poem I'd read in high school."

I searched the bed, feeling for Suzanne's hand. When our fingers touched, she clutched at me. My arthritic fingers complained, but we sat that way, holding hands, until her sobs quieted and her breathing settled into an easy rhythm. My shoulder burned at the odd angle, yet I held on, not rubbing the back of her hand with my thumb like I would with my own children, but returning pressure for pressure. Her hand slipped out of mine as she sat up.

"We have reservations at the Palace tonight," she said.

I stood up. "Lovely place."

"I suppose you think I'm some kind of obsessive-compulsive nut, that having a baby is something to check off my list."

"Nothing of the sort. You want to be a mother to see if you can love someone who poops on you. It's a universal trait of women during the childbearing years."

Suzanne expelled a brittle laugh. "The truth is, I don't deserve a child."

"Nobody does. Children are a gift, a good and perfect gift from the Father of lights."

"He would never—"

I touched her arm. "Then you must get to know him better."

She stepped back and the connection between us dissipated like a mist.

"I think I'll finish unpacking." And I hobbled away.

THE DOOR BETWEEN THE garage and kitchen slammed shut and keys clattered on the countertop. "Ma? Ma, are you here?" The tone of his disapproval stung me. If Chuck had been here—Emory?—he would have told Andy to go back outside and stay there until he could talk to me respectfully.

"I'm in here, reading."

He stood in the doorway, hands on hips. "I rescheduled three meetings to pick you up at the cottage."

I smiled. "Oh dear, Son, I'm sorry. I decided to come home a little early."

"You could have called. Besides, you left Ms. Carlyle in a tizzy. She didn't like you comparing Grand View to Alcatraz."

"I was a little upset when I left. I'm fine now."

Andy ran his hands through his hair, high evidence that I'd pushed him to the brink.

"Have a seat," I said, gesturing to the bed.

"I'm expecting a call."

"I imagine your BlackBerry will ring in here."

Andy leaned against the dresser. "What's up? I'm needed at the office."

Talk about a hostile audience. "Let me try to explain. When we sent you off to college, your father and I knew chances of your doing something stupid or risky was close to 100 percent. I imagined the worst, fretted day and night. I actually lost a few pounds. I'm sure you remember my frequent telephone calls."

"I remember." He crossed his arms. "Is this a long story, Ma?"

"Not so long. Do you have a minute? I'm terribly sorry for the trouble I caused."

He looked at his watch. "Go ahead."

"One morning, after you'd been to college for several weeks, I opened the newspaper to discover Alan Clark had been killed in a car accident. You remember the Clark family? They lived in town just off Pearl on King Street. Alan was a couple years behind you. His sister—"

"I remember the Clark family."

"Anyway, there'd been some drinking. I couldn't cook or sleep or eat. Diane thawed something from the freezer three nights in a row. I shuddered each time the phone rang. Your father thought I'd gone off the deep end. I mourned that boy as if he had been you. It could have been, you know?"

"That was a long time ago." He straightened. "I'm a much more careful driver, I promise."

"I wish I'd understood about faith better back then. God had you in his pocket all along. Of that I'm sure. He still does. But back then, I simply turned fatalistic to protect my heart. I sang along with Doris Day on the radio, "*Que será, será.* Whatever will be, will be."

"You needn't have worried. I spent most of my time in the library."

"My point exactly. The tables have turned. Now you're imagining all sorts of terrible things that could happen to me. Your tenderness warms my heart, but Son, God has me in his pocket too. If something bad happens, he's with me, and for me that's all I need to know."

Andy grunted.

"Yes, well, just know that I absolve you of responsibility for my personal safety and well-being."

"You can't just—"

"Sure I can. You did just that when you went off to college."

"As the eldest, especially with Diane out of the country . . . who else will take care of you?"

"You have plenty on your plate with a child and a wife."

"There may come a day."

"Yes, there may, but not today."

"Will you at least stay until we're sure your ankle is healed?"

"Yes. And I promise, no more donuts."

Chapter 37

Although I was born in New Mexico, the first house I remember living in was an old farmhouse that had been part of the Sugarlands acquisition for Great Smoky Mountains National Park. I'd hoped the farmer had been better at growing corn than plumbing. Black water pipes snaked up and down the walls, delivering hot and cold water to the upstairs bathroom. Pa called the plumbing cantankerous.

Evelyn always woke first, which suited me fine. She came out of the bathroom looking like a painted doll. Most mornings Ma sent her back to the bathroom to wash her makeup off. One morning, I listened for the squeak of Evelyn's bed coils, but I kept my eyes closed and breathed slow and deep. It took her a good long while to gather courage to touch the icy floorboards. As soon as the bathroom door clicked closed, I wiggled into fat wool socks. The cold air rose under my nightie to run an icy finger up my legs. I grabbed a quilt from the bed and headed toward the basement where the only toilet perched thronelike up three steps. With the sound of water rushing through the pipes toward Evelyn, I flushed and ran. The pipes drummed the walls. Inside the shower, the water turned molten and then as cold as lake water in the spring—this I knew from personal experience. I raced up the two flights of stairs to jump under the covers, face toward the wall to hide my flushed cheeks. Evelyn came into the room shivering like Ma's washing machine. She dropped the towel, and I saw her red-hot hiney. I giggled, and you'd have thought I'd lit her hair on fire.

My days of scalding and flash freezing my sister ended abruptly.

By contrast, living in Andy's house was a bit like living in a tomb. Although the family was busy preparing for a coming-home dinner for Suzanne's parents, no pipes pinged. Doors opened and closed with nary a bump. Toilets flushed noiselessly. I ticked up the volume of the iPod and pushed the recliner back, but distracted as I was, I'd missed something of the Flannery O'Connor story I was currently enjoying. I pressed pause until the screen darkened.

Suzanne's parents were snowbirds, escaping winter by scurrying off to the desert—Scottsdale, I think—whereas I welcomed the extremes of weather. The biting cold of winter tested my mettle and kept me as humble as I cared to be. My theory, always calculated, always charitable, is that people fear the quiet of winter more than the cold. Sequestered within the walls of my cabin, memories seeped in, misspoken words haunted, and more lately, a void as menacing as the Grand Canyon reminded me I owned not one original thought. When I could not, in fact, name the day of the week, I rounded up my younger friends for a snowshoeing trip through a nearby ghost town. The need for fresh ideas faded against the startling contrast of sky, snow, and the black green of spruce trees. Trees didn't care if it was Sunday or Tuesday. Instead, they added girth and strength from bending with the winds, growing tougher with each passing winter. I added girth each winter too, with cinnamon rolls at Elsie's Diner and slow-cooked roasts with plenty of gravy, but I could still bend to strap on my snowshoes. Better still, I stayed with the pack of young friends, huffing and puffing up each hill like the little engine that could. I had no choice. I followed Josie's red jacket unwaveringly or ended up sitting in the snow, hoping for someone to notice I'd been left behind. That only happened once.

Andy came to the door, the scent of his aftershave rushing before him. "You're not ready."

I'd prepared myself for his irritation but not for the surprise in his voice. "This is a time for you and Suzanne's parents. They've been away for a long time. I'm sure you have a lot to talk about."

"Martin forwards twenty e-mails daily, mostly ridiculous urban legends about poisoned envelopes or stalking identity thieves, all of which he expects me to reply to. So no, we don't have much to say to one another."

I'd rehearsed my response, attempting to say the words without a hint of bitterness. I filtered the words through a forced smile. "I prefer to stay home. I'm listening to a collection of Flannery O'Connor's short stories. Honestly, they're as terrifying as they are beautiful. I'm going to leave a light on when I go to bed tonight."

"You're still angry about your night at the cottage, aren't you?"

Lord, I'm lowering my son through the roof to you for the millionth time. Catch his gaze and his heart.

"You meant well. I can see that, sweetie."

He sat on the end of the bed, leaned forward. "Really, Ma, you'd be doing me a favor. They talk about their Scottsdale friends as if I know them. They indulge every detail. I hear about so-and-so's chemotherapy and so-and-so's brand-new motor home with four pullouts, and shouldn't we be taking more trips, seeing the world? Martin's completely forgotten what it's like to run a business."

"If your in-laws are that enthusiastic about their friends, perhaps they're worth knowing. I should think a trip to Scottsdale would be delightful in February. Spend some time by the pool, play a round or two of golf to keep your game sharp. That sounds like doctor's orders to me."

He straightened. I'd thrown him a curve, and I loved that he couldn't decide whether to swing or not. He bunted, toddling the ball toward my weakness. "Their cook is amazing. I think he's making lasagna with sausage he made himself."

The pilot light of my anger ignited to flame. "Let me get this straight. You want to hide me away for some—shall we say?—mild eccentricities, but when your in-laws threaten to occupy your precious time with stories of inconsequential people, you have no compunctions about letting your mother take a bullet on your behalf?"

"You are still angry."

"Martin and Gloria are *your* in-laws."

"You're oversensitive."

"Perhaps I am."

Andy waited for my answer, hands on hips, stance at the ready to bolt into action.

Lord, I'm not sure I can hold the rope much longer.

"Do you remember the story of the friends who lowered the paralytic through the roof to see Jesus?"

"A Bible story? What does that have to do with anything?"

"Do you remember the story?"

"I've given up on myths, Ma."

"Jesus saw the faith of the man's friends and healed him."

"I'll take that as a no." He turned sharply to leave.

"You're mistaken. I'll be ready in ten minutes."

"You won't bring out your flannel graph during the entrée, will you?" A smile lightened his voice.

"I'll save it for dessert."

He stepped out of the room. I called him back. "There's something very important I need to talk to you about."

"Can it wait until tomorrow? I could spare a few minutes before I head into the office."

"It's Saturday."

"I'm trying to keep ahead of the curve."

"Just knock on the door when you're up and about."

"Be ready in ten minutes."

"Andy, are you still looking into boarding schools for Fletcher?"

"I've been pretty busy."

"Good."

"That doesn't mean—"

"He's a good boy."

"That's what you keep telling me. Ten minutes."

MARTIN BOWER YAMMERED ON and on about fishing trips to Mexico with senators and walking tours through Tuscany in the company of New York financiers and their take-no-prisoners wives, whom he both loathed and admired, all the while clearing his throat to the point I started counting. During a profile of one of the real estate wives, he cleared his throat thirty-seven times. I attempted to add an anecdote about my travel experiences, only to be talked over and summarily ignored. I was there to serve as an audience, period. I laid my fork and knife down to plot an early exit from this den of tortures. Being old gave me too many choices. Sour stomach? Muscle spasm? Aching joints? Bloating? Gas? My ankle hadn't given me an ounce of trouble for some time. Just as I'd settled on a sour stomach, a hand touched my shoulder.

It was Gloria, whispering in my ear. "Birdie, dear, I'd love to show you my garden before we lose the light." She straightened, raised her voice. "Martin, you don't mind, do you?"

Martin paused his narrative long enough to clear his throat. If any other communication passed between husband and wife, I missed it completely.

Gloria pulled at my chair and offered her arm. "Let's go then."

Under her silk jacket, I held her pulpy arm. As we walked, our hips bumped. Gloria was another pear in the fruit bowl of life, only she camouflaged her shape with sweeps of fabric. The moment she opened the door, the scents of the garden rushed me—lilac, moist earth, mowed grass—life.

"This is my oasis," Gloria said, leading me across a brick patio dotted with purple flowers of my imagination. I scowled at the flowers, willing them to dissipate. They only multiplied. "Martin is forbidden to step foot out here. He has the garage for his precious cars, for which I could not care less."

I sniffed the air. "Which way to the lilacs?"

Gloria hooked a bundle of lilac branches and pulled them to my face. I breathed in and memories flitted in and out, merging and finally sorting themselves for review:

The scent of my Ma, doused with lilac water, bending over my bed to say nighttime prayers.

Playing bride with my school friend Brenda, who lived in town. I was the groom, expected to carry her over the threshold. She was a bossy little thing. She traded me for a more compliant friend the very next day.

My grandmother's funeral where every mourner carried bouquets of the blossoms. The job of cramming the stems into vases and mason jars fell to Evelyn and me, until Evelyn showed Pa the hives that swelled on her neck and arms.

My first and last kiss from Harvey Cornfresher, which happened in a stand of lilacs at the park by the lake.

The nights when the scent of lilacs blew up from the small farms surrounding Great Smoky. I waited until Evelyn fell asleep to inch the window open, then sat, nose to the sill, breathing in the sweetness. I'd known to close the window when Evelyn started scratching her nose in her sleep.

"I only wish they bloomed longer," Gloria said, releasing the blossoms, broadcasting their fragrance. "Martin wanted to stay in Scottsdale for yet another golf tournament. I told him if we missed the blooming of the lilacs, I would make a garden fence of his clubs. I'd never seen him pack faster."

"We all have our Achilles' heel."

"Would you be more comfortable using your cane? I could go get it."

"You're so kind," I said, surprised by my own words. I'd spent the better part of nine years—and it humbles me terribly to admit this—hating her. "I went to see the surgeon yesterday. The bones are healing nicely. The cane is only a security blanket. I don't really need it."

"Glad to hear it." She hooked my arm. "I have a lovely fountain I'd like to show you."

We sat on a stone bench, listening to the energetic gurgle of the fountain. Every once in a while, a droplet hit my face. I closed my eyes to imagine Old Powder Horn Creek rushing past, veiling over boulders, rattling pebbles, exciting my heart.

"I've brought you out here for a reason," Gloria said.

I blinked stupidly. "Your garden is as lovely as you promised."

"Yes, well, that was just a ruse. We have something much more important to discuss. At least, I hope you'll hear me out."

"Go on."

"I'm married to a bombastic, self-important old fool, but you already knew that. You're a sharp woman. I've marveled at your independence since Andrew told us about you. It can't be easy getting by on your own with limited vision. My admiration knows no limits."

She paused. I knew I should acknowledge her compliment, but her words staggered me.

"In fact, Martin's mother claimed he was born a bombastic, self-important fool. She came to my house the night before the wedding to warn me not to marry him, but I married him for reasons of my own, and he hasn't disappointed. That doesn't mean I haven't regretted my decision, but I'm of the generation, as you well know, that sleeps in the bed we've made."

I squirmed. "Gloria, I don't see—"

"I will never forget the look on your face as we ushered little Fletcher out the front door on the way to the country club. You remember the day? He'd just graduated from kindergarten. Such pomp and circumstance for their mild achievement, but you and Chuck drove all the way from Ouray to attend the ceremony. Clearly, we'd ripped your heart in two."

"That was a long time ago."

"You don't have to pretend for my sake. Being left behind hurt you terribly. Martin—and I don't quite know how to say this without being insulting—is too caught up in appearances."

I'd suspected this all along. Having my suspicions confirmed only soured my mood. "Why bring it up now?"

"Your anger doesn't surprise me. I could have stepped in, insisted that you be included in our plans or that other arrangements be made, but I was too interested in self-preservation to do the right thing. I'm hoping that you're a better woman than I am. I'm hoping you can forgive me."

I wasn't the woman she'd hoped for, but I wasn't ready to admit that either. "It sounds like your husband should be out here."

"I believed that, too, for far too long. You see, Martin's behavior has provided a convenient smoke screen for my own selfishness. I'm done with all that."

My face puckered and my bottom lip quivered. I squeezed my

eyes shut to staunch the flow of tears. So forceful did they press, I surrendered to the flow. Gloria held my shaking shoulders.

"Oh, my dear, I'm so sorry. Please, please don't cry."

With no tissues at hand, Gloria offered the hem of her tunic. Even still, her apology seemed frivolous.

She continued. "Although nothing can justify what I failed to do that day, it had been a tough day. We almost didn't go to the ceremony. Martin insisted we attend despite the fact I'd discovered a hotel entry card in the pocket of his trousers when I laid out his clothes. This wasn't the first time. I was a mess. What did I expect? I looked in the mirror every day. I had nothing to offer him. I walked on eggshells for weeks after that, wondering, fearing that one cross word from me and he would turn me out into the streets. And who would want me? My own daughter kept reminding me of that. 'Don't you want your eyes done? Your neck adds years to your age, Mother.' I suppose she meant well."

"What's changed?"

"The most wondrous thing happened at the hospital where I volunteer. I cuddle sick babies. The more cuddling they get, the quicker they gain weight and thrive. And the parents need a break from the constant demands. Looking back on it now, I think I was the one who needed cuddling.

"I'd been cuddling little Marco since he was born. He was just over three pounds. The volunteers and nurses celebrated every ounce he gained with the parents. I almost didn't go to cuddle him that day. Martin had been particularly surly, probably punishing me for putting an end to his latest tryst. I sat in the garage, behind the wheel of the car, for a long time, wondering what I could do to make things better between us. I'd tried everything I could think of. I'd come to the end of my rope. I started the car and drove to the hospital.

"Marco's lids were heavy when I bent over his incubator. Since my last visit, they'd taken the feeding tube out of his nose.

Another celebration. Only one small electrode stuck to his chest. He'd be going home soon.

"I said his name. 'Marco?' His eyes flew open and he turned to me, flailing his arms and legs. That baby was happy to see me. *Me.* The person Martin dismissed as too old and too stale. But this fresh, new human being, who only knew me by the sound of my voice and the beating of my heart, loved me. I fulfilled his every dream just by showing up and holding him.

"I found a quiet corner of the NICU. Marco nestled into my chest, as misshapen as sandbags, and fell into a peaceful sleep. You know, Birdie, that's how we should love one another, pendulum breasts and sagging butts included. Are we present? Are we loving? Are we tender? From that day forward, I knew I was indeed lovable, even if I could play dot-to-dot with my moles. Martin had the problem, not me. But that meant no more hiding behind his poor behavior.

"And so, that brings me back to my reason for asking you out here. Will you forgive me for being too self-involved not to respond to your pain?"

Martin's voice boomed across the garden. "Where in blazes are the pamphlets from the boarding schools?"

"What's he talking about?" I asked, standing.

"Since Suzanne told us about the incident with Fletcher, Martin's been on a mission to find the perfect school for the boy."

I hobbled toward the house. Gloria caught up with me. "What's the rush, Birdie?"

"Tell me what you know about the incident between Suzanne and Fletcher."

In Gloria's version, Fletcher shoved Suzanne when she asked him to take the dog outside. Either Gloria and I were about to end the shortest friendship in history or forge an alliance for Fletcher's benefit.

"First of all, I forgive you. I admire your commitment and your courage."

"But?"

"It didn't happen like that."

IIIIIIIIIIIIIIIIIIIIIIIIIIIIIII

I PETTED THE PLACE on the bed where Bee should have been. "I hope you're being a good dog for Emory. We wouldn't want him changing his mind about us."

My cell phone rang. By the time I upended my purse to find the phone, it had stopped ringing. Without turning on the light, I pressed the redial button. Emory greeted me.

"Did I wake you?" he asked, breathless.

"We had dinner at Suzanne's parents' tonight."

"I'd rather eat glass."

"I tried to stay home, but Andy insisted I go. It was mostly confusing and very upsetting." I fumbled for the button to raise the head of the bed. "But you sound excited. Bee hasn't dug a hole through your foundations has she?"

"Bee? No, she's been great. I hardly know she's around until she's ready to chase a ball."

"Tell her to lie down, and be stern or she'll pester you all night."

"Birdie, Bee's a joy to have around. You don't have to worry."

"You're breathless. What have you been up to?"

"Yes, well, I wish it had been with you, but I couldn't wait to get home to tell you."

"Yes?"

"You know what night this is."

"I do?"

"The tango competition! Don't tell me you've forgotten."

I had. "Of course not. You went?"

"We took first place—Josie and me."

"Josie? Josie doesn't dance."

"She's a fast learner, that's for sure."

"You taught her?"

"We've been practicing four or five nights a week."

If men only knew what the effect of being guided around a dance floor with a firm yet tender hand does for a woman, there would be a dance studio on every corner instead of a Starbucks. It had been the confidence of Emory's steps and the touch of his hand at the small of my back that first woke my sleeping heart. I hadn't recognized the attraction at first, hadn't considered what it meant that my heart beat faster when his Bronco crunched the gravel of the driveway. Now he danced with Josie.

"Aren't you happy for us?" he asked, crestfallen.

Was I? "Congratulations."

"That's it?"

"I'm just surprised, is all. I thought I was your dance partner."

"You are. Josie knew how disappointed I was when you couldn't compete with me."

"She *offered* to dance with you?"

"Is there a problem?"

My throat tightened and tears welled. I was a sixteen-year-old girl again, and Garfield Strutgardt stammered over his words, trying but failing to explain why he'd invited Edith Anne Ganter to the prom instead of me.

"No, no problem," I said as matter-of-factly as my trembling lower lip allowed.

"Would you like to hear about the competition?"

"Not particularly." For the first time in my life, not one word, sarcastic or otherwise, came to mind. A prickly silence filled the broad distance between us.

"I better let you go to sleep then," he finally said.

"It's been a long day."

"You'll call when you're ready to come home?"

"Yes."

"Good night, then."

"Good night."

Chapter 38

Lupe blocked me from the kitchen with upheld hands. "I can't let you bake nothing."

"What are you doing here on a Saturday?"

"It's my job to clean up after the construction guys. You would think their mamas never showed them how to use a broom. Besides taking care of someone else's mess that someone else got paid big bucks to make, I get to run around the house to find things for the decorator lady." She set a cup of coffee in front of me. "Drink this quick. You don't look so good. Maybe you should call your boyfriend. You always smile after you talk to him."

My heart thumped at the thought of him. "I'll call Emory when I'm ready to go home, and I'm not ready yet. It's Bee I miss. There's nothing like a wagging tail to make the heart glad." Did I believe that?

"You better keep that piece of news to yourself. My sister, the one with the apricot poodle who poops in the house, she told her husband she loved the dog more than him because the dog at least listened to her. That very day he packed his bags and left. And he took the only car that runs. I never liked him anyway. He gave me the evil eye every time I came around. You know, like this."

Of course, I missed Lupe's demonstration of the evil eye, but I laughed anyway. It was that or cry. I'd spent half the night picturing Emory and Josie moving with liquid steps around the dance floor, chins tilted up, backs straight, the *slow, slow, quick, quick* steps of the tango. Thighs touched. Knees bumped. Her skirt flipped. His breath warmed her cheek. Teasing. Twirling. Tangled legs. A slow dip as the music faded. My eyes felt like cotton balls.

"My sister's husband? My skin crawls to think about him, and he thought he was so much better than me. He managed a Carl's Jr., bragged all the time that his store sold more Star Burgers than any other Carl's Jr. in the whole wide world, like this is brain surgery or something. Who knows? Maybe all that grease clogged his pores. I never knew a man who sweated so much. And he smelled like a pig. I hear he got fired for pulling cash out of the register. Now he drives a truck for a—what do you call it?—the place where they take dead animals. Anyway, my sister has a new boyfriend who brings her gifts all the time and keeps her car running. That's more than I can say for *mi esposo*."

"Lupe . . . ?"

"Don't look at me like that. You want to pray again, don't you?" She threw up her hands. "Okay, but first you have to tell me about Miz Doctor Lady's parents' house."

"It was nice."

She leaned across the island. "More."

"They have black-and-white marble floors, like a giant checkerboard, in the entry, which, by the way, is bigger than my whole cabin. And they had two staircases, one curving to the left and one to the right, the kind Cinderella walked down. Lots of mirrors. Furniture polish. We walked a city block from the front door to the dining room. It was all rather cold, if you want my honest opinion, although the garden was lovely. The lilacs are blooming."

"Did you see the doctor and his miz's bedroom?"

"I didn't even see the kitchen. The wait staff came in and out of a swinging door."

Lupe slammed her hand on the counter. "I knew it! Mrs. Bower, she always has something to say about how this dining room is too small and how Miz Doctor Lady can't have a real dinner party with the kitchen in the middle of the house like it is, not that Miz Doctor Lady ever gives a party or anything, but she tries to explain to her mama that tastes have changed, that entertaining is more casual, but the mama, she says her daughter shouldn't read so many magazines. There's a proper way to do everything. After the mama leaves, Miz Doctor Lady stomps up to her room and slams the door, just like my Veronica when I made her change her clothes into something more decent before she went out. I never knew nobody more eager to show off their belly button. Now it's sticking out so far, people have to turn sideways to move past her. She's fat. She doesn't do—"

"Lupe!"

"What's the rush? Does God have somewhere he needs to be?"

"Dr. Bower had brochures for boarding schools all up and down the east coast. He's talked to friends, some of them senators, for goodness' sake, who promised to pull strings to get Fletcher into their alma maters. Gloria—Mrs. Bower—tried to intervene, but Dr. Bower isn't a man who takes suggestions well. It's only a matter of Andy and Suzanne making the choice." I swallowed hard, hoping to tame my emotions. "Lupe, Fletcher isn't a boarding school kind of boy. They'll eat him alive. They teach the boys how to shoot rifles at those schools and go out on bivouacs. Dr. Bower says it's all about making a man out of a boy. I tried to tell him about Fletcher, how he has ambitions to do great things, but Dr. Bower isn't big on listening either. And poor Fletcher, he didn't say a word."

"You got a better plan?"

"He wants to live with me."

"The boy?" Lupe let out a long whistle. "And what do you think?"

"Of course I want him. He's my grandson."

"Maybe you should have brought this up before you burned the kitchen down and took the boy driving."

I buried my face in my arms. "I know."

She pulled on my sleeve. "Let's go. I know you. You'll feel better after we pray."

I followed Lupe into the bedroom. She knelt beside the bed and bowed her head. "Hurry up. It's almost time for Jerry Springer."

I knelt beside her.

"You know, my husband's brother's wife who had all those miscarriages? Well, she had a baby girl last night."

"A baby girl?"

"They named her Rosalita Guadalupe, after me. I told them we prayed for the baby. You don't suppose God had anything to do with that, do you?"

"'Wherever two or more are gathered . . .'"

Lupe fished a rosary out of her pocket. The beads rattled in her hands. "There he is in your midst."

ANDY, DRESSED IN TAILS and white tie, bowed low after opening the door for Fletcher and Mi Sun. "How was the ball, Master Fletcher? Miss?"

Mi Sun entered. Fletcher stayed beyond the threshold. "Dad? What's this all about?"

"May I take your wrap, miss?" Andy helped Mi Sun out of a hoodie and laid it over his arm. "Your hostess this evening is Mrs. Margaret Tobin Brown, noted philanthropist and reformer.

You may know her as Molly Brown, the tenacious survivor of the *Titanic* disaster. This way," he said, extending a gracious arm into the house. "The mistress of the house awaits you in the drawing room."

Fletcher mumbled, "Is she wearing a life vest?"

"Master?"

"Never mind."

I waited for the couple in the great room. A fire and burning candles provided the only light, which diminished my vision considerably. I did, however, catch the sheen of Mi Sun's gown though not the color. Andy introduced us. "Madam, your guests have arrived, Master Fletcher and Miss Mi Sun. May I present your hostess, Mrs. Margaret Brown?"

"Grandma, is that you?"

I didn't expect him to recognize me, wigged as a red-haired Gibson girl and wearing enough rhinestones to blind Zsa Zsa Gabor. I fluttered myself with a fan. "So good to see you again, Master Fletcher. Welcome to my home, Mi Sun."

Mi Sun extended her hand. "Mrs. Brown, I've always wanted to meet you. You're so much more than the *Titanic*. I most admire the work you did to improve working conditions for miners." She bent toward me to whisper. "I wrote a paper about you in the eighth grade."

Fletcher sat on the couch, face in hands. "I can't believe this is happening."

"This is great." Mi Sun sat beside him. "My parents would never think to do anything like this."

"That's because they're normal."

"Of all people, Master Fletcher, I would expect you to understand that normal is highly overrated," I said.

Suzanne entered with a silver tray, wearing a long black dress with a lacy apron and cap. "May I pour you a spot of tea, mum, before dessert is served?"

"Only if my honored guests will join me."

Mi Sun clasped her hands over her heart. "I would love tea."

When Suzanne withdrew, Mi Sun lifted her skirt to reveal high-topped sneakers. "My mom nearly croaked, but no way was I going to wear spikes."

"Tell me about the ball," I said. "How did Fletcher do with the waltz?"

"It's hard to waltz to rap, Grandma."

"You didn't waltz?"

Andy appeared from the darkness. "Dessert is still some time off. Shall I gather the musicians, mum? It hardly seems a ball can be considered complete without a waltz."

Fletcher's hands went up. "That so won't be necessary, Dad."

"Cool," Mi Sun said, standing.

"Oh man."

In a matter of moments, "Moon River" played on the stereo and the rug had been rolled away. Fletcher talked Mi Sun through the basics. They counted together and off they went. Skirt swaying. Music swelling. Fletcher counting, "One, two, three. One, two, three . . ." At the last strains of the violins, Fletcher and Mi Sun dropped their arms and shuffled about, studying their feet as we applauded their performance.

Suzanne entered and curtsied smartly. "Dessert is served, Master Fletcher."

After dessert Andy helped Mi Sun into her sweatshirt. He asked, "What time does your mother and father expect you home, miss?"

"Midnight," she said and giggled.

Andy looked at his watch. "Splendid, we have time for a turn about the park. The city lights are lovely."

IT TOOK LONGER THAN usual to go through my nighttime ritual. I stood before the mirror with every light blazing, admiring myself with red hair. I dimmed all the lights before I pulled the wig off and tousled my curls.

In bed, I lay in a delicious happiness. Andy and Fletcher returned home, laughing with much backslapping. "Thanks, Dad, that was fun. How did you know that was a replica of Martha Washington's garden?"

"I didn't." There was a moment of silence, presumably awkward as it passed between two males trying to be grateful without showing emotion. "Son, I want you to know this was all Suzanne's doing. It was her idea. She's the one who rounded up the costumes and suggested we create a dance floor."

"I wasn't so sure about it at first."

"Neither was I."

Chapter 39

Andy strode past me and Lupe watching *The Dr. Phil Show* to stand at the bottom of the stairs. "Fletcher, get your butt down here! We have work to do."

Lupe snapped the television off and scurried for the kitchen. Fletcher walked slowly to the railing. "What's up? Is there a problem?"

"I talked to your teacher. What's his name? Mr. Cherry? I got an extension for your lit project. The lumberyard will deliver supplies within the hour."

Fletcher walked tentatively down the stairs, stopping midway. "You talked to Mr. Cherry?"

"He gave us a week."

"To do what?"

"Son, if you're going to build a raft, make something you can actually float on. Everything we need to build a full-scale Mississippi River raft is on the way."

Andy took the steps two at a time past Fletcher. "I'll be down as soon as I change. If the delivery guy comes, tell him to dump everything in the driveway. I won't be a minute." Andy stopped.

"I got the dimensions off the Internet. Do you have a picture or something we could work from?"

"In my room."

"Don't just stand there. We have a raft to build."

My heart caught on a beat. Andy sounded exactly like Chuck. He leaned over the rail. "Mom, a couple of hardworking men need sustenance, something to hit the spot, like a strawberry-rhubarb pie. Can you do something about that?"

When I hesitated, he said, "Go ahead and burn the kitchen down, as long as you save the pie."

I baked that pie and one for every day Andy and Fletcher spent out in the garage working on the raft. Saws screamed. Hammers pounded. More than a few times Andy and Fletcher butted heads over details, like where the wigwam should go and how to protect the deck from the fire pit. Andy did a fair amount of acquiescing to Fletcher, which surprised me more than anything the two had accomplished to that point. All that, and Andy stole minutes from his workday to build the firebox and experiment with tiller shapes. Unprecedented. Best of all, I felt reconnected to my son. As the raft took shape, words flowed freely. We ribbed each other with no offenses taken. Silences became comfortable. My lungs expanded to breathe deeply for the first time in a very, very long while.

With only one evening left to work on the raft before its due date, Andy came home at lunch, asked for a peanut-butter-and-jelly sandwich, and headed for the garage. I followed him.

"This is Fletcher's project," I said.

"Finals are next week. Fletcher needs time to study." Andy sanded a rough spot on the tiller and stopped. "Do you suppose this baby will float, Ma?"

"There's only one way to find out."

When I turned to estimate the raft's seaworthiness, Huck lay on the deck, his knees bent, his arms pillows for his head, lost in thought as boys are prone to be, feeling the rush of the current carrying him along. I ignored the boy as much as any woman can ignore something wondrous and mysterious. Even inside the garage, Huck closed his eyes against the Mississippi sun. He tapped his foot and whistled "Camp Town Ladies." He stopped and sat up straight. "Thar ain't no use in building a raft if you ain't going to set it on the water. Where's the nearest river?"

"Andy, is there someplace you can test the raft?"

"The rivers are swollen with snow melt. Heck, I'm not even sure how we're getting this baby to the school."

Huck kicked the firebox. "This here firebox won't hold a fire worth startin'."

"How about Dillion Reservoir?" I asked.

"Too far. Too deep."

"Cherry Creek?"

"Too fast."

"How about the park? I see paddleboats out there all the time."

Huck dropped his jaw. "If I'd a-wanted to act like a girl—a pond?"

Andy rubbed at another rough spot. "Too illegal. Private boats aren't allowed on the lake. Only the vendors with city permits can rent out canoes and those paddleboats you saw."

"You know, Huck traveled at night," I said. "Traveling with a runaway slave was dangerous business. By day, he and Jim tied the raft in the towheads of willows and spent the day sleeping. Otherwise, they'd have been headed for the hanging tree."

Huck pulled at an imaginary noose around his neck, bulged out his eyes, and stuck out his tongue. I chewed on my lower lip to stave a laugh.

Andy stopped sanding. "What are you saying?"

"Oh, nothing really."

"Ma?"

"It seems to me, for Fletcher to share what Huck experienced, this raft must be launched under some degree of danger."

Huck widened his stance and hooked his thumbs in his suspenders. "The river is mighty dangerous. Watch out for them liars, the ones who made Jim and me believe they was a duke and a dauphin. Although their premature balditude gave them a regal air, all their talk about being snaked down wrongfully out'n a high place warn't nothing but lies."

Andy stepped onto the deck. Huck jumped back. I reached for the edge of the raft to steady myself and closed my eyes. *Go away now, Huck.*

Andy kicked at the boards with his heel. "She's solid, that's for sure."

Huck sat smack in front of me and swung his feet over the edge. "I ain't seen nothing finer. This raft's ready to shove off for the big water."

"They rent flatbed trailers, don't they?" I asked, knowing better than to agree with Huck, although I was awfully proud of what Andy and Fletcher had built.

"It would have to be a big one," Andy said, swiping the sweat from his forehead.

"I could call around for you."

Andy hopped off the raft. "That won't be necessary."

Huck lay down on the deck. "I think I'll just lazy myself off to sleep."

You just do that, young man. "Andy," I called, wondering where he'd gone off to.

From the kitchen door he said, "Ma, I'm here."

"I'm very proud of you."

"I head a business that manufactures and sells top-of-the-line golf equipment on five continents, and you're proud of me for building a raft?"

"It's the little things that mean so very much."

"Thanks," he said and turned to leave.

"There's something else, Andy. If you have the time, there's something very important I have to ask you."

He stepped back into the sunlight where I could see that he hooked his pockets with his thumbs, something he used to do as a boy when he was lost in thought and long before he wore a watch. "Suzanne and I talked until midnight last night," he said. "You can set your heart to rest, Ma. Fletcher's staying with us."

I stopped myself from clapping. "That's good to hear, son."

"Partly it's because we've seen a change in Fletch, and partly it's because we'll have to do some belt-tightening around here." Andy leaned against the workbench. "They laid me off, Ma. They didn't feel like I'd responded quickly or decisively enough to the economic downturn. The board brought in a new man."

"I never dreamed . . . you've poured your life out for that company."

"I figured I'd die in my office chair. I spent most of the morning walking around Cherry Creek Reservoir. At one point I sat on a bench and my whole body went limp. I almost cried, for heaven's sake."

"Relief?"

"Yes. Maybe. I think so. I don't know."

"What will you do?"

"I don't know, maybe pick up a small business on the cheap. Fortunately or unfortunately, lots of companies are failing. I'll pick one up and nurse it back to health."

"Are you open to advice from your mother?"

"Do I have a choice?"

"Not really, and it's nothing earth-shattering: Don't rush into anything, will you?"

"There's a custom cabinet shop in Englewood I've been keeping my eye on."

"Do these sorts of opportunities come along often?"

"With the economy the way it is, you can count on it." He crossed his arms, the international sign for *back off.* He knew his ma better than that. "This place has a golden reputation, and the shop foreman said he'd stay on."

"You already talked to him?"

"I talk to people all the time."

Time for a conversational shift. "Fletcher is counting the days until he leaves for college."

"I did, too."

"Do tell." Well, now, that smacked like a swinging branch. But this was the very reason I'd come out to the garage in the first place. "We need to talk."

"This sounds serious. Are you feeling okay?"

"It's nothing like that." I patted the edge of the raft, and Andy moved to sit next to me. "Son, I loved your father very much." Andy stiffened. I patted his leg and continued. There would never be a good time to say this. "He wasn't a perfect man. Once he got a burr under his saddle, there was no soothing him. At first, I saw this as strength and determination. When you kids came along, he softened—"

"He did?"

"In some ways, yes. But we both know he was assigned to the backcountry for a good reason. Your father wasn't a people person."

"He could be when it suited him."

"There's truth in that."

"I couldn't please him no matter what I did."

"You pleased him more than you'll ever know, and that's the tragedy." This wasn't going the way I'd planned. In and out, down and dirty. Say it: "When you turned sixteen, and you inched past Chuck, I saw a change in how the two of you related to one another. You pushed for independence, like every child does, but for some reason Chuck took something very natural—incredibly terrifying, but natural—too personally. You pushed all the harder, and yes, he bullied you. I can see that now."

"I got plenty tired of being yelled at."

"I imagine you did."

"I felt guilty about leaving you alone with Diane. Good night, she was a handful!"

"We weren't your responsibility."

"You got awfully lonely, I know you did."

"There you go, turning this into something about me, but this is about you. Andy, I should have stepped in, told Chuck to leave you alone. Maybe you wouldn't have that scar on your back if I had."

"Mom, you're forgetting how stubborn he was."

"Was he that bad?"

"Worse."

"I can be stubborn too."

"What is this about, Ma?"

"I need your forgiveness."

Andy expelled a long breath and massaged his temples.

I touched his arm. "Can you say without any hesitation that you never wished I'd stepped in to help?"

He stood, paced back and forth. "What good is this?"

"Someday, I hope you'll forgive your pa. I don't have much of a say in what you do about that, but I hope you will for your own sake. Bitterness is poison."

He stopped. "Were you afraid of him?"

"Never."

"Then I wish you'd told him it was you who pulled off the truck fender."

"Don't get cute with me."

Andy looked at the ground. "I should be asking you to forgive me. I mean, I've been pretty selfish."

"One thing at a time, Son. Will you forgive me? Will you?"

I don't know why Andy couldn't say yes to me that day, not with words anyway. I suppose a woman could live to be a thousand years old and never know what pops and sizzles inside the male mind, but Andy and me blubbered all over one another for a good thirty seconds. That has to be some kind of record for a grown son crying on his mother's shoulder. I took it. I treasured it. I thanked the good Lord for catching Andy's gaze.

Huck had taken his leave by the time I thought to look for him.

Chapter 40

My heart hadn't raced this hard since I'd found a bear in the kitchen. Back then I plopped baby Diane, all wide-eyed and anxious for her bottle, into the sink and shooed the bear out the door with two clanging pots. I told that bear where to go, but he'd ambled down the road, sure to enjoy the vittles of a careless camper. *Good riddance!*

Nothing so wild or odorous as a bear shot adrenaline through me as I stood wrapped in a blanket with Suzanne. No, this was something grander, much more glorious. In fact, Jesus turned his gaze on me as Andy and Fletcher set to launch the raft onto the tiny lake in the park, and maybe he winked. I liked to think he did. I laughed like a schoolgirl.

"Mom!" Suzanne pulled me closer. "We have to be quiet," she whispered in my ear with coffee-tainted breath. "I am not ending up on the front page of the *Denver Post* tomorrow morning."

The midnight chill seeped through the blanket. I dabbed at my nose with my cuff and filled my lungs to embrace the night. The lake smelled stale and lifeless, nothing at all like a mountain lake, where the stew of life rose to sting one's nose. Leaning out the window of his new truck, Andy backed the trailer with the very large, very heavy raft into the water. "Fletch, are we in yet?" he called in a forced whisper that wasn't much of a whisper at all. Suzanne tensed.

Fletcher motioned his father deeper into the water. "The truck's wheels are in about three inches."

"Stop me before the tailpipe gets wet."

Andy eased the trailer farther down the ramp.

Fletcher yelled, "Keep coming, Dad!"

Suzanne moaned. How easily the young forget caution.

Darkness is the most frustrating of situations for a macular degenerate like me. Once the sun goes down, the world grows thick and viscous. No details. This night Andy's taillights stabbed at my eyes.

Fletcher yelled, "Stop! The raft's touching the water."

Andy wasn't satisfied. He left the cab to investigate. A sloppy launch meant terrible risks, all enumerated by Andy before we'd left the house. The raft was more than capable of crushing anyone who got in its way if it slid off the trailer sideways. Andy ordered Fletcher into the cab.

"Are you sure, Dad? I mean—"

Andy put a hand to Fletcher's shoulder. "Take it nice and slow."

Fletcher climbed into the cab. The truck shuddered as he shifted into reverse and eased toward the lake.

"Nice and easy, nice and easy. Keep it coming. Stop!"

The raft rolled on scraps of pipe Andy had purchased at the plumber supply store. He'd thought of everything, but that was my son. "Get out here, champ," he called to Fletcher. "Your raft is about to float off without you."

"It's floating?"

"Grab the poles from the truck bed. Let's get this baby into the big water."

Suzanne clutched my hand.

"Tell me everything," I said, nearly spitting my partial into the lake. "What's happening?"

She gasped.

I squeezed her hand tighter. "What?"

"The raft tilted, but it's level now."

"What are they doing?"

"Andrew and Fletcher are standing on each side, pushing the raft away from the shore with the poles. Uh-oh, now the raft is turning to the left."

"To port," I said.

"Yes, to port. Andrew has moved to the *port* side to help Fletcher pole. They're going straight now. Can you hear them counting?"

I couldn't.

"They're poling together, in unison."

"How far out are they?"

"Not very far, only thirty feet or so."

"And the raft is level?"

"Like a pool table."

As if Suzanne's words opened the door to another world, the raft appeared to me, not as it was—I knew that—but as I dreamed it would be, floating on the ink-black water of the mighty Mississippi with Andy at the tiller and Fletcher casting a fishing line into the water. The moon hung low where no moon hung in our world, a ribbon of light writhing on the swirling current. Embers sparked from the fire pit, ready for the catfish Fletcher would pull off the bottom. Willows bowed over the river and cottonwoods swayed with a breeze I couldn't feel. A lantern winked a yellow light. Another figure rose from the wigwam and stretched as if to tickle the stars. *Huck!* Of course he wouldn't resist the chance to hop a raft, in big water or small.

"They're in the middle of the lake," Suzanne said, her voice tight with apprehension. "They should turn back."

The image of the broad river and the content threesome faded into my perpetual grayness. I caught a tear with the blanket. "They'll be fine. There's no other place Andy or Fletcher would rather be right now."

"How do you know that?" Suzanne said, releasing my hand.

"They're testing themselves and the work of their hands. Men thrive on that kind of stuff."

"This is the twenty-first century, for heaven's sake. What kind of nonsense is this? The 'work of their hands.'"

It was no small miracle that Suzanne had come to be wrapped in a blanket with me, a woman whose presence she had once despised, watching her husband on what she'd declared a fool's errand. Explaining the nature of men or mentioning her quest for motherhood seemed unnecessarily provocative. I entertained no claims to having tamed my tongue, but this small victory is counted among the string of miracles from that night that I hold up to the light now and again, not the least being our common purpose. Anyone stopping to look out their window toward the lake that night as they pattered to the kitchen for a second slice of pie would call us a family. That's a miracle.

The boys made it back to shore without attracting the attention of the law. Getting the raft out of the lake proved more difficult than launching it. Andy called a tow truck to hoist the raft onto the trailer, and he slipped the driver a hundred dollars to turn off his flashing lights.

Back in the kitchen, Fletcher held out his coffee cup to his father. Andy hesitated before filling it. Suzanne served muffins she'd bought at a boutique bakery across from the hospital. Fresh from the microwave, the chocolate chips coated my tongue.

"Oh man, we totally forgot the life vests," Fletcher said around a hunk of muffin.

"We'll use them, don't you worry," Andy said.

After slaps on the back for the boys and wishes of sweet dreams all around, I hobbled off to my bedroom. Under the blankets, I waited for the warmth to ease the pain in my joints. I patted the spot where Bee should have been. "It's a good thing you weren't here tonight. You would have barked your head off, and the neighbors surely would have called the police." Thinking of Bee reminded me that Emory had a new dance partner, my best friend.

"You can have him."

I turned toward the wall, and after a considerable amount of shifting to ease the pressure on my hip and shoulder, I let silly half dreams usher me into sleep.

Chapter 41

I'd only seen Josie talk on the phone one time. She'd held the receiver at arm's length and shouted for the plumber to come to her house. She gave him her address and hung up. He showed up before lunch. Wouldn't you?

"Don't be an idiot!" she said. "There's nothing going on between us! Emory loves you! Good-bye!" The phone line clicked a few times before it buzzed incessantly. I hit the off button and sat on the edge of the bed.

Lupe stepped into the room. "So, this Emory guy loves you. He's got a good job, right? What you going to do?"

"You heard that?"

"Me and everyone from here to Kansas. Even my sister Jacinta could hear that, and she doesn't hear so good." She planted her fist on her hips. "You're avoiding the question: So what are you going to do about Emory?"

I felt myself smile. "Maybe I'll call him."

"Maybe?" She pointed an accusing finger at me. "Love is not so easy to find. You should know that by now. I think that maybe you should wake up and smell the . . ."

"Coffee?"

"Nah, you smell the coffee just fine. What you need to smell is something rare and beautiful, like . . . ah, like an agave. *Mi abuela tiene un agave—*"

"In English, please."

"When I talk about home . . . well, I forget." She shuffled across the room and sagged into the recliner. "My grandmother waited and waited for her agave to bloom. Her mother, my great-grandmother, she planted the agave in the garden of *mi abuela* when my mother was born. She hauled water from the house. My grandfather, he made fun of her. The kids, my brothers and sisters and all the cousins, we hated that plant. It had thorns like fish-hooks all along the edges. The boys, they liked to chase the girls with the leaves like they were pirates with long swords.

"I'd just had my *quinceanera* when my parents moved us to the United States, and still that agave didn't bloom. I got married, had children. Still no flower. The spring my grandfather died, a shoot as tall as a telephone pole grew out of that agave. *Mi abuela*, she made us all come home to see it blooming. We had a party. The newspaper came and took a picture."

"Did it smell good?"

"Who would know? The flower was too tall."

"You said—"

"I said you needed to smell something rare and beautiful, not something that smelled good."

I would call Emory, beg his forgiveness, and tell him it was time for me to come home, but first there was something I had to do.

Chapter 42

Before popping the shu mai open, I used my cane to walk around the house. It wouldn't do to have an audience. Satisfied that the house was empty, I opened the take-out box. The steam bathed my face with ginger and garlic. I popped a whole dumpling into my mouth.

"Come on out here, Huck. We need to have some words."

Only the gray orb floated in front of me. Perhaps I needed to sweeten my words.

"I want to thank you, Huck, for providing my family with a grand adventure. I hope you enjoyed floating on the raft."

He walked out of the bedroom. "I can't see how you're any better off, seeing I'm so ignorant and so kind of lowdown and ornery." Huck lounged on the leather sofa like a king being carried on a litter. I half expected him to flip an offhanded salute to the peasantry. And why not, there had been an amazing transformation in Huck. His hair was combed and clean, streaked with highlights from endless days in the sun, and his feet were scrubbed pink. He pulled at the collar of his shirt, a blue calico.

"What you gawking at?" he asked like he'd swallowed a spoonful of castor oil.

"New shirt?"

"It might as well be a feedbag for how it sets a body itching. Aunt Sally has a mind to adopt me and civilize me, but I had a taste of that before."

"I'm surprised she'd want anything to do with you with all the trouble you and Tom dished out at her expense. You nearly drove the woman crazy."

"She wanted to tan the Old Harry out o' the both o' us."

"You look awfully handsome in your new clothes, Huck."

He stood and pulled the hem of his shirt out of his pants, scratching his belly and back. "I'm lightin' out for the territory first chance I git and dumpin' these clothes in the ditch. I have my old things holed up under a rock down by the river."

"Huck, I need you to sit down and give me your attention for a minute."

He plopped on the sofa, arms and legs bouncing from the fall. He huffed and looked at me through his eyebrows.

"Sit up, and don't be giving me any of your lip."

"I never said nothin'."

"You didn't have to. Now, I must admit to enjoying, for the most part, our visits, but they have to come to an end."

"It gets powerful lonesome on the river."

"You might rethink Aunt Sally's offer. You liked her pies well enough, and the river isn't so far that you couldn't take a line down there to catch yourself some dinner now and again."

"There's nothing like the bullfrogs a-cluttering through the night when you're floating down the river, but she warn't that bad of a cook neither."

"There's nothing like three hot meals a day and someone to keep an eye out for your well-being."

He pouted now. "She smiles about as much as a ham."

"She's willing to put up with your shenanigans. Getting on in the world means learning to do the same for others. It's called love, Huck."

"You ain't willing to put up with me no how."

"Visiting with you filled a need, I can't deny it, but I'm determined to have those needs met by flesh-and-blood people, friends and family, and the Good Shepherd who doesn't give a lick that I'm a lunkhead. I'm asking you, as a friend, to move on. But please consider Aunt Sally's offer."

Huck stood, his head hung low, and I just about told him to sit back down for a spell. He looked at me with those sky blue eyes of his and drew a finger across his lips. He scuffed across the floor toward the front door, and the closer he got to the door, the lighter his footfalls. By the time he touched the doorknob, his movements made no sound. He turned, set his ratty old hat on his head, and winked.

Chapter 43

"I thought you *wanted* to come home," Emory said, breaking the ragged silence on our drive from Denver back to Ouray. "That's what you said. That's what you told me."

"Yes, I did ask you to come."

"You've changed your mind?"

Bee whimpered from the cargo area.

"We'd better stop." The canyon hugged the interstate, so I knew we'd entered Glenwood Canyon, but that was about all. "Where are we?"

"We just passed the Bair Ranch exit."

"Grizzly Creek exit then. That'll do." I turned in my seat toward Bee. "You better cross your legs, little missy."

Waiting for the exit, I did my best to wink away the tears, but they streamed down my cheeks and dampened my T-shirt. I finally swiped at my eyes and made like I was cleaning my glasses. We drove on as silent as two fence posts—me in my hole and Emory in his. As he pressed on the brake to exit, he said, "You told me to come. I came. Now . . . now you're all sappy and weepy. I thought you'd be happy."

I didn't understand the brew of doubt and anticipation that bubbled inside me. How could I explain it to Emory? A heart doesn't move from one place to another just because the rest of the body logs miles on the interstate. As for me, I'm well acquainted with the strange things that tether a heart in place, like when my family left the farmhouse in the Smokies. I was ten years old. I barely waved good-bye to Leslie, my best friend, but I ached for months for the dependable water stain on the ceiling and the way the house accompanied the wind with snaps and creaks. Being homesick for a water stain? That's a fickle heart. Walking away from Andy, Suzanne, and Fletcher? That was a different story all together. I was straining against the most primal of instincts: to run through fire and brimstone to be with my family.

Emory opened the car door, and the rush of the Colorado River bounced off the canyon's towering walls to welcome me. "Wait here while I get Bee," he said.

"Wait!" I grabbed at his sleeve. "Do you hear that? Oh my, I'd almost forgotten."

Emory offered his elbow, and Bee pulled hard at the leash. Fletcher had taught her to heel and to heel smartly.

"Are you sure you can manage both of us?" I asked.

"I've learned to hold on for dear life when I'm around either one of you."

Bee sniffed every square inch of the rest area. All of our pleading for her to hurry her business only made her more determined to find the perfect spot to mark. "Good grief, Bee. We don't have all day!"

"Don't we? What's the rush? I have a rope in the car. It's long. Bee can sniff around as she pleases, and we can sit here and admire the scenery."

I laid my head on his shoulder. "You're right. This is a lovely place." Emory handed over Bee's leash. I pushed Bee's rump toward the pavement. "Sit! I won't be tugged at, you bamboozler.

See if I ever stop a car for you again." Bee lay at my feet, and I considered feeling sorry for sassing her. Instead, I closed my eyes to listen to the river's song and the rattle of aspen leaves overhead.

Do you trust me?

My eyes popped open. I closed them against the disappointing fog.

Do you trust me?

"Emory!"

"I'm here, I'm here," he said, drawing me into his arms. "Did something startle you?"

"What should I do? I haven't a clue. Andy doesn't have a job. They have that big house to take care of. Fletcher has so many questions. We talked for hours after every youth group meeting. And Suzanne—well, she really is a fragile thing. How will she manage all of her new responsibilities?"

"Without you?"

"Now that I'm getting around better, I could—"

"Answer me this, Birdie: Can God accomplish good things without you dabbling your fingers in everything?"

I sat up. "What are you trying to say?"

"It's a question we all have to answer sooner or later, some of us many, many times. When you were off in Denver, it seems like the question came to me a hundred times a day in one form or another. I agonized over being so far away. Who could take care of you as well as me? In case you're wondering, the answer was no one."

"I didn't realize . . ."

"Birdie, I want to take care of you every minute of every day from now until forever, but I know that's not possible. You'll fly off with your Round Robins, or I'll have to deliver insulin to Crazy Bill up to Beaver Lake, or—and this is the toughest separation of all—one of us will enter forever before the other."

"I was hoping for a two-seater blaze into glory."

"That would be just fine with me." He stroked my cheek. "But we both know . . ."

"Only too well."

"Loving you has introduced me to a whole new kind of faith. It's not enough for me to believe my Savior loves me. Now I have to believe he loves you too, that he can do wonderful things in your life, with or without my help." He sat quietly for a moment. "I will treasure every moment we do have together. I can promise you that."

"That's enough for me."

Chapter 44

I used a painter's brush to drench the sky penciled onto the watercolor paper with pools of water. Evangeline grunted from her infant seat. Bee sniffed her, whimpered, and then slunk away into the house. I swirled a fat, round brush in cadmium red and tapped the point into cerulean blue before blending the colors on the palette. Suzanne slept in the hammock, shaded by a stand of aspens flittering in the breeze.

"Hey there, Grandpa, it's time to go to work," I whispered.

Emory looked up from a pharmacological journal. "Huh?"

I loaded the brush with fuchsia and dipped it into a puddle on the paper. A firework of color exploded on the page. "You can't smell that?"

"What?"

"Evangeline's been busy, and as I remember, our agreement was Suzanne rests, I paint, you change."

"Already? When are Andy and Fletcher back from the river?" He lifted the baby from her seat. "Oh my, you have been busy. Wow. I say it's bath time." And off they went, a bundle of pink over Emory's shoulder.

Painting with watercolors required too much patience, and yet I loved the movement of color the technique brought to my work. I rinsed the paint out of the brush, tapped it dry on a paper towel, and considered my options. Cadmium yellow with red? Cobalt violet? Ultramarine with Indian yellow? I lifted my eyes to the far horizon to catch the dance of the dragonfly sky. I loaded the brush with ultramarine and cadmium yellow. Yellow and red. Violet. And then I stood to stretch my back and to wait, wait, wait for the paper to dry.

A coyote yipped nearby, so I closed the door. Sure enough, Bee barked to be released within a heartbeat. "Don't go sassing me, you old hound," I whispered through the glass.

Woof!

I slipped into my painting smock against the seeping chill and covered Suzanne with a blanket. The sky turned soft, and the first star twinkled over Amphitheater Ridge. The crickets chirruped. A breeze lifted the curls from my forehead.

Home.

Epilogue

Had I the slightest inkling how troublesome writing a book would be, I never would have started. Once the folks at Elsie's Diner found out what I was about, they asked me every single day, "What page are you on, Birdie?" It got so that I wondered if a piece of pie was worth the haranguing they dished out—but only for a minute or two.

Although I learned how to make shu mai, I've never seen Huck again—not that I haven't looked for him, maybe even hoped that I'd see him. I can't explain his showing up like he did, except that he may have been nothing more than a Charles Bonnet hallucination, at least to start with. What gave him words is something I find myself wondering about whenever I get dirt under my fingernails or come across a fine bolt of calico fabric, something Huck would throw in a ditch but I would use to make a tablecloth, the brighter the better.

I'd like to tell you everything's hunky-dory with my family, but then I wouldn't be talking about a family now, would I? Fletcher stayed at home until he graduated from high school, just as he'd planned, then he headed for college in Nebraska of all places. That had something to do with a girl he met in youth group. While at home he butted heads with his father, as sons do, but I never once heard him recite another baseball statistic. I took this as a good sign.

My editor insisted on a touch of romance in my story. Please forgive me for all the tickling tummies and flushed faces, especially for a woman my age, but Emory is almost as good as I portrayed him. Maybe better. Anyhow, I married him when I could walk down the aisle without limping, although the aisle was in a meadow at Carpenter Reservoir. We waited until July for all the snow to melt from under the trees and the wildflowers to bloom.

I'm at least that romantic.